Wopper

HOW BABE RUTH LOST HIS FATHER AND WON THE 1918 WORLD SERIES AGAINST THE CUBS

Volume 2

The Show

Touch 'em all!
Salt & Light
Frank Amoroso

By Frank Amoroso

simply francis publishing company
North Carolina

Library of Congress Control Number 2017900274
ISBN: 978-1-63062-013-4 (paperback)
ISBN: 978-1-63062-014-1 (ebook)

Publisher's Cataloging-in-Publication
    Amoroso, Frank L., author.
        Wopper : how Babe Ruth lost his father and won the
    1918 World Series against the Cubs / by Frank Amoroso.
        volumes cm
        Includes bibliographical references.
        CONTENTS: Volume 1. Pigtown -- Volume 2. The Show --
    Volume 3. The Series.
        ISBN 978-1-63062-013-4 (Volume 2)
        1. Ruth, Babe, 1895-1948--Fiction. 2. Ruth, Babe,
    1895-1948--Childhood and youth--Fiction. 3. Ruth, Babe,
    1895-1948--Friends and associates--Fiction. 4. World
    Series (Baseball)--(1918)--Fiction. 5. Baseball players
    --United States--Fiction. 6. World War, 1914-1918--
    Evacuation of civilians--United States--Fiction.
    7. World War, 1914-1918--German Americans--Fiction.
    8. Biographical fiction. 9. Historical fiction.
    I. Title.

    PS3601.M668W67 2017   813'.6
                QBI16-900097

For information about this title or to order other books and/or electronic media, contact the publisher:

simply francis publishing company
P.O. Box 329, Wrightsville Beach, NC 28480
www.simplyfrancispublishing.com
simplyfrancispublishing@gmail.com

OTHER BOOKS WRITTEN BY FRANK AMOROSO

Behind Every Great Fortune®

". . .boldly imaginative historical novel that is sumptuously detailed and filled with intrigue, betrayal and plot twists that surprise and entertain the reader."

Dread the Fed

". . . a gripping story of a crime so bold, so ingenious and so perfect, that a century later, the plunder continues and the People venerate the banksters who commit it."

Behind Every Great Recipe
From Latkes to Vodkas & Beets to Meats

". . . a charming and unique companion book containing delicious period recipes and vignettes featuring the characters from the historical novel *Behind Every Great Fortune*®."

Wopper - How Babe Ruth Lost His Father And Won The 1918 World Series Against The Cubs Volume 1 Pigtown

". . . a fantastical Ruthian novel based on the life of Babe Ruth!"

Wopper - How Babe Ruth Lost His Father And Won The 1918 World Series Against The Cubs Volume 1 Pigtown YOUNG ADULT VERSION

Dedication

The author between sons Jason and Louis

The Show is dedicated to my wonderful sons, Louis and Jason. Our legacy is defined more by our children than any worldly success. The values that we impart endure long after our victories have faded and our monuments have crumbled. I have been fortunate to pass to my sons the gift of baseball that I received from my father. The time spent coaching my sons and sharing my love of the game with them is one of the true joys of my life.

I recall as a youngster attending a doubleheader at Yankee Stadium with my brother and father to watch Mickey Mantle play. My father raved about Babe Ruth as the greatest ever. After the Mick pounded three homers that day, my Dad conceded that Mantle was pretty good. A generation later I was having a similar conversation with my sons over the relative merits of Derek Jeter and Mariano Rivera compared to former Yankee greats. Priceless.

FOREWORD

The Show is volume 2 of my series entitled *Wopper -How Babe Ruth Lost His Father and Won the 1918 World Series Against the Cubs.* It picks up the story at the point where the nineteen-year-old George Herman Ruth, Jr. becomes a professional baseball player with the Baltimore Orioles.

In *Pigtown*, volume 1 of the series, young George's family is plagued by multiple infant deaths, his mother's alcoholism, and the family's economic struggles. Nicknamed Jidgie, he turns to a life of truancy, vandalism, and petty crime. Jidgie's relationship with his father is volatile and tumultuous. After a childhood filled with petty crime, alcoholism, and death, Jidgie's behavior is so rebellious that he is declared incorrigible at the age of seven and committed to a reform school. He spends most of the next twelve years as an inmate at St. Mary's Industrial School for Orphans, Delinquent, Incorrigible and Wayward Boys. There, Jidgie's life changes when he meets Brother Matthias, the prefect of discipline. The genial brother mentors Jidgie on self-discipline, hard work, and the finer points of the game of baseball.

At a time when Jidgie's prodigious baseball skill blossoms, he falls in love with a brave young girl named Colina. She introduces

Jidgie to the wonderful singing of Enrico Caruso and, by strange coincidence, Jidgie and his friends meet Caruso at the Central Park Zoo. Jidgie's childhood comes to an abrupt halt when his mother dies, and his father reveals the details of her alcoholism and the traumatic divorce that had been kept secret. Amid these shocking revelations, Jidgie is offered an opportunity to play professional baseball. *Pigtown* ends with Jidgie struggling to choose between his first true love and possible fame and fortune as a professional baseball player.

In *The Show,* we learn more about the developing relationship between Caruso, the great superstar, and, Ruth, the budding superstar. How Ruth gets his nickname and begins his career with legendary performances in North Carolina entertain the reader. He is traded to the Boston Red Sox and soon becomes a dominant pitcher. As the world teeters toward war, Babe experiences discrimination as an American of German extraction. War hysteria flames through the nation capturing his father, friends, and many others in the conflagration.

In the course of this turmoil, Babe loses friends and struggles to find himself on the baseball field. Is he a dominant pitcher, or, an everyday position player who wields a powerful bat? While dealing with these issues, Colina re-emerges in his life. The ensuing conflicts over love, family, war hysteria, and career demands buffet the young man toward an explosive conclusion in the final installment of *Wopper*, entitled Volume 3, *The Series.*

One of Babe Ruth's records that is often overlooked is the unprecedented amount of ink used in recounting the life and times of this sports hero. I have endeavored to provide a fresh and imaginative look at his life by developing new revelations about his family and exploring his relationships with the fathers, real, surrogate, and imagined, in his early life. While the events depicted in *Wopper* may have actually occurred, I have used the novelist's tools to create a plausible narrative that I hope is entertaining, evocative, and intriguing. Some of the characters are fictitious; others are used fictitiously. At the end of the day, Babe Ruth is a great American icon whose exploits on and off the field are timeless and deserve re-interpretation.

As Babe remarked:

Listen, kid, there's heroes and there's legends.

Heroes get remembered, but legends never die.

Enjoy this historical novel about Babe Ruth, an immortal whose legend will never die!

Frank Amoroso

Wilmington, North Carolina

Ruth Family Tree

Paternal Grandparents

John Anton Ruth (1844 – 1897) Babe's paternal grandfather.

Mary E. (Strodtman) Ruth (1845 – 1894) Babe's paternal grandmother. Both were born in Maryland of German heritage. John's parents were born in Prussia, and Mary's parents were born in Hanover.

Maternal Grandparents

Pius Schamberger (1833 – 1904) Babe's maternal grandfather.

Johanna Schamberger (1836 – 1900) Babe's maternal grandmother. Both maternal grandparents were born in Baden, Germany.

Babe Ruth's Parents

George Herman Ruth, Sr. (1871 – 1918) Babe Ruth's father

Katherine "Katie" Schamberger Ruth (1873 – 1912) Babe Ruth's mother. She lost 6 of 8 children and two brothers.

Children

George Herman "Babe" Ruth (1895 – 1948)

Augustus Ruth (1898 – 1899) who was born on March 15, 1898, but died at the age of 1 year and 1 day.

Mary Margaret "Mamie" Ruth (August 1900 – 1992) Babe's sister. "See, there were many children in our family, but they were all deceased, other than Babe and I. Babe was the firstborn. I'm the fifth. There was a sister to me, a twin. Twin girls and a set of twin boys. But Babe and me were the only ones to survive."

William Ruth (1905 – 1906) Babe Ruth's youngest brother who died when he was one.

Babe Ruth's Wives

Helen Woodford Ruth (1896 – 1929) Babe's first wife who died mysteriously in a house fire while cohabiting with another man.

Claire Hodgson Ruth (1897 – 1976) Babe's second wife.

Babe Ruth's Children

Dorothy Helen Ruth (1921 – 1989) according to her book, *My Dad, the Babe*, Dorothy was the daughter of Babe and his mistress Juanita Jenkins. Dorothy was adopted by Babe Ruth when he married Claire Hodgson.

Julia Hodgson Ruth (1916 –) Claire Hodgson's natural born daughter from her first marriage. Julia was adopted by Babe Ruth when he married Claire Hodgson.

Julia, Babe, & Dorothy Ruth

People, Places, and Things

Archduke Franz Ferdinand (1863 - 1914) nephew of Emperor Franz Ferdinand and heir apparent of the Austria-Hungary Empire, assassinated with his wife Sophie on June 28, 1914 by Gavrilo Princip, generally acknowledged to have sparked the outbreak of WWI.

John Franklin "Home Run" Baker (1886 –1963) played third base in the famed "$100,000 infield" of Connie Mack's champion Philadelphia Athletics. Baker led the AL in home runs and RBI in 1911, 1912, and 1913. He was elected to the National Baseball Hall of Fame in 1955.

Baltimore Terrapins, franchise in the Federal League that outdrew the Baltimore Orioles which was a major impetus for the trade of Babe Ruth to the Red Sox.

Black Hand, secret military society formed in 1911 by officers in the Serbian Army seeking independence of Bosnia-Herzegovina from Austro-Hungary and favoring a union between Bosnia-Herzegovina and Serbia.

Blind Tiger drinking and gambling establishment in Wilmington, North Carolina, operated in defiance of temperance and anti-gambling laws.

Cherry Bounce alcoholic beverage made with corn whiskey, sourwood honey, and wild sour cherries associated with moonshiner Amos Owens of Rutherford County, North Carolina.

Yo-na Brighthorse (1896 – 1916) Native American of the Cherokee tribe who was a waiter at Hot Springs Country Club. He befriended Babe Ruth and later served with distinction in the Canadian Expeditionary Force during World War I.

Enrico Caruso (1873 – 1921) world's greatest opera singer in early 20th Century and lead tenor for the Metropolitan Opera.

Soldano Cefalo (1892 – 1957) cousin of Colina Petronilla and protègèe of Enrico Caruso.

Edward "Eddie" Trowbridge Collins, Sr., (1887 – 1951) played second base in the famed "$100,000 infield" of Connie Mack's champion Philadelphia Athletics. He was one of the most skilled players of the Deadball Era. He was elected to the National Baseball Hall of Fame in 1939.

Jack Dunn (1872 – 1928) successful manager and magnate of the Baltimore Orioles in the International League who signed Babe Ruth from the schoolyard of St. Mary's Industrial School.

Ben Egan (1883 – 1968) catcher for the Baltimore Orioles under Jack Dunn who was traded along with Babe Ruth and Ernie Shore to the Boston Red Sox in June 1914.

Harry Frazee (1880 – 1929) made his fortune as a real estate manager and stock broker. He later became a theater impresario who purchased the Boston Red Sox and Fenway Park in 1916 and notoriously sold Babe Ruth's contract to the New York Yankees before the 1920 season. Many baseball fans believe that this transaction spawned the 'Curse of the Bambino' that prevented the Red Sox from winning the World Series until the curse was broken in 2004.

Fenway Park home field of the Boston Red Sox completed for the 1912 season.

Oscar Gnarltz (1884 – 1961) major league infielder, manager of the Baltimore Terrapins in the Federal League, and later third base coacher for the 1918 Chicago Cubs.

Hollow Leg Club after hours drinking establishment in Wilmington, North Carolina, circa 1914.

Byron Bancroft Johnson (1864 – 1931) former professional ballplayer and sports journalist who founded the American League and ruled it authoritatively for fifteen years.

Dougal "Bubba" MacDongle (1890 – 1949) local pool shark, blacksmith, and third generation Wilmingtonian of Scottish descent.

John Phalen "Stuffy" McInnis (1890 – 1960) played first base in the famed "$100,000 infield" of Connie Mack's champion Philadelphia Athletics. McInnis gained his nickname as a youngster in the Boston suburban leagues, where his spectacular playing brought shouts of, "That's the stuff, kid."

Billy Morrisette (1984 – 1966) graduate of St. Joseph's College who engaged in legendary sandlot pitching duel with George Ruth of St. Mary's Industrial School who along with Ruth played for Jack Dunn's Baltimore Orioles.

Herb Pennock (1894 – 1948) left-handed pitcher and teammate of Babe Ruth who pitched for the Philadelphia Athletics, the Boston Red Sox, and New York Yankees. He was elected to the National Baseball Hall of Fame in 1948.

Colina Petronilla (1896 – 1954) New York native and contemporary of Babe Ruth who spent her summers in Baltimore and became a member of the Bunny Hole Gang. She was Babe's first, and most haunting love.

Rodger Pippen (1888 - 1959) young sportswriter covering the Baltimore Orioles during Babe Ruth's first spring training in 1914. In subsequent years, he was the sports editor for the *Baltimore News-Post.*

Gavrilo Princip (1894 – 1918) Serbian nationalist whose assassination of Archduke Franz Ferdinand in Sarajevo on June 18, 1914 sparked the outbreak of WWI.

Bill "Bojangles" Robinson (1878 – 1949) iconic Black dancer, actor, and vaudeville performer who, among other things, co-founded the New York Black Yankees and friend of Babe Ruth.

Jacob Ruppert (1867 – 1939) wealthy brewer, Congressman, and National Guard Colonel who purchased the New York Yankees in 1915 and turned the franchise into a dynasty.

Lewis Everett "Deac" Scott (1892 – 1960) shortstop and teammate of Babe Ruth with the Red Sox and Yankees.

Ernie Grady Shore (1891 – 1980) right-handed pitcher signed by Jack Dunn and traded with Babe Ruth to the Boston Red Sox in 1914. During the off-season, he taught math at Guilford College in North Carolina.

George Sowers (1883 – 1940) ne'er-do-well bartender hired to work at Ruth's Saloon.

Samuel Steinman (1869 – 1923) scout and coacher for the Baltimore Orioles who is generally credited with assigning the nickname "Babe" to George Herman Ruth, Jr.

List of Images*

*The poor quality of some of the images provided was unavoidable due to limited availability of early pictures of Babe Ruth and his environs.

Wopper

HOW BABE RUTH LOST HIS FATHER AND WON THE 1918 WORLD SERIES AGAINST THE CUBS

Volume 2

The Show

By Frank Amoroso

simply francis publishing company

North Carolina

OPENING

The bench was cracked, worn, and featured the carved initials of previous occupants of the bullpen. Light reddish-brown dirt filled the cracks with dusty intensity. The wood had started out smooth and perfectly planed. Over time, the elements wore at the surface and small fissures developed into full-scale cracks in the wood. When it rained some of the players would stand on the plank with their iron spikes to avoid the mud forming on the ground. Their weight and the water further chipped away at the surface smoothness.

Once a pitcher from Goldsboro named Travis actually got a splinter in his buttock when he slid across to make room for one of his buddies. It took a full season of ribbing for him to live down the mortification of having the Doc lower Travis' uniform pants and remove the offending sliver in plain sight of his teammates and the curious cranks.

The uniform pants of the players who inhabited the bullpen were stamped with a distinctive, soiled swath of North Carolina clay residue. To some it appeared like a terracotta track across the back of the thighs. Due to his unbridled enthusiasm for the game, Babe's pants were stained more than any other player – reddish-brown across the rear, grass-green on the hips from sliding for balls in the outfield, and frayed at the knees from his ferocious slides into bases.

The stains were permanently embedded in the thick flannels and the coaches viewed them as marks of distinction and hustle. As coach Steinman said, "No one ever made the Orioles in a clean uniform."

Ruth was a tall, rangy player who was bursting with vim and vigor whenever he was on the field. Manager Dunn liked Babe's jinegar. Actually, Babe's energy was boundless whenever he was awake. This afternoon he waited in the bullpen. He was the first pitcher to be used in relief and would pitch if the starting pitcher faltered.

He spent the first few innings carving the letters C-o-l-i-n-a into the bench. Before he completed embedding the name in the wood, it was the sixth inning and the opponent was threatening to score against the Orioles. In anticipation of the call to get ready, Babe fidgeted, eyes intent on the action on the field. He stood on the bullpen bench and narrated each play to his mates while he performed the stretching routine that Brother Matthias taught him. A signal from the dugout directed him to begin throwing.

Jimmy Deittrich, a catcher who hailed from Canton, Ohio, grabbed his catcher's mitt and warmed up Babe. A lump of chaw filled Jimmy's cheek and he spit a stream of slimy brown juice in front of the bullpen platter with every return throw. After just a few pitches, Babe was humming the ball to Jimmy at glove-popping velocity. When Babe was ready to go, he waved to Jimmy and watched the manager approach the pitcher's mound. It was time.

"Are you ready to give 'em hell?" said Jimmy in a fiery voice.

"Almost," replied Babe.

Looking incredulously at his reddening hand, Jimmy said, "Whattaya mean almost?"

"There's one more thing that I got to do. Here, pull my finger," said Babe, offering his left index finger to Jimmy. The boy hesitated. Then Babe nodded that he was serious and it was okay.

As soon as Jimmy tugged on Babe's finger, Babe unleashed a loud, smelly, fart of epic duration. The guys in the bullpen broke out into hysterical laughter. Jimmy was so shocked that he held his grip on Babe's finger. Once the gaseous crescendo concluded, Babe winked, pivoted toward the field, and said in a relieved voice, "Now, I'm ready!"

Jack Dunn stood at the mound staring uncomprehending at Babe, as he double-timed onto the field amid whoops and howls from the bullpen creatures.

Jack Dunn

Babe Ruth

February 1914
Baltimore, MD and Fayetteville, NC

> "Two roads diverged in a wood, and
> I took the one less traveled by,
> And that has made all the difference."
> ~ Robert Frost, *The Road Not Taken*

Groggy, he picked up his pillow for the umpteenth time. He rammed the edge of the pillow between his ear and elbow and creased the remainder over his other ear. His feet protruded from beneath the sheets, hanging over the edge of the bed. His plans, to the extent that he had thought them through, did not include going to Fayetteville to become a professional ballplayer. No, he had a vague, hazy idea that, even under the most generous definition of plan, this could not be termed a plan. Simply put, Jidgie figured that he would get a job in the Garment District in New York City and hang out with Colina. To him, it made perfect sense. Jack Dunn had just thrown a baseball-bat sized monkey wrench into his future.

Jidgie wondered whether Colina would want to go with him to Fayetteville, even though he was sure that she had no idea where Fayetteville was located. On the other hand, maybe he would be an abysmal failure and get cut by the Orioles. In that case, he could head north to the City. What did the Boss always say – No harm, no foul? No, no, he would not fail. He was the best player around, it was not even close. Jidgie knew that he was destined to succeed.

Brother Matthias seemed to want him to go with Mr. Dunn. The ease with which he dismissed the importance of the custody paper left Jidgie with an uneasy feeling. He thought that the paper meant that the Xaverians were his parents. Since his mother was gone, the brothers were in a legal sense his mother and father. Or, were they? What would his father say? Would he even care? OK, he reached a sleep-infused decision. He would go talk to Big George about it. With that procrastinating approach resolved, Jidgie lapsed into a deep sleep.

When the mail was delivered to the Ruth household the following morning, Big George's hopes were raised. He fingered an envelope bearing the bright, new logo of the Baltimore Terrapins. Earlier that month, he had written to the Terrapins' manager seeking a tryout for his son. Big George's heart raced. This must be a response from Gnarltz to his letter. Ruth was encouraged by the heft of the envelope. Maybe it included a contract. Tearing open the letter, the first thing he encountered was a flyer promoting the sale of season's tickets for the major league Terrapins. Tucked behind the flyer was an artist's rendering of the new ballpark Terrapin Park that was under construction along 29th Street, stretching through to 30th, east of Vineyard Lane and the 2900 block of Guilford Ave.

Hidden under the promotional material was another missive. Like rejection letters since the dawn of rejection letters, Gnarltz' response was succinct and definitive. Thank you for your inquiry. We regret to inform you that we have no need of your services. Since our objective is to build our fan base, we are only seeking candidates with major league experience and demonstrated accomplishments in professional baseball. The letter ended with the obligatory best of luck in your future endeavors. George hung his head in disappointment. He had convinced himself that his son would use baseball to lift himself out of Pigtown. The bartender had suffered too much disappointment in his life to hope that the closing of one door might lead to the opening of another.

The following day, Jidgie boarded the trolley on his way to visit his father. He arrived after lunch to take advantage of the saloon's slowest time. When George saw his son get off the trolley, he removed the Gnarltz letter from the counter. No need to share the bad news with the boy.

"Hey, Pop."

"Hi, Jidge, what are you doing here? Need money?" he said with not a small dose of sarcasm.

"Naw, I wanted to tell you about a meeting I had yesterday."

"Who'd you meet with?"

"Do you know who John Dunn is?"

"Do you mean Jack Dunn, the Orioles' magnate?"

"Yeah, that's him. Well, yesterday he offered me a job."

"As what, the team janitor?"

Jidgie paused, second-guessing his decision to come to see his father.

"Will you just stop it for once? I'm trying to get your advice and all you want to do is belittle me," said the son, his voice rising in spite of every effort to control it. He tried to remember one serious discussion that they had ever had. The only one he could recall happened when his father talked about the travails his mother had suffered during the course of their marriage. Jidgie learned things that he had never known about his parents. The friction caused by the multiple deaths of their infants savaged their marriage. Perhaps, the treatment of the boy and his rebellious reaction was a manifestation of the family sorrows.

"Son, you gotta live your own life. Whatever choice you make is the right one. Just realize that once you make it, there is no going back."

Back at St. Mary's, Matthias went about business as usual. He figured that it was the type of decision that Jidgie alone had to reach. For his part, Jidgie struggled with how to get to know Colina's feelings. He lacked the time and money to go to the City. He wished that there was a speedy, convenient way to discuss it with her. Neither had access to a telephone that would assure them the needed privacy. He concluded that the best way was to use the method that had sufficed through the ages. He would reveal his dilemma in a letter. This decision had the same, predictable results – it was slow, letters crossed in the mail and actual communication was thwarted.

Spring training was scheduled to begin in March. Jack Dunn told Brother Matthias that the team was leaving from the Keenan Hotel on March 2nd. The brother said that he would tell the boy, but, that the young man had yet not decided whether he would be on the train. Dunn was about to fly off the handle when Matthias told him give Jidgie time to reach the most important decision of his young life.

"Why don't you just tell him to get his ass on that train? You know he'll never have another opportunity like this."

"That may be what you think, but he's got to reach that conclusion on his own."

"Right. After Monday, if he's not on that train, no deal," said Dunn, his eyes nearly bugging out of his head. He left the brother's office muttering to himself and shaking his head.

Meanwhile, back at Ruth's Saloon, Jidgie stared out the window searching for the letter carrier. It was almost two weeks since he had sent a letter to Colina explaining his options and requesting her guidance.

Actually, he was desperate for her to tell him to come to New York to be with her. As fate would have it, on the day the letter was delivered, Colina's father had thrown the day's mail onto the kitchen table. Jidgie's letter was on top and had slid off the table and had fallen behind the radiator. No one noticed.

On the Sunday before the drop dead date, a frantic Jidgie went to St. Mary's to use the phone to call Rosina's Trattoria in a last-ditch effort to reach Colina. High winds and heavy snow battered the trolley over the entire four mile trip. The worst winter storm in his lifetime had already dumped almost a foot of snow. There was no sign of a let-up.

The wind nearly yanked the door out of Brother Mathias' hand when he let George in. The grounds were covered white. Snow had drifted along the outfield fences to cover all evidence that a ball field existed there. Matthias listened to George's plea and ushered him into his office. He dialed the phone number that George gave him and handed over the receiver. Jidgie pressed the device against his ear so hard that Matthias saw a white circle develop on the boy's skin. With a look of intense concentration, his lower lip lost under his upper teeth, Jidgie listened as the circuits crackled through the connections up the coast to the City. The next thing he heard was voice of an operator.

"I'm sorry, sir, we are experiencing a severe winter storm, lines are down in New Jersey. We are unable to complete the connection. Try back tomorrow."

The phone went dead.

"Tomorrow will be too late!" he screamed at the phone.

A bear with its leg caught in sharp teeth of a bear-trap could not have had wilder eyes than Jidgie. His conflicting emotions were tearing him apart.

"It's your fault. You can't just sign me over to Dunn like I'm a piece of meat. I should have another year before I have to decide," shouted Jidge, who bolted for the door. A stunned Matthias thought he heard George mutter under his breath something that sounded like '. . . just like my Pops.'

The retreating young man probably did not hear Brother Matthias say in Latin, "*Noli timere,* Don't be afraid. George, you'll make it."

Another night where sleep evaded him. He had lost count. All he knew was that his pillow felt like a stone, providing no comfort. Attempts to shift his position yielded no relief for the dull headache that had taken up residence in this skull. He knew that until he made his decision the headache and sleeplessness would persist. He thought, maybe the armchair in the living room might be comfortable enough to induce sleep. Naw, he had tried it a few hours ago and the smell of his father's tobacco and the ever-so-faint aroma of his mother's perfume that Mamie wore when she was feeling blue, robbed him of slumber. A clock ticked in the kitchen, he heard the wind slipping through the alley like a burglar escaping. The shutters creaked.

He roamed the apartment quietly, slowly. From the kitchen window he saw dim illumination. It came from the direction of the railyards. There were men working the night shift throughout the city – in the relentless darkness mechanics, bakers, brewers, and teamsters kept the metropolis machine repaired and prepared for the next day. Bored and anxious he decided to take a walk in the darkness. No destination, just something to do.

Wandering the streets aimlessly in concentric circles, he drifted toward the railyards. Subconsciously, he knew that the yards would facilitate his fate. Within the next day or so he would board a train – whether it would take him north to New York and Colina, or south to Fayetteville and Jack Dunn was the question.

Before long his meandering had taken him to Bailey's Wye. The wind buffeted him as he trudged toward the railroad roundhouse located there. He pulled his cap down tight and lifted his collar in a vain effort to stay warm. Steam, light, and noise emerged from the roundhouse. He could hear the shouts of men working at the turntable. Drawing closer he saw a crew attaching a large wedge-shaped plow to the front of a locomotive.

The foreman of the crew saw Jidgie eying the operation and approached him.

"We could use an extra hand to steady the plow while the mechanics attach it to the front of that there jack," he said gesturing toward the locomotive. The plow hovered before the engine like some gigantic, menacing parasite.

"Sure, I'll pitch in. What do I have to do?"

"Go over with Tom and the boys and help them with that block and tackle to raise or lower the plow when needed."

Jidgie welcomed the distraction of physical exertion.

Later when the operation was done, Jidgie learned that another jack would be attached to the first engine to form a doubleheader. For some reason, he found the use of the same term for two locomotives paired together and two baseball games played back-to-back on the same day comforting. Thus equipped, the train would make its way north through the snow-blocked tracks to New York. Jidgie wondered whether he would be on that train.

All through the night and next day he vacillated over which direction to travel. North to Colina? Or, south to the Orioles?

Twenty-four hours later, on March 2nd, George H. Ruth, Jr. arrived at the Keenan Hotel carrying a borrowed suitcase. Amid a tangle of wrinkled clothes, he had placed his most valued earthly possessions - a thin worn baseball mitt, his hymnal, and the Caruso postcard from Colina. The day following their cruise on the Staten Island Ferry, Colina had sent him a love letter promising her eternal devotion. Inside the envelope was a postcard of *Signore* Caruso that was marked on the back with a lipstick imprint of a perpetual kiss from his Colina. He craved a return to the warmth of her breath as she kissed him that night. It was not meant to be.

Like an automaton, Jidgie trudged through the snow to the train station. He was so overcome with frustration and anger that he barely heard the introductions to his new teammates. Uncharacteristically somber, he boarded the south-bound train without a trace of joviality.

1914 Spring Training
Fayetteville – Wilmington

"I hope he lives to hit one-hundred homers in a season.
I wish him all the luck in the world.
He has everybody else, including myself, hopelessly outclassed."
~ Frank "Home Run" Baker

As the train chugged south toward Fayetteville, North Carolina, reflections flickered across the windows of the passenger car. Accelerating, the train whizzed by factories, the rowhouses, then barns and then telegraph poles as it escaped from the city into farmland and wilderness. With an unfocused gaze, the young man registered the reflections as ghostly images passing before him. First, the face of Colina rushed past, then, Brother Matthias, then, his father, then Jack Dunn, then his mother, on and on, the faces flashed before him like the cards of a deck being shuffled. With each flicker, Jidgie's emotions twitched, rising and falling in rhythm with the staccato thrum of the train. He found the experience exhausting.

After what seemed like an eternity, the locomotive hissed to a stop in Fayetteville, North Carolina. It was a small town whose main distinctions were that it was named after Marquis de Lafayette, a hero of the American Revolution who visited there in 1825 and it was home to the Fayetteville Independent Light Infantry, the oldest militia unit in continuous existence in the U.S., having been established in 1793. Other than that, it was a dreary place made drearier by the gloomy weather.

Although warmer than the weather in Baltimore, the weather in North Carolina was windy, rainy, and raw, hardly conducive to practicing baseball. Jack Dunn and most of the veteran players were hampered by the snowstorm that blanketed the northeast and would not arrive for another week. For the next few days, the Orioles practiced inside at a local armory. The ballplayers occupied themselves playing catch, handball, and basketball. When team activities concluded, the weather trapped the team in the Lafayette Hotel, a bright yellow building. It was a brick and steel building, replete with modern amenities such as elevators, steam heat, glass porches, gas and electric lights, abundant fireplaces, and state-of-the-art bathroom facilities. Compared to the spartan conditions at St. Mary's, Jidgie was in the constant state of marvel at his new surroundings.

"Mind if I join you, Jidgie?" said the tall young man. He was dressed in grey sweatpants and sweat shirt that bore jagged salt lines from yesterday's workout.

"Sure. Have a seat, Billy," said the seated boy between bites of his breakfast. The neck and the armpits of his grey sweatshirt were dark with moisture.

Both young men were members of the Baltimore Orioles, a professional baseball team owned and managed by Jack Dunn. They were sitting in the hotel dining room. Billy was a right-handed pitcher and sometimes outfielder, who was in his second year with the team. Just like the other boy, Jack Dunn had signed him from the sandlots of Baltimore. Jidgie was a lanky, angular youth who had recently signed. For now, his friends called him Jidgie; however, that nickname would soon be replaced by one that would become one far more famous.

"How come your shirt is soaked? Have you been out working already?"

Not wanting to interrupt his chewing, the other just nodded.

"It's barely 6 A.M. Why are you out so early?"

Nudging the remainder of his meal onto his fork with his finger, Jidgie scooped the food to his mouth, chewed it and washed it down with a healthy swallow of coffee.

With a satisfied grin, he replied, "After practice yesterday, I bought me that bicycle over there." His grin widened as he cocked his head toward a mud-splattered bike that was leaning against the window of the hotel dining room. "I got up at first light and rode my bike all around Fayetteville. Some of those roads out in the country are still muddy from the rain we had the other day."

He beckoned to a passing waiter and gestured that he would like another order. Then, he raised two fingers and pointed toward his companion. The waiter acknowledged the request amiably.

"Did you just order two?"

"Yep, one for me and one for you, Billy."

"I promised him a ride on my bike if he took care of me," said Jidgie with a wink.

Within minutes, the waiter returned with two platters piled high with food. Billy stared at the plate set before him and looked at Jidgie in disbelief.

"Don't tell me that you've already eaten one of these?"

"Sure, why not? Mr. Dunn told me that I could order whatever I wanted and the club would pay for my feed bill," said Jidgie. Billy mused to himself that there was no way that Dunn anticipated this.

"I've never seen anything like this on the menu. What is it?" asked Billy with a hint of mild revulsion in his voice.

"Do you remember the other day when Coach Steinman was working with the pitchers on fielding?"

Billy nodded.

"Remember that drill where we had to cover first base on every ball hit to our left? And then we had that scrimmage and on the first ball grounded to the pitcher's left, Darby stood on the mound and watched the first baseman field the ball. He never moved to cover first. Do you remember what Steinman did?"

Billy shrugged quizzically.

"He stopped the scrimmage and yelled at the top of his lungs at Darby for failing to cover first. Aside from cursing him for being stupid and lazy, he called him a ham-and-egger. Well, that got me thinking about breakfast and I decided to create this dish. With the help of my waiter friend and the cook, we stacked a ham steak on a large flapjack covered it with another flapjack and topped it with three fried eggs. Now, that's a real ham-and-egger!" smiled Jidgie, tilting the plate proudly.

Across the dining room two men followed the hostess to a table.

"Sam, have you heard from Dunn and the veterans?" asked the younger man. Rodger Pippen was a reporter with the *Baltimore Sun* who was assigned to Orioles for spring training.

"They are still snowbound and probably won't arrive until Saturday," said Sam Steinman, one of the coaches for the team. The reporter nodded.

"So what's the plan until then?"

"Now that the skies are finally clear, we'll have some scrimmages between the veterans and the yannigans this afternoon. We may need help with numbers, but we'll figure something out."

"You know, Sam, I was a pretty fair ballplayer in my day. I could play the field if you need an extra body."

"Can you play the outfield?" asked Sam.

"Sure, just give me a uniform and I'll show those yannigans how to patrol the garden."

"Ok, you're in."

They were interrupted by their waitress who took their orders with a look of absolute boredom. She tucked her order pad into a pocket on her apron and sauntered slowly toward the kitchen. When she passed the table where the two ballplayers sat, her posture straightened and a friendly smile transformed her previously sour face.

"Can I get you boys some more coffee?" she asked. Billy and Jidgie responded enthusiastically, extending their mugs appreciatively.

"Hey, Patsy, why don't you come out to the ballfield this afternoon and watch us scrimmage?" asked Billy.

She touched his arm lightly and said sweetly, "I just might do that."

A few minutes later, she delivered breakfast to the coach and the reporter. Rodger eyed the grizzled coach who radiated gruff baseball acumen.

"You know, Sam, I know that a yannigan is a term for inexperienced, rookie players, But I don't know where it comes from. I heard from one old-timer that in the last century there was a first baseman named Con Yannigan who played with a cork leg. By all accounts he was a solid player. Nobody knows if he is connected with the term as it's used today."

Sam chewed pensively as if rummaging through his memory banks. After a long pause punctuated by draining his coffee cup, he smiled.

"When I was coming up, I remember competing against a fellow named Yannigan. He was from Connecticut. I don't think the term refers to him. No, there's a better explanation," he said.

"Connie Mack once told me that the term was coined by his catcher Mike Grady who Mack put in charge of the second team to scrimmage against the regulars. After one particularly severe drubbing Grady disparaged his team as a bunch of yannigans, applying a Celtic word used by his Irish mother for something that is easily beaten like an egg or a worn carpet. The name stuck. Now, we use it for any rookie or second rate player."

"What do you think of the yannigans in camp here?"

"Too early to tell," responded Sam between sips of coffee.

"That one over there," said Rodger nodding toward Jidgie, "He sure can mash the agate. He hit some drives in batting practice yesterday that still have not landed."

Sam chuckled as he stood to leave. He dropped a few dollars on the table and walked away. Over his shoulder, he remarked, "The magnate is high on that kid; I told the other players not to mess with the big rookie because he is one of Jack Dunn's babes. Jack knows superior talent when he sees it!"

As soon as the coach disappeared out the door, the reporter pulled out his notepad and wrote, "You heard it here first - the next great star for the Orioles is a southpaw named George "Babe" Ruth. This Babe hits the horsehide with such force and distance that the

Orioles have yet to find a ballpark that can contain him. Watch out for the Babe this season."

To relieve the boredom of a morning off, Ruth and the other rookies ventured into the city. When Jidgie and a couple of the young Orioles passed the Bubble & Squeak Food Emporium on Donaldson Street, he saw an intriguing placard taped to the front window:

The Bubble & Squeak is proud to serve the Thorpe Thunder Sundae in honor of the longest home run ever struck in Fayetteville by that indomitable athlete, Jim Thorpe. The ball travelled 115 yards.

The rookies entered and Jidgie asked to see the manager.

"I'm curious about the Thorpe Thunder Sundae. How was it created?"

The store manager, an amiable merchant named Hyman Fleishman, explained that, "A couple of years back, we had that Indian Olympian Jim Thorpe playing for the Fayetteville Highlanders and he mashed a ball so high and far that it brought down the thunder. We decided to name a sundae after such a prodigious blast. We had a contest to name it and the entry with the most votes was the Thorpe Thunder sundae. Would you boys care to try one?"

"I believe I will, sir," said Jidgie to the astonishment of his teammates who had just seen him polish off two orders of his ham-and-egger special.

When the sundae arrived, Jidgie asked Mr. Fleishman, "What happens if someone hits a ball farther than that Thorpe fella?"

The store manager gave him a look that combined pity, surprise, and condescension.

"Oh, that will never happen. No one is stronger than Jim Thorpe. He won gold medals in the Olympics in the decathlon and pentathlon. Now, he is a garden tender for the New York Giants. That blast will never be topped."

"Wanna bet?" said Ruth.

Mr. Fleishman did a double take.

"You think that you can out-distance Jim Thorpe, son?"

"Most definitely."

"I'll take that wager, son. If you hit a ball farther than Thorpe, I'll gladly name a sundae after you."

Except for Billy Morrisette, the boys poked each other in the ribs in disbelief at Jidgie's arrogance. The young pitcher from St. Joseph's College in Baltimore had been personally victimized by the power of Jidgie in the famous showdown against St. Mary's the previous fall. The others would have to see for themselves. No one could anticipate that they were about to witness history that would still be talked about more than a century later.

The Orioles practiced at the Cape Fear Fair Grounds. The baseball diamond was situated inside the horse track. That afternoon there was an intra-squad game – the Buzzards versus the Sparrows. Ruth started at shortstop for the Buzzards and batted fifth.

With the game tied at one after the first inning, the Buzzards broke the game open. The big blow came off the bat of George Ruth. With one mighty swing, Ruth turned on a fastball and launched it high and far over the right fielder Bill Morrisette's head. As soon as the ball left the bat, the umpire heard Morrisette unleash a string of expletives while shouting, "Not again." The ball travelled so far that it exited the field of play, landing in a neighboring cornfield. Many years later, some putative eye-witnesses attested that Babe's blast landed beyond the cornfield, splashing in Mallet's Mill Pond. Jidgie waltzed around the bases and was in the dugout before Morrisette had reached the ball.

The game halted while sportswriter Rodger Pippen measured the distance from home plate to where the drive had landed in the muddy field. He blinked at the tape measure, trying to process what he was seeing.

"Four hundred and five feet . . . why that's sixty feet farther than Jim Thorpe's drive," Pippen shouted in disbelief. In his written report of the historic clout by the Babe, Pippen was effusive in his praise for the youngster from Baltimore, noting that he can play every position and can hit from either side of the plate.

In the dugout, Jidgie, rubbing his tummy, walked over to the batboy.

"Hey, kid, you are Mr. Fleishman's boy aren't you?"

"Yes, sir, my name is Maurice."

"Well, Maurice, you can tell your Daddy that Mr. Ruth just destroyed Jim Thorpe's record for the longest ball ever hit in Fayetteville," bellowed Jidgie. "Tell him that he can call my new sundae the Hokie Pokie."

He laughed so hard that tears came to his eyes. The rest of the Buzzards joined in the hilarity.

"Oh, yeah. Tell your Dad that I want the sundae made of strawberry ice cream, covered with crumbled Berger cookies. Got that? Crumbled Berger cookies."

Much later in his career, Ruth described this feat, 'I hit it as I hit all the others, by taking a good gander at the pitch as it came up to the plate, twisting my body into a backswing, and then hitting it as hard as I could swing.' [i]

The pace of spring training picked up once Dunn and the veterans arrived. Soon, the drudgery of repetitive practice drills gave way to actual games against major league teams. After a few exhibition games, the Orioles were scheduled to play the Philadelphia Phillies. Coach Steinman informed Babe that he would be the first relief pitcher if needed. Babe trudged down to the bullpen with a mounting sense of excitement at the prospect of facing major league hitters. He caught his shallow breathing and admonished himself to breathe deeply and not get too revved up. After all, it could be another hour or more before he would get his chance. As Brother Matthias had schooled him, it was important to relax and treat every situation as if it was an ordinary occurrence. A slight whistle escaped his lips as he exhaled slowly. He looked for something to distract him until his turn came. His eyes alighted on the perfect object.

The bench was cracked, worn, and featured the carved initials of previous occupants of the bullpen. Light reddish-brown dirt filled the cracks with dusty intensity. The wood had started out smooth and perfectly planed. Over time, the elements wore at the surface and small fissures developed into full-scale cracks in the wood. When it rained some of the players would stand on the plank with their iron spikes to avoid the mud forming on the ground. Their weight and the water further chipped away at the surface smoothness.

Once a pitcher from Goldsboro named Travis actually got a splinter in his buttock when he slid across to make room for one of his buddies. It took a full season of ribbing for him to live down the mortification of having the Doc lower Travis' uniform pants and remove the offending sliver in plain sight of his teammates and some curious cranks.

The uniform pants of the players who inhabited the bullpen were stamped with a distinctive, soiled swath of North Carolina clay residue. To some it appeared like a terracotta track across the back of the thighs. Due to his unbridled enthusiasm for the game, Babe's pants were stained more than any other player – reddish-brown across the rear, grass-green on the hips from sliding for balls in the outfield and frayed at the knees from his ferocious slides into bases. The stains were permanently embedded in the thick flannels and the coaches viewed them as marks of distinction and hustle. As coach Steinman said, "No one ever made the Orioles in a clean uniform."

Ruth was a tall, rangy player who was bursting with vim and vigor whenever he was on the field. Manager Dunn liked Babe's jinegar. Actually, Babe's energy was boundless whenever he was awake. This afternoon he waited in the bullpen. He spent the first few innings carving the letters C-o-l-i-n-a into the bench. By the time he completed embedding the name in the wood, it was the sixth inning and the opponent was threatening to score against the Orioles. In anticipation of the call to get ready, Babe fidgeted, eyes intent on the action on the field.

He stood on the bullpen bench and narrated each play to his mates while he performed the stretching routine that Brother Matthias taught him. A signal from the dugout directed him to begin throwing. Jimmy Deittrich, a catcher who hailed from Canton, Ohio, grabbed his catcher's mitt and warmed up Babe.

A lump of chaw filled Jimmy's cheek and he spit a stream of slimy brown juice in front of the bullpen platter with every return throw. After just a few pitches, Babe was humming the ball to Jimmy at glove-popping velocity. When Babe was ready to go, he waved to Jimmy and watched the manager approach the pitcher's mound. It was time.

"Are you ready to give 'em hell?" said Jimmy in a fiery voice.

"Almost," replied Ruth.

Looking incredulously at his reddening hand, Jimmy said, "Whattaya mean almost?"

"There's one more thing that I got to do. Here, pull my finger," said Babe, offering his left index finger to Jimmy. The boy hesitated. Then, Jidgie nodded that he was serious and it was okay.

As soon as Jimmy tugged on Babe's finger, Babe unleashed a loud, smelly fart of epic duration. The guys in the bullpen broke out into hysterical laughter. Jimmy was so shocked that he held his grip on Babe's finger. Once the gaseous crescendo concluded, Babe winked, pivoted toward the field, and said in a relieved voice, "Now, I'm ready!"

Jack Dunn stood at the mound staring uncomprehending at Babe, as he double-timed onto the field amid whoops and howls from the bullpen creatures.

He snuffed out the threat and became the pitcher of record when the Orioles won the game in the bottom of the ninth inning by a score of 4 – 3. When the Orioles gathered on the field to congratulate themselves on the victory, the jubilant pitcher made his way down the gauntlet of teammates shaking hands. As Babe approached Jimmy Deittrich, the pitcher held out his index finger. The catcher cringed and waved sheepishly. Babe and the bullpen creatures guffawed.

One week after the sundae blast, as the players called it, the Orioles were at full strength and aboard a train to Wilmington, North Carolina to face their stiffest challenge of the spring, and perhaps, the season. Dunn had arranged for his team to play the defending World Champion Philadelphia Athletics who had won three of the previous four World Series. Managed by Connie Mack, their veteran manager and owner, the A's had steamrolled over the New York Giants (four games to one) the previous fall to win the 1913 World Championship. They defeated the legendary Giants' pitcher, Christy Matthewson in the clincher, 3 – 1.

Heading into the 1914 campaign, the A's were heavy favorites to repeat as champions. Led by the "One Hundred Thousand Dollar Infield" comprised of second baseman Eddie "Cocky" Collins, third baseman Frank "Home Run" Baker, shortstop Jack Barry and first baseman Stuffy McInnis, the team was a powerhouse. Although the game was only a preseason exhibition game, it was notable for the presence of seven future Hall of Famers were on the field that day: Frank "Home Run" Baker, Chief Bender, Eddie Collins, Connie Mack, Herb Pennock, Eddie Plank, and Babe Ruth.

In addition to the normal antagonism that might be expected in a game between the World Champions and the underdog minor league challengers, the air was rife with tension caused by two extraneous factors. The drumbeats of an impending war in Europe reverberated through the ranks of young ballplayers preparing for the baseball season, knowing that soon their country might need them to go to war. Restive segments of the population resented the fact that many of their sons had been called to serve in the military while major leaguers continued their careers without interruption. The Secretary of War vowed to study the issue and exempt from service only those working in essential industries.

Next, the emergence of the rival Federal League caused havoc for existing teams that watched as players were paid exorbitant sums to defect to the new league. The renegade Federal League directly challenged the supremacy of the American and National Leagues. Uncertainty and a fatalistic 'who's the next to leave' permeated major league clubhouses. The Orioles were in a particularly precarious competitive position because the Federal League Terrapins had lured an impressive roster of accomplished major league players to compete in the Baltimore market with Dunn's minor league roster. Although Dunn had assembled a talented team with a combination of former major leaguers and superior young players, the Terps would trounce his Orioles at the box office. As one beat writer phrased it, during the 1914 season, the Orioles could not draw flies.

The Athletics had just completed training in Jacksonville, Florida and were traveling north, playing along the way home to stay sharp. They were unbeaten over the previous two weeks and were primed to defend their title.

The cleanup hitter for the powerful A's was the big leagues' reigning home run king, Frank "Home Run" Baker. He had earned the nickname for his heroics in the 1911 World Series when he blasted a go-ahead homer in game two and a dramatic ninth inning game-tying home run off Christy Matthewson in game three. In an era where the home run was a rarity, Frank Baker led the American League four straight years starting in 1911 with eleven dingers, 1912 with ten, 1913 with twelve, and 1914 with nine homers. Little did

Baker know that on that memorable day in Wilmington, he would be batting against the man who would obliterate his home run records.

In contrast to newspaper hype about the luminaries on the A's, stories about the Orioles focused on second baseman, Neal Ball, a thirty-three-year old, whose main claim to fame was that he was the first major leaguer to record an unassisted triple play. The unbeatable feat occurred while he was playing for the Cleveland Indians. With two men on and a full count on the batter, the opposing manger signaled a hit and run. The runners broke on the pitch. Second baseman Ball caught a screaming liner, stepped on second base for the second out and then tagged the runner from first. It happened so fast that Cy Young, who was pitching for the Indians, asked Ball where he was going as he headed for the dugout. The laconic Ball replied, " 'That's three outs.' " [ii]

On the morning of the game, the Orioles took the Palmetto Limited to Wilmington from their training base in Fayetteville. Ruth was an unknown rookie who had signed his first professional contract one month earlier, just days after his nineteenth birthday. His first start as a pitcher on a professional baseball team would be memorable.

The Athletics started pitcher "Boardwalk" Brown, a lean, righthander whose colorful nickname came from his days playing on the sandlots of Atlantic City. He was in his third year with the Athletics having played on the American League pennant winners in

1911 and 1913. Before the crowd had settled into their seats, Brown was in trouble. Baltimore's leadoff batter reached first on an errant throw by shortstop Barry and scampered to second on the wild throw. With two outs, centerfielder Birdie Cree, a former Yankee, broke the ice by singling in the first run of the contest. When the Birds threatened to blow the game open by loading the bases, Collins called time and ran in to encourage his pitcher. His advice worked and Boardwalk escaped the jam with only one run scored.

The first time through the A's batting order, Ruth protected his one-run lead by pitching deftly with zippers, curves, and fades. Then, in the third inning, his inexperience surfaced.

Collins opened the third with a frozen rope bingle. The ball was hit so hard that he had to hold at first. As if awakened from a stupor, the crowd came alive and gave Frank "Home Run" Baker a huge ovation in anticipation. The catcher for the Orioles was the thirty-year old team captain, Ben Egan. He called for the ball as it was returned to the infield. With crooked fingers, he massaged the ball as he ambled to the mound.

"How ya doing, boy?"

"I'm fine. That little sonofagun got lucky."

Egan spit a stream of tobacco juice onto the ground and mused, this kid is either the most fearless pitcher I have ever caught, or, the most ignorant. He thought of asking Babe whether he knew that the little sonofagun on first was, in the words of the venerable John

McGraw, "the best ballplayer I have seen during my career on the diamond.'"iii

"Alright, let's get this next guy and keep our lead. He likes the ball down and in, so we will work him away with that darter. Once we get ahead in the count I want you to throw a waste pitch. Remember if we get him 0–2, throw a waste pitch."

Ruth nodded.

The first two pitches were perfect strikes that Baker took. Egan pumped an encouraging fist at Babe, then, settled into his crouch. The pitcher set, checked the runner, then, hurled the ball. Egan's eyes opened wide, his mind screamed "No!" With a sinking feeling, he watched a batting practice fastball approach. He could almost hear Baker's brain exult as it recognized a pitch that he would crush. Baker loaded his swing and uncoiled perfectly, lashing his bat at the incoming ball. A loud crack erupted as the sweet spot of the bat connected with the ball, sending it skyward toward center field. The baserunner Collins knew that no one would catch that drive and was at full speed in two steps. With determination guided by experience, he rounded the bases heading for home with the tying run.

For his part, Baker paused to admire his handiwork before galloping out of the box. A perfect throw by Beal, the cutoff man, nailed Baker at second.

When Babe returned to the mound from his backup position behind the plate, Egan walked next to him.

"What the hell was that?" he demanded.

Babe gave him a quizzical look.

"I told you that if we got ahead two strikes and no balls to throw a waste pitch."

"I did exactly what you said. I threw the sonofagun a pitch right at his waist like you called," said Babe.

Egan stared to make sure that the youngster was serious. He was. Too bad he did not know the difference between waste and waist. To his mind, throwing a pitch down the middle, waist high was what Egan wanted and that's what he got. The catcher made a note to make sure that the next time he called for a waste pitch, to make sure that the pitcher could spell.

With the score tied in the fifth inning, Connie Mack replaced Boardwalk with lefty Herb Pennock. The Orioles treated him roughly. They poured on four runs in the next inning to take a 6 – 2 lead. The teenage Ruth kept the Athletics at bay with guts and guile. In the words of A's star Eddie Collins, "Ruth is a sure comer. He has the speed and a sharp curve, and believe me, he is steady in the pinches. "[iv]

In the bottom of the ninth, the Athletics tried to rally against the rookie left hander. Baker got it started when he drove the ball against the top of the right field fence that was destined to be a double. However, he got only a single because as he was rounding first, he "stumped his toe" and returned to first. The crowd stirred in anticipation of a dramatic comeback against the tiring rookie. Their hopes were deflated in the next instant. With a deft pickoff move, Ruth caught Baker napping off first base for a rally-killing out.

After the final out, Dunn bounded out of the dugout to congratulate his protegée. The manager pointed toward the big rookie and shouted, "How about that for a mere babe!"

The Orioles picked up the refrain and started chanting, "Babe, Babe, Babe!"

Then, Babe was mobbed by his teammates who understood the magnitude of his accomplishment much more than he did.

Afterwards the boys went to local Wilmington saloons to sample the robust beer culture of the area's German immigrants. With a simple nod, Dunn appointed Ben Egan as unofficial chaperone of the newly-Christened Babe. Although Babe's naïve antics in Fayetteville had amused his teammates, they would soon learn that he knew how to handle himself in a saloon.

Like much of North Carolina, Wilmington had a love-hate relationship with alcoholic beverages. In 1909 the state of North Carolina had enacted statewide prohibition. This was ten years before the prohibition of alcohol would become the law of the land nationwide. North Carolina's attempt to curtail the production and consumption of alcoholic beverages came into direct conflict with the state's tradition of distilling moonshine.

Since the Whiskey Tax of 1791, the brainchild of Treasury Secretary Alexander Hamilton, the German and Scotch-Irish immigrants who settled North Carolina exercised what they considered was their God-given right to brew their individual formulation of White Lightning without sharing their proceeds with the government. They considered taxation on alcohol to be a gross infringement on their freedom. Battles between the tax revenue collectors, known disdainfully as revenuers, who attempted to track down moonshiners and prevent them from delivering their illegal hootch was the stuff of legends. Indeed, those epic motor vehicle chases would spawn the preeminent stock-car racing organization known today as NASCAR.

In any event, Wilmington was no stranger to alcohol and the sale of beer and liquor was an open secret. As one historian observed, speakeasies and "blind tigers," that sold illegal liquor, sprang up "like mushrooms in the rain.'" So when the Orioles went out to celebrate their victory, there was no shortage of watering holes. They ended up at an establishment known as the Blind Tiger. The proprietor was a stout German immigrant named Dieter who recognized a celebration when the Orioles entered. After ascertaining that the team was celebrating the victory over the World Champions, he ordered the bartender to serve a round of beers on the house. That gesture brought cheers and assured that the boys would stay for the duration.

Babe had started the evening intending to call Colina at Rosina's, but was quickly sidetracked by free beers purchased by his appreciative teammates. No stranger to the rhythms of a waterfront saloon, Jidgie picked up a pool cue and hit a few balls. Seeing that the lefthander had a deft touch, one of the locals, a fellow named Bubba MacDongle, challenged Babe to game of eight-ball. There were no stakes, just a friendly game.

A third generation Wilmingtonian of Scottish descent, Bubba ran the local blacksmith shop. His pool cue looked like a twig in his massive hands. Due to his mop of red hair and a full beard, his complexion appeared ruddier than working before a furnace might suggest. He fancied himself an expert at billiards owing to a string of victories going back almost a year.

The game started with good-natured banter. To show how magnanimous he was, Bubba allowed Babe to break. That was his first mistake. On the break, the striped three-ball rolled into the right corner pocket. Babe methodically cleared the table of striped balls with a variety of banks and combination shots, until the only ball left for him to sink was the eight-ball. The shade of red of Bubba's face and neck increased with each shot. Sensing an inevitable explosion, Ben Egan positioned himself near Bubba in case it became necessary to protect his pitcher. Ben thought he smelled smoking wood coming from Bubba's pool cue as he twisted it tighter and tighter with each made shot.

Babe stood back to assess his shot. He would have to call the correct pocket and sink the eight-ball to win the game. But first he had to navigate around all the solid balls on the table. The bar was quiet as all the patrons watched the match. Bubba's fuming created such tension that one onlooker told the cops later that he heard that there was one thousand dollars at stake.

Over his shoulder, Babe asked Dieter in German for a boilermaker to celebrate after he won the match. Bubba snapped at the language. As Babe turned toward the table, Bubba sprang.

"You lousy, mother- f_ _king Kraut!"

He whipped the handle of his cue at Babe's head with murderous ferocity. For an instant, Babe froze, then, he ducked. If he had not had a crewcut, the pool cue would have mowed his hair down. Fortunately, it passed over his head without making contact. The blacksmith charged Babe. Before Egan could tackle the blacksmith from behind, Babe was on his feet hurling the cue ball. It struck Bubba right between the eyes and he went down in a heap just like a modern-day Goliath.

Babe gulped down the boilermaker as Egan and the other Orioles ushered him out of the Blind Tiger before Bubba regained consciousness.

March 1914

Hollowleg Club, Wilmington, North Carolina

"He reverently believed that while bread was the staff of life, whiskey was life itself. That it was the chief end of man to raise enough corn to make whiskey, and convert the remainder into bread."

~ M. L. White, describing Uncle Amos Owens

1914 would be a year for the ages. While Jidgie and the other young ballplayers sweated, grunted, and competed on the baseball diamonds of North Carolina for roster spots, power-blinded men were devising battle-plans which, when set in motion, would disrupt the fragile equilibrium in Asia Minor and Central Europe and the world. Suffering from systemic injustice, misplaced priorities and intellectual atrophy, several centuries-old autocratic monarchies were on the verge of collapse. While the drumbeat of war was growing more intense, rational thought faded. Within the next decade the Emperor of the Austria-Hungary Empire, the Kaiser of Germany, the Sultan of the Ottoman Empire, and the Tzar of Russia and their dynasties would all be deposited into the dustbin of history. None of this mattered to the young Orioles, nor, to a young girl in love.

Colina was heartsick when her mother found Jidgie's letter that was sent prior to his decision to accept Jack Dunn's offer to sign with the Orioles and board the train to Fayetteville. The envelope was slightly yellowed and covered with dust and the remnants of a spider web. When Colina saw the postmark on the letter, she was blinded by rage. How could such an important letter gather dust under a radiator for weeks? After hurling venom at her mother, Colina retreated to her room to read the message. She cried over Jidgie's expressions of love and indecision; she was on the verge of hyperventilation. Her emotions ricocheted from elation to despair to resolve.

She knew that he had to go – it was his chance to escape the specter of doom that enveloped his life with the Ruth family. She knew that; yet, it did not make accepting his absence and the changes he might undergo while chasing his dream any easier. Still, she was young and did not understand that not all surprises are for the best. She would soon find out.

Her cousin had been sending her news accounts from the local Baltimore papers about the exploits of one George "Babe" Ruth. From his titanic blasts to his endearing 'discovery' of mechanical elevators, her beau was fast becoming a folk hero. Colina gasped when she read about his near decapitation when he stuck his head from the elevator car to hail his teammates while operating the hotel elevator. Only the frantic shouting to watch out saved him from disaster.

Colina immediately posted an apologetic letter to her Jidgie. When it arrived, he was overwhelmed by emotion. His spirits soared, resembling the trajectory of his mammoth blasts on the ballfield. He responded to the sudden flood of Colina's letters with equal speed. Soon the pair was corresponding on an almost daily basis. As the weeks passed the stream of Jidgie's letters lessened, she attributed it to the increasing demands of the team as they travelled to play a greater number of exhibition games later in spring training. Nevertheless, his missives were funny, interesting, and consistent in their devotion to their future together. His cursive hand was so beautiful, she treasured each letter.

A newspaper clipping announcing that the Orioles would be playing the World Champion Athletics in Wilmington, North Carolina in the latter part of March sparked a plan in her mind. She had been there once as a child to visit relatives. Recalling a youthful train ride, she checked the schedule. Sure enough, she could travel from New York City to Wilmington and arrive on the day of the game.

Alighting from the train at the Atlantic Coast Line Railroad Terminal she walked along North Front Street to the Orton Hotel. One of her cousins was a maid there and had told Colina that she could flop in her room at a nearby boarding house. Colina dropped her overnight bag with the bellman even though she had to use some of her scarce funds to tip him. She couldn't wait to see

Jidgie. When she asked where she could find the Oriole players, one of the young bellhops told her that he had seen them enter the Hollowleg Club down the street past the alleyway. She wore a fashionable mint green dress that was Jidgie's favorite. He always remarked about how the dress brought out her beautiful green eyes. Colina straightened her hat in a lobby mirror, pinched her cheeks to bring up some color and ventured out into the night.

A slight breeze blew in from the Cape Fear River. The air was redolent with the smell of brackish water mingled with animal odor from the nearby holding pens for the livestock that would soon be loaded on vessels headed for metropolitan ports up north. The chef at Rosina's Trattoria always insisted on pork from North Carolina. He used it as a substitute for wild boar to make his signature recipe from Tuscany, *Pappardelle al Ragù di Cinghiale*, Fresh Pasta with Wild Boar Ragù. Colina realized that, although she had not eaten for hours, she was not hungry - her stomach was too filled with butterflies in anticipation of reuniting with her Jidgie. She glanced at the garnet ring on her finger and smiled at its power to reconnect separated lovers. Sometimes myths are valid she mused. Sometimes not.

Walking carefully on the uneven sidewalks, Colina slowed as she neared the Club. Was it a place for a respectable girl? Suddenly, her confidence wavered – had she made a dreadful mistake? What if he was not even there? Would he resent her intrusion on his new life? What would she say? A voice in her head told her that she had come this far and it was too late to turn back. Then, realizing that she was in a seaport in the south, she recalled the admonition of the Union Admiral David Farragut, 'Damn the torpedoes full speed ahead!' She resolved to follow that advice. Unfortunately, she was not as successful as Farragut.

An hour earlier, Ben Egan and Neal Ball who were the senior members of the Orioles, both in age and experience, had decided that the rookie phenom had earned a night to remember. After all, not only had he defeated the World Champion Athletics, he had thoroughly dominated the local tough at pool and in the ensuing fight. Both veterans agreed that a special reward was warranted, but were uncertain of exactly what might be appropriate.

"What'll be, gentlemen?" asked the bartender of the Hollowleg Club. He was a sandy-haired rake with a handlebar mustache that rode atop a Cheshire Cat-like grin. No one knew his full name; he called himself Skeet.

"What do you recommend? We are celebrating a great victory tonight," said Ball.

"You are in luck. We just received a shipment of Cherry Bounce today. It comes with the special label of Uncle Amos Owens himself. He's a legendary moonshiner from Rutherford County"

"What is Cherry Bounce?" asked Egan.

"It's a heavenly mash of moonshine, black-heart cherries, and a touch of sourwood honey to make it go down real smooth," purred Skeet, producing a bottle from beneath the bar with so much pomp that he might well have been presenting a Fabergé egg.

After tasting the blend for themselves, the veterans called their teammates together and shared the elixir with a toast to Babe. The jug quickly emptied. Skeet replaced it amicably. Nodding toward the person of honor, Skeet whispered in Egan's ear, "Do you really want to give the boy a night to remember?"

"Absholutely," slurred Egan.

"Bring the boy out to the alley and I'll have Bridgette take care of him so that he will come back in here as a man," said Skeet wickedly. He tilted his head toward an attractive blonde who was stationed on Birdie Cree's lap while he leered into her slightly-open blouse. Egan slipped some currency over the bar and Skeet nodded to the voluptuous Bridgette. To the hoots of his teammates, she kissed Cree on the top of the head and sidled over to Skeet. Bridgette eyed the sturdy youngster while Skeet whispered in her ear. She nodded and slipped out the back.

Meanwhile, Egan took Babe by the elbow and steered him outside to a bench in the alley courtyard that was used for overflow patrons during the warm, summer weather. Egan instructed Babe to close his eyes and wait for a surprise. Wobbling slightly, the boy complied. Egan returned to the speakeasy sporting a huge grin and signaling a thumbs-up to the guys.

Colina traversed the sidewalk in front of the Hollowleg Club several times trying to muster the courage to enter. Primal noises from within and outside the club weakened her resolve. It all changed when she heard a familiar voice.

"Come on, Toots, one more time, come on," he implored with an animal urgency.

"I told ya . . . ."

Bridgette stopped, sensing a presence. The woman turned toward Colina who gasped in shock and horror at the sight of her Jidgie partially disrobed and his dark, tanned hands holding the white cheeks of the woman's bottom. His face was pressed against her chest. He was unaware of the interruption until he heard a voice that he recognized. Through the fog of his alcohol-addled brain, he heard Colina scream.

"Jidgie, my God, Jidgie, what the devil are you doing!?"

The following morning, on the Palmetto Limited during the return trip to Fayetteville, the Orioles' manager gave Babe the news that every young player craved.

"Congratulations, Babe, you have earned yourself a spot on the Orioles," said Jack Dunn. "You will be on the opening day roster. And . . . we are going to double your original salary. You'll be making $1200 for the season!"

He paused in happy anticipation to enjoy the youngster's reaction. Dunn's face turned into a mass of confusion at Babe's wooden response. Dunn felt that the youngster almost would have preferred to learn that he had been cut. Indeed, Ruth fantasized about turning the clock back to where he could simply be a tailor hanging out with Colina. He was learning the hard way that life does not work that way.

Jidgie's pounding head was nothing compared to his depressed emotions over losing Colina. After the shock and shame of the courtyard encounter, Babe had unsuccessfully pursued Colina back to the Orton. She had disappeared into the recesses of the building like one of the ghosts that haunted Wilmington.

For her part, Colina spent the night crying in her cousin's room. Babe returned to the Hollowleg and drank himself into oblivion. He awoke dreaming of Oinky, his childhood pet, which was fitting because he was in the holding pens with the hogs destined for slaughter up north.

When he returned to the Orton to prepare for the trip back to the training camp, no amount of scrubbing could remove the filth he felt. To make matters worse, his cranium ached more than it did when he was clocked by Mick Flanagan at the plate at Old Bethpage. He was bruised, confused, and ashamed. Babe was totally confounded. He had no idea how Colina had appeared in the alley. He wondered whether or not it was just a manifestation of his Catholic guilt over his licentious behavior. No, it was real – her blazing eyes and heart-piercing tone of voice were emblazoned in his brain. The pervading shame over the way he had crushed Colina's love would remain with him for a long, long time.

No one was happier than Babe when the Orioles broke spring training camp and returned to Baltimore in early April. He was heartsick, homesick, and heedless toward more exhibition games. He spent his waking hours and a good measure of his sleeping hours tormented by Colina's absence and berating himself for his behavior. Despite his concerted efforts to communicate with her, he was spectacularly unsuccessful. All of his letters were returned, marked "Addressee Unknown. Return to Sender."

His phone calls to Rosina's Trattoria seeking Colina were answered with derision or ignorance of any such person. Even his friend Dante was cool and unhelpful when Babe spoke to him. Babe studied the Orioles schedule to see when they would travel to the metropolitan area to play the Newark Indians and the Jersey City Skeeters. Maybe he would be able to sneak into the City and try to find Colina. He knew that it was a long shot, but the possibility buoyed his laggard spirits.

Meanwhile, Jack Dunn spent much of his spare time closeted with coach Sam Steinman strategizing about how to counter the growing enthusiasm for the Baltimore Terrapins of the outlaw Federal League. Dunn fumed over the Terps' audacity to build a new stadium called Terrapin Park almost directly across the street from his Oriole Park. It seemed like on a daily basis the Baltimore newspapers reported some new signing of a major league player, or, extolled the virtues of the sightlines of the wooden grandstands at the Terp, as one wag dubbed it. The Terps had wisely scheduled their opening games a full week before the Orioles opened. Already there were reports that the city of Baltimore was so excited about the return of major league baseball after more than a decade that the first series had been sold out for weeks in advance. Dunn correctly sensed that any residual enthusiasm for his club would be minimal.

However, all this paled to the real possibility that his players would jump to the upstarts. Rumor had it that the Terps were offering outrageous sums to his Orioles. Dunn did his best to disguise his concern over the existential threat to his franchise. The economic reality of his plight would force him to take drastic measures by mid-season.

1914 Baltimore Orioles – Babe Ruth on far right

1914
Baltimore, MD and Sarajevo, Bosnia

"I turned it down because we were told by organized baseball that if we jumped we would be barred for life. But nobody was barred for life and I just got jobbed out of $20,000 without a thank-you from anybody."
~ Babe Ruth

He had experienced many firsts in Fayetteville during that spring training. His first paycheck, his first elevator ride, his first professional home run, and first victory over a World Champion team were all treasures. It was the first time that he was able to tame the hunger in his belly. He relished all of the firsts except one. Although he was unable to articulate it accurately, it was another first that would have the greatest impact. His first broken heart, the loss of Colina, would haunt him and cause him to seek solace in every bed he could find.

There was another impact from his broken heart. His relationship with his father intensified. Without Colina in his life, Babe shared his triumphs and disappointments with his father. Big

George made plans for Babe to live with him when spring training concluded and the Orioles returned for the season. The elder Ruth had left the saloon business and was trying another, more stable occupation. He hoped that his new endeavor would provide a more conventional lifestyle for his son.

For his part, Big George reveled in his son's accomplishments and new-found fame. George started a scrapbook in which he dutifully clipped and pasted the stream of articles about the lefty phenom from Baltimore. The father anxiously awaited his son's return and did everything he could think of to make this return better than any of the previous disastrous returns home. He also did something that threatened to destroy the progress of Babe's career.

"Wait right here, sir," instructed Gladys Withers, the secretary to Ned Hanlon the president of the Federal League Terrapins. She eyed the visitor's workingman's apparel with disdain and wrinkled her nose at the faint smell of stale beer that wafted across the reception area of the offices at Terrapin Park. The odor clashed with the smell of freshly sawn pine that permeated the new building. As secretary to "Foxy Ned," she was used to attending to potential investors, a decidedly more refined clientele than the hoi polloi that were descending on the office now that the team had returned from spring training.

With Opening Day barely a few days away, Baltimore was infected with Terrapin fever. In order to process the deluge of ticket requests for Opening Day, all the office personnel except for Gladys had been conscripted to assist the box office. The cranks were so obsessed with the Terps that over thirty thousand tickets for Opening Day had already been sold. Gladys grumbled to herself as she entered the temporary office of the short, stocky manager of the newly-formed ball club.

Gladys grimaced when she saw Oscar Gnarltz, smoking a cigar with his feet comfortably propped on Mr. Hanlon's custom mahogany desk. He was on the phone recruiting star pitcher of the Philadelphia Athletics, Chief Bender.

"Listen, Chief, we are selling tickets like hotcakes. I know that you are stuck with your current contract but, next year we want you to play for us. We will definitely have a big enough stash to satisfy your needs. OK, buddy, you have a great season and we'll be together next season. Listen, while I have you on the phone, do you know of a kid southpaw on the Orioles named Root, or Ruth?"

Gladys stood at attention before Gnarltz, waiting for his call to conclude. He nodded his head and scribbled some notes on a pad. Finally, he said, "That's quite an endorsement, Chief. I appreciate it. When someone with your eye for talent says that this kid is special, then I have to sit up and take notice. Thanks, gotta go."

"Your eleven o'clock appointment is here, Mr. Gnarltz."

"Bring him in, but come back in ten minutes. I gotta be on the field for practice by noon," said the manager.

George Ruth stood before him, eyes lowered. With strong, large hands, he clutched a large cloth-covered book.

"I won't take much of your time, Mr. Gnarltz. I wrote to you over the winter about my son George Ruth from St. Mary's Industrial. You wrote back saying that you wanted only established major leaguers for the Terps. I respect that . . . "

"What has changed?" said Gnarltz, feigning impatience.

"Well, sir, my boy has beaten the Athletics and the Phillies in spring training," said George who stepped forward and handed the scrapbook to the manager.

Gnarltz perused the crude book and read the articles with quotes from respected big leaguers about the kid's pitching prowess.

"Listen, I gotta get out on the field. Where can I get in touch with you? I'd like to see your son in person," said Gnarltz, rising to signal the end of the meeting.

"I run a harness business on Columbia Avenue. My son will be home this weekend. Maybe you can see him then?"

"OK, I'll be in touch," said Gnarltz, ushering George with him out the door.

The following Wednesday, George Herman "Babe" Ruth made his first appearance on the mound in a regular season game. His chest swelled with pride from wearing the uniform of his hometown Orioles sporting a capital B within a large diamond on the left sleeve. Unfortunately, attendance was abysmal. Although years later many more would claim to have witnessed the Babe's debut, only two hundred paid customers pushed the turnstiles to see the Orioles take on the Buffalo Bisons. The newspapers were no help. The reporters were excited to have the major league Terrapins in Baltimore after a ten-year hiatus of big league baseball. They denigrated Dunn's Orioles as a poor substitute for the real thing that was right across the street in Terrapin Park.

None of that bothered Babe. He was having the time of his life. He was getting paid, quite handsomely he thought, to play the game he loved. When he was on the field competing, nothing else mattered. It was like living inside a protective bubble where he was safe from outside dangers, just like the snow globes from the old country that his Grandpa Pius used to describe – safe and perfect. Off the field, he would hang with Gunny or go to St. Mary's and play with one of the school's many teams. Anything to avoid the void left by Colina's absence from his life.

His debut at Oriole Park came early in the season. Standing tall on the mound, Babe scanned the crowd for his two biggest supporters. He nodded to Brother Matthias and his father who had settled in behind the Orioles dugout. A twinge of sadness swept over him when he thought that Colina should be here. The umpire shouted, "Play," and pointed at him. The next few hours were a blur. When it was over, his teammates pounded him on the back for pitching a complete game shutout for a 6 – 0 victory. He had even stroked his first safety, a single in his first plate appearance.

Two days later, after observing Babe in a secret early morning workout, Gnarltz offered the senior Ruth twenty thousand dollars if his son would join the Terps for the 1914 season. When his father relayed Gnarltz's offer, Babe was overwhelmed. For a kid from Pigtown, twenty thousand dollars was an incomprehensible sum of money. Big George berated his son for hesitating even for a moment.

"But, Pop, Mr. Dunn told us that Commissioner Johnson had declared that any player who jumps to the Federal League will be banned from major league baseball for life. What if the Federal League collapses and goes out of business? Where will I be then?"

"They're running scared, boy. The Federals have filed a lawsuit and they are going to win. The Terps drew 30,000 cranks to their opener. The Orioles could not even draw one tenth of that. You just pitched to what, a couple of hundred cranks? Imagine what it would be like to pitch before thirty thousand. Son, the handwriting's on the wall. You gotta go with the hot hand. The Terps own Baltimore. Sorry, but that's the way it is."

"I just can't do it, Pop. I gave Mr. Dunn my word. I like the Orioles. Tell Mr. Gnarltz that I'm going to stay with the Orioles. The money is tempting, but I gave my word. Brother Matthias taught me that a man's word is his bond. Anyway, Mr. Dunn has the guardian paper. Mr. Dunn has promised to take care of me and I know that he will."

"Someday soon you will learn not to trust people – they will always disappoint you," said Big George, grimacing at the mention of Matthias.

The Orioles got off to a good start to the 1914 season. Dunn had put together the best team in the International League. It was a balance of veterans with major league experience and young, hungry players. The Orioles raced into first place. Sadly for Dunn, so did the Terps. To make matters worse, the media, politicians and fans flocked to support the Terrapins. The Terps were outdrawing the Orioles by a factor of more than one hundred. This, of course, led to the kind of financial stress that caused Dunn to lose sleep at night. He feared that his best players would be lured away by promises of higher salaries. He was most worried about his Babe. To keep the young man in the fold, Dunn doubled his salary in the first month, and in June tripled it to an annual salary of $1800.

When the Orioles were home, Babe lived with his father and took the Greenmount-York Road streetcar line to the ballpark. When the team visited the International League teams in New Jersey they stayed at the Forrest Hotel, near Broadway a few blocks above Times Square. In a vain attempt to find Colina, he frequented Rosina's Trattoria and spent his spare time scouring the City. The futility of his search was as complete as it was puzzling. It was as if Colina had entered a secret society of ghosts that protected her whereabouts no matter what. On several occasions, he was closer than he could have imagined. Yet, when she observed him from behind a two-way mirror or a rooftop, she only felt revulsion due to the image of betrayal from that night in Wilmington. Her broken heart had not healed and she shunned him.

On the ball field, the Orioles and Babe were making it look easy. Jack Dunn had stacked his team by paying former major leaguers handsomely. The investment in players did not produce results at the turnstiles. Despite a comfortable lead in the International League, the Orioles were a flop at the gate.

In those days, major league baseball was governed by a three-person National Commission. It was headed by Ban Johnson the dictatorial president of the American League who was joined by John K. Tener, the president of the National League and Garry Herrmann, the magnate of the Cincinnati Reds. The Commission rejected Dunn's plea for assistance in combatting the Terps. This refusal left Dunn embittered and desperate. Unless there were a dramatic reversal of the relative fortunes of his team soon, Dunn would be forced to sell off his most attractive assets. He was already in constant contact with Connie Mack of the Philadelphia Athletics and owner Joe Lannin of the Boston Red Sox. The owner/manager of the Orioles entertained offers for his pitchers, especially the young southpaw from Baltimore.

Somewhere in the foothills outside Belgrade, the capitol city of Serbia, a young man prepared for his role in world-shattering events. He and Babe were both nineteen years old. He and Babe were both survivors in families where multiple infants died in infancy. As youths, he and Babe had antagonistic relationships with their fathers. He and Babe impacted the world in ways that could never have been foretold or imagined.

Toward the end of May, Gavrilo Princip and two companions left Belgrade by river steamer on an arduous sojourn to Sarajevo for a rendezvous with other Black Hand zealots. They carried four FN Model 1910 Browning semi-automatic pistols and six hand grenades supplied by the Serbian Army officers who trained them in terrorist tactics. The gravity of their mission was underscored by a parting gift of cyanide capsules to be consumed in the event of capture.

En route, one of the group was indiscreet regarding their mission and was summarily abandoned. Gavrilo and his remaining companion proceeded to Sarajevo, using a secret network of trails and safe houses. The objective of the group was the assassination of the presumptive heir to the throne of the Dual Monarchy of Austria-Hungary. The Serbs feared and hated the Austrians. Six years earlier, in 1908, Austria Hungary had unilaterally annexed Bosnia-Herzegovina. The Serbs chafed under this act which clashed with their dream of uniting the region under Serbian control. A series of events, fortuitous for the assassins, placed the Archduke within their sights.

Sunday, June 28th was St. Vitus Day, a patriotic Serbian holiday commemorating the assassination of a foreign invader by a Serbian knight during the Battle of Kosovo in 1389. It was the ideal day to attempt to assassinate the future Emperor of Austria-Hungary. Oblivious to the intensity of the danger, the regional governor persuaded Franz and Sophie to ride in an open car through Sarajevo. Eight assassins lined the parade route.

As the Archduke's motorcade wended its way through the city, a young terrorist hurled a grenade at the Archduke. Out of his peripheral vision, Franz Ferdinand saw the grenade and batted it away. It bounced under the automobile following and exploded injuring several people. The Archduke's car sped to the Town Hall in an effort to escape.

"What is the good of your speeches? I come to Sarajevo on a visit, and I get bombs thrown at me. It is outrageous!' "xvi roared an agitated Archduke at the Mayor of Sarajevo when they arrived at the Town Hall. After conferring with members of his party, the Archduke decided to abandon the remainder of his planned itinerary. Instead, they would make a quick stop at the hospital to visit those who had been injured in the grenade attack.

The plan was to proceed on the main road directly to the hospital. Franz Ferdinand and Sophie again boarded the open, third car of the motorcade. The revised itinerary was never communicated to the chauffeur of the Archduke's car because the officer responsible for the motorcade was in the hospital as a result of the earlier grenade blast. This critical failure of communication became deadly when the motorcade mistakenly turned off a wide avenue onto the narrower street. An official in the lead car shrieked at the driver to stop and return to the main road. When the driver of the lead car tried to reverse his course, he was blocked by the other cars in the convoy that were following closely behind him. The car transporting the Archduke and his wife was struck between the halted vehicles while it waited for the cars behind it to back out onto the main drag.

At that precise moment, Gavrilo Princip emerged from Schiller's delicatessen only to find his prey directly in front of him. He seized the opportunity, drawing his Browning. He tightened the grip safety and calmly squeezed the trigger twice. One bullet struck Archduchess Sophie in the abdomen, severing her vena cava. The other bullet struck the Archduke in the throat, piercing his jugular. Both Franz and Sophie died before they could get to a hospital. The assailant turned the pistol on himself in an effort to end his own life but was immediately wrestled to the ground and disarmed. He was arrested for treason and murder.

Over the next month there was frantic diplomatic activity and an ultimatum to Serbia followed by cascading mobilizations of European armies. By August, Europe was aflame in a war that would have twenty million casualties.

Back in the United States, Babe was facing his own crisis.

"I'm sorry, boys, but the cranks have abandoned us. As you probably heard, attendance is way down. The Terps are stealing our cranks and drawing big crowds while we play before a couple of dozen people," said Jack Dunn.

He was sitting in his office. His hat was tipped back on his forehead. His salt and pepper hair was noticeably more salt than it had been when Babe first met him last winter. He wore an unbuttoned Orioles jersey. His undershirt beneath was dark with sweat. As he spoke, the chaw in his cheek moved erratically as if inhabited by a live critter. In between sentences, he expectorated a stream of black juice into a spittoon. Off in the corner of the small office, Billy Wicks, the Orioles' traveling secretary, stood grim-faced with his arms crossed over his chest.

Standing in front of the manager's desk were catcher Ben Egan, Ernie Shore, and Babe Ruth. They were sweaty and dirty from the game they had just completed. In the last two days, Dunn had traded their centerfielder, shortstop, and leftfielder. The three men surmised the reason for the meeting was to advise them that they had been traded – the only question was to which team. Egan had been traded before so he was relieved by the prospect of being traded; he did not want to be stuck on a sinking ship. Shore had just graduated from college and considered being traded as another part of the adventure before his actual career. Ruth was as green as they came, being totally unfamiliar with the business side of the game. He considered the Orioles simply a replacement of his friends at St. Mary's Industrial School. Babe shifted uncomfortably, the scraping of his spikes made an irritating shriek on the concrete floor.

"I did the best I could for you boys. I'm sending you to Boston in the AL. Congratulations, as of Saturday you will be major leaguers. Billy, here, has your train tickets for the evening train for Boston after tomorrow's game."

Wicks smiled and patted his chest pocket where the tickets rested.

"Billy here will take you through the paperwork. Then, tomorrow, he will accompany you on the trip and help you get to Fenway Park where you will meet your new teammates. Best of luck, I'm sorry," said Dunn, who rose to shake their hands.

Egan and Shore shook hands with the manager, muttering "Thanks, Skip," or a similar sentiment. Babe hung back, waiting for the room to clear. Wicks closed the door behind them as he left.

"I don't understand, Mr. Dunn. There must be a mistake. Baltimore is my home. I've always lived here. I can't leave," said the big pitcher who wore a crestfallen expression.

"I'm sorry, son. Sometimes we have to make sacrifices," said Dunn.

"But, what about the paper? I'm too young to be traded to Boston," said a distraught Babe.

"The brothers gave me full authority to act in your best interests. Trust me. This is for the best. You're going to the Show. Don't be downcast. You'll do great. By this time next year, you will own Boston," said Dunn, ushering a dazed Babe out of his office. Dunn leaned back against the door and rubbed his eyes. That kid is going to be great and I'm going to miss it all, he thought wistfully.

Word of the trade was carried in the morning papers. The sports editor for the Baltimore Sun mourned the sale of Ruth. He wrote, "He is a wonder and his performances have been followed by fans all over the country. During the past four months, his shoots have made the whole baseball world sit up and pay attention.' [xvii]

The following morning, he no sooner settled into his office to figure out how he would field a competitive team, when there was an insistent knock on his door. He listened quietly, hoping that the visitor might give up.

"Come on, I know that you're in there. I saw you enter. Open up!" said an irate voice.

Dunn vaguely recognized the voice, but it was deeper and less playful than that of his young pitcher. Time to face the music. He opened the door.

"What are you trying to pull, Dunn?" demanded George Ruth, Sr.

"What do you mean?" said Dunn, retreating behind his desk.

"My son; you can't trade my son. He's all I've got."

"Mr. Ruth, you've been to our home games. You have seen the empty seats. You have heard the roar from the huge crowds across the street at Terrapin Park. The Orioles are losing money faster than Holiday, the winner of this year's Preakness Stakes can gallop," said Dunn.

"Don't hand me that malarkey. The paper says you can't trade him. You are the guardian and you have to keep him," growled George.

"Actually, it says right here," said Dunn, pointing to the verbiage on an official-looking document.

"That John Joseph Dunn, that's me, 'shall have full and complete discretion to act in the best interests of George H. Ruth, Jr. Any action taken by the aforementioned Mr. Dunn shall be final and not subject to challenge.' So, you see, you have no say in this. As of midnight tonight, Babe is under contract with the Boston Red Sox."

"Why you conniving son-of-a-bitch," roared George, Sr. as he hurtled over the desk and began throttling Dunn. Fortunately, coach Steinman was on his way to visit the manager to go over the day's assignments. He grabbed Ruth from behind, but, not before he had landed several blows to Dunn's face. Ruth shrugged Steinman off his back and walked out of the office, cursing a blue streak.

Later, Dunn greeted reporters with an ice pack on his left eye. After explaining his clumsy fall down the stairs, Dunn provided details of the trade and explained how the Orioles were destined to win the International League title.

1914 Baltimore Orioles in Fayetteville – Babe Ruth, back row center, wearing cap

June 1914
Baltimore, MD and Boston, MA

*"I do not feel that I am a piece of property to be bought
and sold irrespective of my wishes."*
~ Curt Flood

When Babe entered the waiting room at Baltimore's Pennsylvania train station, he was in a foul mood. His Orioles had lost the last two games since the trade was announced and now he was boarding a sleeper for the overnight trip to Boston. His last meal with his Dad had been joyless and perfunctory. George senior kept his right hand wrapped in ice. Although they barely talked about the altercation in Dunn's office, Babe was surprised at the odd pride that he felt because his father had stood up for him. Now that Babe was near the end of his teenage years, he finally had the support that he had always wanted.

In the time since Dunn told him of the sale to the Red Sox, he had visited St. Mary's and said his goodbyes. The inmates were thrilled that he was going to the big leagues. While Babe concealed the ache in his heart from his fellow students, he could not hide it from the Boss. Brother Matthias encouraged him to consider the event a promotion and to try his best to succeed in the major leagues. He reminded him that he was capable of playing with the best players on the planet. The big mentor cautioned him to steer clear of the many temptations that he would encounter.

In a less than convincing manner, Babe assured him that his only interest was baseball. Earlier that day, Orioles' shortstop, Claud Derrick, had regaled Babe about the elegant brothels that reserved the most attractive female talent for Red Sox players. A slip of paper with the names and addresses of the best madams in Boston seemed ready to combust in his pocket as he sat with Brother Matthias.

Babe had experienced so much in the four months since his original signing in February. He reflected on the good and the bad, but always came back to the devastating loss of Colina. Maybe, just maybe, his new status would help him find her and they could reconcile. As with many young lovers separated by time and distance, Babe developed an idealized version of Colina in his mind. She was beautiful, alluring, and most of all, always agreeable. The longer the estrangement, the more perfect the idealized version became. He vowed that, along with succeeding on the field, reconnecting with Colina would be his mission.

The three ballplayers and their chaperone boarded the Federal Express for an overnight train ride to Boston. After an uneventful dinner and a spirited game of bridge dominated by the erratic and unpredictable play of the young rookie, the group retired to their berths in the sleeper car. Babe and Ernie were paired with Babe taking the top bunk.

The berths were built to accommodate normal-sized people. By any measure, the ballplayers were abnormal-sized. Babe was almost six-foot-three and Ernie Shore was six-foot-four. Babe did not mind the short berth because of his preference to have his feet protrude from his bed. On the other hand, Shore was miserably uncomfortable in the standard berth. He moaned and tossed and turned all night. Shore's nocturnal noises haunted Babe's sleep. He dreamed that he was in a foggy alley following a female form that had to be Colina. Whenever he overtook the figure, she turned and Babe beheld the distorted face of his berth-mate. That was enough to drive anyone into a state of turmoil.

When the train finally pulled into Back Bay Station in Boston, the ballplayers debarked into a cloud of steam released by the engine. Billy Wicks led them across Dartmouth Street to Landers Coffee Shop. Through the hazy condensation of the front window, Babe spied a female figure wearing a mint green uniform. She was a thin brunette. From his vantage point looking through the steamed glass she looked like his lost love. Babe thought that it was strange that Colina would be working in Boston. Maybe that was why he couldn't locate her in New York City.

With a surge of excitement, he pushed into the shop just in time to see her slip through swinging doors into the kitchen.

"May I help you?" asked the hostess. She gathered four menus in the crook of her elbow.

"Booth or counter, gentlemen?"

Staring at the porthole of the wooden door to the kitchen, Babe was dumbfounded.

"Excuse my young friend," said Egan to the rescue. "I think he's been on the overnighter too long. We'll take a booth."

She led them to a booth and distributed the menus, advising that their waitress would be right with them. Babe's attention was on the kitchen door. A slender figure reminiscent of Colina emerged. Her face was obscured by the large tray that she was carrying. Babe craned his neck to see around the tray. He started to rise but realized that Egan had crammed him into the booth toward the window. A comedic bumping and wedging routine ensued until Egan pinned Babe in place with an elbow.

"What's gotten into you? Sit still! You're acting like a toddler," hissed the big catcher.

Babe ceased squirming because the waitress was getting ready to approach their table. When she pivoted toward them, Babe's disappointment was palpable as he studied her face. She was pretty with dark, yet delicate features. The name Helen was embroidered on her uniform. She could have passed for Colina's twin, but, her eyes were smaller, softer and her cheeks were plumper. All doubt was removed when she opened her mouth and spoke with a decidedly Boston accent. As Babe withdrew into a silent shell, Egan shook his head. The rookie had so much to learn.

After breakfast, the group decided that traveling secretary Wicks would register them at the Brunswick Hotel and the players would go directly to Fenway Park to get sized for uniforms and prepare for that afternoon's game. Egan tried unsuccessfully to lift the gloom from Babe's expression. The catcher had never seen the usually exuberant pitcher so morose. Perhaps a stint on the mound would cure whatever girl trouble was bugging him. Five hours after arriving in Boston, Ruth made his major-league debut pitching against the Cleveland Indians on July 11, 1914.

Behind drifting clouds, the sun burned hot on the solitary figure on the mound at Fenway Park. Babe did not remember warming up in the bullpen. He was in a fog when his new manager and catcher came to the mound in the top of the first inning of his major league debut. Nicknamed "Rough," Bill Carrigan was an Irish Catholic ballplayer who was known for his toughness around the plate. Square-jawed with rugged features, Carrigan could have been a model for a Marine recruitment poster. Blessed with a powerful lower body, low center of gravity, and strong hands, he starred in college as a football halfback. As a catcher on the baseball field, he never backed away from contact or a scrap. As one respectful opponent, Jimmy Callahan the manager of the Chicago White Sox, said, "You might as well try to move a stone wall."

With a steely glare, Rough pounded the ball into Babe's glove and growled, "Let's get these bastards, kid!"

The role of concentration needed to pitch at the highest level is often underestimated. Babe's ability to focus intensely was one of his greatest attributes. In the first inning of his major league debut his mind was distracted by the vision of Colina's virtual double. It would not take very long for Babe's concentration to be tested.

Leading off for the Cleveland Naps was the Canadian-born outfielder, Jack Graney. Known as a patient hitter who worked the count, Graney waited for Babe to make a mistake. After falling behind to the lefty batter, Ruth grooved the next pitch. Graney slapped the ball into leftfield for a single.

After inducing the second batter to ground out, Babe faced the fearsome Shoeless Joe Jackson with Graney at second base. The sight of Jackson at the plate eradicated any remaining cobwebs from Babe's consciousness. The lanky man from South Carolina had a reputation as the greatest natural born hitter to ever play the game. Babe would later say that he admired Shoeless Joe's sweet swing so much that he tried to emulate it. On that afternoon, Jackson's sweet swing would connect with one of Babe's slants so hard that the ball nearly knocked his cap off as it whizzed by for a base hit.

Boston's All-Star centerfielder, Tris Speaker, was off at the crack of the bat and charged the sinking liner. As Graney approached third base, he wisely decided to stop rather than be gunned down at the plate by one of Speaker's rocket throws. Jackson rounded first running full tilt and watching Speaker's throw. Babe alertly cut off the throw and winged it to second in an effort to nail Jackson. A surprised Jackson put on the brakes and scrambled back to first to avoid the throw from second. At that instant, Graney took off for home. The throw from the first baseman reached Carrigan before the runner. Carrigan blocked the plate and applied a bruising tag on Graney.

Carrigan walked the ball out to his pitcher. He handed him the ball and patted him on the rump as if to say way to go, rook. His work was not done. The clean-up hitter for the Naps was Napoleon Lajoie, one the greatest hitters of all time. To build tension on the rookie pitcher, Lajoie took his time digging his spikes into the right-handed batter's box. Ruth did some tending of his own around the pitching slab and hatched a plan of his own. He ignored Jackson as he stretched his lead off first base. Babe deliberately threw wide for a ball, making sure that it was high enough for Carrigan to execute a good throw to second if Jackson bolted. The trap had been set.

Jackson touched his cap, indicating to Lajoie that he would attempt to steal while Lajoie hit behind him to the area that the second baseman would vacate in order to catch the peg from the catcher. Babe did not lift his right leg when he delivered the pitch; instead he took a slide step and rifled a throw to first. His move caused Jackson to hesitate for a fraction of a second, which was the margin between the ball and the glove arriving on his hand and his hand reaching the base. The base umpire, Silk O'Loughlin, emphatically called, "You're Out!" as Shoeless Joe sprawled in the dirt. The flamboyant ump then made his signature gesture. With the enthusiasm of Karl Muck, the conductor of the Boston Symphony Orchestra, O'Loughlin pumped his hand bearing a large, multifaceted diamond ring and gloated, "Ha! I flashed Shoeless Joe some crushed ice with that call."

Babe had survived his inaugural first inning by demonstrating resourcefulness and moxie. Carrigan noted the talent of the nineteen-year old and his fearlessness under pressure. Whatever distractions had plagued Babe before the game disappeared in the heat of competition. The young man used speed and guile to thwart the Indians into the seventh inning. Nursing a 3 – 1 lead, Babe finally weakened. He yielded three straight singles allowing the Naps down to break through with two runs in the seventh inning to tie the game at 3.

In the bottom of the inning, manager Carrigan pinch hit for Babe. This move helped to produce the go-ahead run, as pinch hitter Duffy Lewis reached base safely and came around to score. Relief pitcher Dutch Leonard kept the Naps off the board and Boston held the lead to earn Babe the win in his first major league game by a score of 4 - 3. After the game, Babe celebrated with the blue plate special at Landers and then proceeded to the Brunswick Hotel where he collapsed onto the bed fully clothed and slept for twelve hours straight.

As the Scottish poet sagely observed, "The best laid plans of mice and men/ go oft awry.' ”[viii] Perhaps Jack Dunn had tried to live up to his obligation as Babe's guardian. Perhaps Ben Egan was included in the transaction between the Orioles and the Red Sox to act as Babe's surrogate guardian. Perhaps the thirty-year-old Egan would have been the perfect person to keep Babe on the straight and narrow. Whatever Egan's role was to be with respect to Ruth, it never materialized. As a catcher, he was superfluous to the Red Sox who had ample talent to handle the tools of ignorance. Within two weeks, Ben Egan was traded to the Cleveland team, leaving Babe to his own devices.

The Red Sox of 1914 were a veteran bunch. Most of the players were in their late twenties or early thirties and had little time or inclination to mentor a boisterous, unsophisticated rube like the nineteen-year old Ruth. Ernie Shore was the closest in age to Babe and he was four years older. At that point in his life, Shore was a college graduate who had taught math for several years. He was more cerebral than Ruth who was impulsive and instinctive. Later in life, the reserved Shore would remember Ruth bragging that he did not graduate from St. Mary's he was acquitted. Without adult supervision, Babe followed his most basic appetites for better or for worse.

Babe was lonely and homesick. His father and Brother Matthias were far away in Baltimore. His girlfriend had all but vanished. The Bunnies and his St. Mary's teammates were becoming a distant memory. It was great to have money, youth and freedom, but, without someone to share it all with, it just did not seem worth it. Then, a light came into his life.

He was an early riser. Every morning he left the hotel and meandered through the streets toward the Charles River to watch the water traffic. On the day after his first victory, he attended early morning mass at St. Joseph's Catholic Church. From there he went to Landers' Coffee Shop for breakfast. He tried to convince himself that it was for the food, but he acknowledged there was an ulterior motive to his culinary choice. Babe made sure that he was seated at one of the tables assigned to Helen, the cute waitress who had served them on their first morning in Boston. He had finished his third omelette when he was interrupted.

"Can I get you some more coffee?"

"Sure . . . It's Helen, right?" he said peeking at her name tag.

"Yeah, I'm Helen," she giggled. "And you are one of those Sawx. What name do you have sewn on your uniform?"

"You know, that's an excellent idea. We should have our names on the uniforms, so the cranks can tell who is who."

"So, what would your uniform say?" she said, pouring the coffee.

"Babe."

"Really? That's your name? Naw, it can't be. Tell me true. What's your name?"

"The players on the field call me Babe. My friends call me Jidgie."

"What should I call you?"

"You can call me Hon," said Babe, reaching his arm around her waist.

"And why would I do that?" she replied, without wriggling away like he expected.

"Because I want you to come out with me," said Babe.

"Where do you want go?" asked Helen.

"We could find a duckpin alley."

"What's that?" said Helen wrinkling her nose.

"It's a game where you roll a ball down a lane and knock down wooden tumblers shaped like ducks. You score points by knocking them down."

Helen tossed her head back and laughed loudly. A confused look covered Babe's face.

"Silly, we call that candlepin here in Boston," said Helen.

"Well, it's called duckpin in Baltimore where I'm from."

"I'm game," she said a little too quickly.

"OK, when do you get off?"

"I get off at 3," said Helen. "I'll meet you here. We can walk to Pinhead Alley."

"OK, three it is," said Babe smiling broadly.

He spent the intervening hours watching sculls rowing on the Charles River. Before he knew it the time arrived and he was walking along with Helen to the bowling alley. As they wended through rows of brick tenements, the neighborhood reminded him of home. He was surprised at how easy it was to converse with Helen. Perhaps it was because she was close to him in age. She was only sixteen. Perhaps it was because she was a student and he had been one so recently. Most likely, it was the physical attraction between young people that leads to infatuation. The physical resemblance to Colina was remarkable, but her manner was softer, less New York edge, more puritan reserve. He reminded himself to call her Helen.

Babe followed her into a low brick building and was immediately assaulted by a cacophony of wood smashing into wood as balls struck pins. The dark interior was a welcome relief from the summer sun. He soaked in the atmosphere. His Pops could easily be the proprietor of a joint like this. Babe paid to use a lane and rent shoes. In the dim light, Helen's brown eyes glimmered with excitement. She led the way to an empty lane when all of a sudden, she was whisked into the arms of a dark-haired young man who wore a bowling uniform shirt. He whirled her in the air. Babe's initial reaction was to protect Helen. He lurched forward. When she twirled around he saw that her face was filled with delight. His heart sunk.

"Come here, Babe, I want you to meet my older brother William."

Babe shuffled over, slightly embarrassed for his quick offense.

"So, it's Babe, is it?" said Will, giving an exaggerated wink to his mates. "Will Woodford." They shook hands.

"Will you look at that! His hand is like the paw of a baboon," said Will, lifting Babe's hand for his teammates to see. Babe yanked his hand back and walked to the ball rack. Will mimicked a simian gait behind an unsuspecting Babe. Howls and catcalls filled the alley. Babe heard someone hurl the word *pavian* in his direction. He bristled at the German word for baboon. Fuming, he tried to maintain his composure. There were at least eight of them. He repeated Egan's mantra, "You are a professional ballplayer now. You have to let insults slide off your back. Take it out on the ball."

He and Helen settled in to the lane adjoining Will's team which was engaged in a spirited match. Both teams were imbibing copious quantities of beer. The decibel level of the contestants had increased with each frame.

Candlepin bowling was invented in Worcester, Massachusetts towards the end of the previous century. The game derived its name from the way the oblong pins resemble candles with a slight convex taper in the middle of the pin. The pins are arrayed in a triangular formation at the end of a long alley. Points are scored when the bowler knocks down the pins by rolling a spherical ball toward them.

Babe bounced two balls in his hands, assessing their balance and density. They were made of the densest wood and were about the size of a grapefruit. These bowling balls had no finger holes. He preferred a red and blue striped ball. A good omen, he thought, team colors. He watched Helen take a practice shot and admired her form.

He followed with his practice shot, using a powerful, fluid motion. Bending low with full extension, he unleashed the rock with all his might. When the ball reached the pins, an explosion akin to a thunderclap filled the alley. The only thing missing was the smell of ozone that follows a lightning strike.

The owner rushed from behind the bar to see whether his alley was still standing. As a dazed pinboy emerged from his perch above the pins, the sound reverberated through the structure. His ears were still ringing. The pinboy dropped several splintered pins before the owner and mouthed the words, "I quit."

1914 Babe Ruth wearing Red Sox uniform

Providence, RI and Baltimore, MD

"Marriage is a wonderful institution,
But, who would want to live in an institution?"
~ H. L. Mencken

The 1914 Boston Red Sox were as bigoted, nasty, and contentious group of individuals as Carrigan had ever met. Their clubhouse was a toxic cauldron of prejudice – the Protestants despised the Catholics, the Northerners harassed the Southerners, and the nativists hated anyone who could not trace their lineage to the *Mayflower.* The animosity flowed equally in all directions. If there was a person who could forge this motley crew into a cohesive team, it was Rough Carrigan.

Born of Irish Catholic stock in an unforgiving section of Maine, he knew the value of hard work. His family scratched out a living on the family farm. His father worked as a deputy sheriff to supplement the family income. The youngest of three children, Carrigan realized early on that athletics was his ticket out of subsistence farming. He earned a scholarship to Holy Cross College and starred in baseball and football.

Although he was not blessed with great size, he got the most out of his five-foot nine, one hundred seventy five pound body. It was his sharp mind and astuteness in judging a man's character that made him an effective leader. Carrigan would need every ounce of savvy, guile, and resoluteness to command this group. As he confided to his coaches, his main job was to keep the twelve players who hated him away from the twelve who were not sure.

Carrigan understood all too well how fast things could change in the major leagues. He liked to use the phrase in a major league minute to describe the rate of uncertainty and change in the big leagues. Rough had seen many a talented player wash out when they could not adjust to the speed of the game at the highest level. He had been a mainstay behind the plate when the Red Sox won the World Series in 1912. Then, in a major league minute, the team was in disarray.

It got so bad in 1913 that they fell into the second division, scuffling and listless in fifth place. That was when the team president, Jimmy McAleer, fired the manager and persuaded Rough to assume command. Carrigan saw first-hand the vagaries of the game when McAleer sold his interest in the Red Sox to Joe Lannin, a Canadian real estate magnate, in 1914. Rough could sense that the magnate was not in it for the long haul, so, Carrigan and his wife Beula wisely planned for life after baseball. Right now, he was determined to win the 1914 pennant.

The new owner was an aggressive opportunist who was bent on assembling a powerhouse team in Boston. Lannin was shrewd enough to understand that baseball favors youth. In this regard, he was helped by his silent partner, Harry Frazee. He was a good judge of talent (probably more so with respect to baseball talent than theatrical). Frazee had been so impressed with the young pitcher's performance in the game in Old Bethpage, that he convinced the team owner to obtain Babe. In addition, Lannin was astute enough to take advantage of the disruption caused by the Federal League. Lannin preyed on Dunn's financial fears and convinced him to sell Babe and Ernie Shore, another young pitcher who together with Ruth might just help Boston win the pennant.

As catcher/manager, Rough had a unique perspective on the two rookie pitchers that the Red Sox magnate had acquired from the Orioles. Ernie Shore was wicked fast and, at twenty-four, had the maturity to step right in and spark a winning streak that moved the Sox within striking distance of the first-place Athletics.

In the nineteen-year-old Ruth, the manager saw dazzling raw talent. He especially liked the kid's competitiveness in a pinch. Babe seemed to have the rare ability to rise to the occasion – it was almost as if he drew energy from the crowd in a big moment. The boy had charisma and endeared himself to Rough because Babe loved the game. He would spend hours talking inside baseball – never tiring of analyzing the subtleties and nuances of the game. While Carrigan knew that Babe was special, he also recognized that the young man could be moody and inconsistent.

In most organizations, newcomers must learn the unwritten protocols that shape relationships within the group. This is especially true in major league clubhouses where young men compete physically and mentally against opponents and each other in a tough, unforgiving, environment where reputations, playing time, and livelihoods are at stake. Newcomers are particularly prone to innocent transgressions of established norms that spark the ire of senior members of the tribe.

As a rookie, Babe was oblivious to the sense of hierarchy that prevailed in the Boston clubhouse. His most egregious infraction was his insistence on participating in batting practice with the position players. He did not appreciate the code that hitters hit and pitchers pitch. Babe took particular pride in the bats that had been issued to him. He spent hours boning the surfaces; a tedious process of rubbing a bone or a bottle against the bat to seal the grain of the wood thereby hardening it and generating greater power.

In retaliation for his effrontery, his teammates decided to send him a clear message. Prior to warming up for his second start, Babe entered the dugout to prepare for batting practice. When he reached the bat rack, he discovered that someone had sawed his bats in half. His anguished bellows at the carnage to his equipment were met with stone-cold silence from the veterans. When Babe finally calmed down, it was almost game time. He barely warmed up.

Predictably, Babe so distracted that his second start against the Detroit Tigers was a disaster. They pounced on everything Babe threw and knocked him out of the game in the fourth inning. He lost his first game.

Bill Carrigan empathized with the youngster, but recognized that he could not intervene on Babe's behalf lest he create an even more toxic backlash against the rookie. Babe would have to find his place on his own. For his part, the homesick young man sulked. The manager's dilemma was how to teach the young man to tap into his potential and not succumb to the dark moments of doubt that besiege every ballplayer.

In contrast to Babe's rough transition, Ernie Shore the affable young man from North Carolina thrived. He pitched a two-hitter in his first outing and won four games in his first month. Of equal importance, his self-effacing manner earned him acceptance with the veterans who saw him as a weapon to earn extra money in their quest for a championship. On the other hand, the veterans viewed Babe's raw talent as a harbinger for future success, but of little use now.

Rough Carrigan understood the importance of team chemistry and realized that it would be difficult for the youngster from Baltimore to suffer a season-long baptism by fire. The manager went with the hot hand and inserted Shore into the starting rotation. Ruth became the forgotten man on the pitching staff and did not play for a month.

Magnate Lannin was a rookie owner who saw an opportunity to not only win the American League pennant, but also win the International League championship with the Providence franchise. The magnate conceived a plan to assign Babe to the Providence Grays for the remainder of the minor league season. It fell to manager Carrigan to break news of the demotion to the young man from Baltimore. Given

Babe's state of mind, Carrigan did not relish that conversation. Fortunately for all concerned, the answer to Carrigan's dilemma just walked into the manager's office.

"Morning, Skip," said Charles Francis Wagner, better known to his friends as 'Heinie' in honor of his German ancestry. From 1906 to 1912, Heinie had been the team's shortstop and captain. However, over the past winter, Wagner had suffered an attack of rheumatism so severe that he was forced to retire. In late June, his good friend Bill Carrigan prevailed upon Heinie to help the Sox as third base coacher. Heinie had the perfect temperament for the job and he and the team thrived.

"Orders from Lannin," said Carrigan, handing Heinie a packet. "I need you to break the news to Babe."

Heinie gave the manager a knowing nod.

It was early August and the team had just returned from a long road trip. Babe crossed the locker room to the row of pitchers' lockers and sat down before his locker. It was hard to believe that more than five months had passed since his departure from St. Mary's Industrial School. To call it a roller coaster ride would be an understatement. From Baltimore to Fayetteville to Wilmington and back to Baltimore for his professional debut was a blurry dream. The disastrous encounter with Colina outside the Hollowleg Club was the nightmare low point. It would not be the last – the invisible web of life would repeatedly impact his life for better and worse.

At the ballpark, Babe experienced baseball in a way that he never had before – from the bench. After a couple of starts with mixed results,

Babe was relegated to the bench. The principal reason was the outstanding pitching of his former Oriole teammate. Ernie Shore would win ten games in 1914, pitching to a low, 2.00 earned run average.

Babe missed Baltimore sorely. Earlier in the season when Babe was playing for the Orioles, he often played for St. Mary's after pitching for the Orioles. He had no such outlet in Boston. Boredom and loneliness dominated his mood. Babe released his frustrations by writing diatribes to his father and Brother Matthias. The responses were as different as the two men. Matthias counseled patience and hard work, while George Sr. urged him to be combative, aggressive and to remember Pigtown pride (whatever that was, thought Babe).

When in Boston, Babe spent most of his free time with Helen. His relationship with Helen blossomed. Babe ate every meal possible at Landers and spent his paycheck lavishly on outings with Helen. It helped him dull the pain of inaction on the field. Helen considered it her obligation to show Babe all the sights that Boston had to offer. With the Red Sox facing a long road trip out west, the couple's touring efforts increased.

One of the activities that Babe enjoyed the most was attending rehearsals of the Boston Symphony Orchestra. Parker, a friend of one of Helen's girlfriends, worked as a stagehand at Symphony Hall. He would lead them to one of the shallow side balconies before the musicians arrived. They would remain hidden during the rehearsals. The Hall was long, narrow, rectangular-shaped shoebox that was configured to provide world-class acoustics. The music reminded Babe of the classical pieces that formed the palette for Caruso's masterpieces. Unfortunately, the music made him melancholy over Colina. Whenever Helen sensed him slipping, she would squeeze her nubile body closer.

For Babe the best part of the rehearsals was the banter among the musicians during breaks. In the few weeks since his sale to Boston, the situation in Europe had deteriorated rapidly. One month after the assassination of Archduke Franz Ferdinand, Austria-Hungary declared war on Serbia and Germany declared war on Russia. The so-called Great War had begun. This was the topic of lively discussion. Maestro Karl Muck professed to be a good friend of Kaiser Bill. The conductor had been born and educated in Germany. Now in his mid-fifties, he was opinionated and surly. His craggy features were set off by thin, pursed lips that made him look like he had just imbibed a Berliner *weissebier*, an extremely sour beer unique to northern Germany.

Muck harassed the Russian and French orchestra members with predictions that Germany would be victorious by Christmas. Within weeks, the orchestra was divided into three camps – the pro-Germans, the anti-Germans, and the neutrals. The Germans were divided into pro- and anti-Kaiser factions. Babe enjoyed listening to the musicians argue in German. He quietly whispered translations to Helen. Since they were located quite a distance from the pit and Babe's German was, at best, rusty, his translations were a humorous contrast to the serious discourse below them. On one occasion, he translated a boast that the German Wehrmacht would grind the French Army into sausage, into a statement that the Kaiser was a hot dog. Helen thought Babe was brilliant.

Of course, the debate was spirited and often consumed much of the rehearsal time. By Babe's unofficial count nearly half of the musicians spoke German. No doubt this was due to recruiting by Dr. Muck. Babe's favorite musician was an oboist from Chicago named Hans Spieler. He was a fearless defender of the United States and told Dr. Muck that Kaiser Bill had better watch his manners or Uncle Sam would have to cross the ocean and spank him. Muck responded that der Kaiser's U-boats would prevent the Americans from leaving North America. Before Spieler could retort, the conductor raised his baton and the musicians assumed the ready position with all attention focused on the conductor.

It was Saturday, August 15th and the Red Sox had just defeated the Yankees to avoid being swept at home. Babe was looking forward to the Sunday off day with Helen when his plans were shattered by coach Wagner. When the game was over, Wagner steered Babe into the trainer's room.

"Listen, kid, I know that you've been unhappy on the bench these last few weeks."

"Coach, I ain't been in a game in a dog's age. What gives?"

"In this game, you gotta be patient. Your time will come. For now, we got a special request from Mr. Lannin to get you some playing time."

Babe's countenance turned radiant at the prospect of returning to the mound at Fenway.

"The bad part of this is that you cleared waivers. You are being sent to Providence to help the Grays win the International League pennant. Mr. Lannin believes that you will be the difference," said Heinie, his voice inflecting slightly to communicate enthusiasm.

Babe barely heard the coach say how much Mr. Lannin thought that Babe had the hoodoo over the Buffalo Bisons because of his 3 - 0 record against them earlier in the season when he was with the Orioles. He definitely did not hear the part about revenge against the Orioles and the chance to see more of his father. All Babe could think of was that the demotion meant failure. He hardened his heart against the pain of being a commodity in a game where the rich man jerked the strings. His hands folded over the packet of information and tickets that Wagner handed him. Train tickets to Providence were nestled in the envelope. He stared at the ducats in disbelief. He would spend his day off on a train, instead of spending Sunday afternoon with Helen.

The next morning, he went to mass with Helen and then boarded the train to Providence. Helen promised to visit him frequently and she was true to her word. Before he knew it, she was traveling on the Boston & Providence Railroad a distance of forty miles, over the Seekonk River Bridge into Providence.

In his first start for the Grays, Babe stumbled and lost to a Buffalo team determined to break the hoodoo Babe had held over them by virtue of three early season victories. In the next six weeks Babe thrived in Providence, winning nine games and losing only one other game. Babe's exploits on the field made him an instant fan and media favorite. After one notable victory over the Newark team, the *Providence Journal* reported that, "Babe Ruth appears to have gotten in on the ground floor with the fans as a result of his baffling southpaw brand of pitching and his ability to give the horse-hide vigorous punishment with the wagon tongue.' "[ix]

Babe spent much of his salary buying train tickets for Helen who visited often. The Grays won the championship and the Red Sox recalled Babe to Boston. He was so elated that he proposed to Helen.

Now, he was on the train returning home to Baltimore with his young fiancé snuggled at his side. He had been through so much over the last six months. From the sandlots of Baltimore to the rarefied heights of Boston's modern big league palace with a detour in Providence, Babe had compiled an impressive pitching record of 23 victories against only 8 losses in 1914.

"Do you think your father will approve of me?" asked Helen. Ever since boarding the train in Boston, her stomach had been aflutter with the reality of their situation – two teenagers announcing that they were getting married. True, Babe seemed to have a lucrative job, although it was unpredictable and could disappear in the blink of an eye with a serious injury. She was abandoning her education and would be left only with her waitressing skills.

"Will my father like you, Hon? I'm sure he will. He's always looking for a good waitress," said Babe laughing in that open-mouth way that made him so endearing.

As it turned out, Helen's worries were ill-founded. She and Babe settled into life sharing an apartment with Big George and his second wife, Martha. As a real live major leaguer, Babe became a something of a local celebrity. When he wasn't helping his father at the harness shop, he could be found at St. Mary's where he regaled the inmates with stories of big league life, or, as one jealous rival put it, "Babe held court for those who idolized him."

After a few weeks in Baltimore, Helen and Babe tied the knot at St. Paul's Catholic Church in nearby Ellicott City. The setting was enchanting – a rustic, granite building set on Mulligan Hill above a verdant valley whose foliage was tinged with vibrant oranges, reds and yellows. The bright sunshine reflected off the silver Celtic cross atop the church's distinctive spire. The Indian summer sun illuminated the tinted glass panels giving the interior of the church an ethereal glow.

A small group of Helen's relatives had traveled from New England for the occasion. An equally limited number of Babe's family attended. Babe's teenage sister Mamie was the maid of honor. She was joined in the wedding procession by the best man, Henry "Gunny" Gunther, former Bunny and now banker. On the third Saturday in October, Babe and Helen stood before the Scottish marble altar and agreed to love, cherish, and obey 'til death do they part. The bride and groom spent a few idyllic days honeymooning in the Patapsco River Valley. Babe enjoyed hiking and fishing while Helen tagged along.

The only blemish on their special week was an argument between her brother Will and Big George at the outdoor wedding banquet. Will baited George by boasting about the superiority of the German U-boat fleet. George responded by proposing a toast to the German shepherd that had spawned Kaiser Bill. Will's face turned into a grotesque mask of *Kreigs-Gott*, the god of war.

"German Americans had better understand that this is the great German time, *die größe Deutschlandzeit*, and America must support the Fatherland," shouted Will.

"That's blatherskite," replied George. "America bows to no nation, certainly not to a mad Hun named Kaiser Wilhelm!"

This comment enraged Will who charged George. The would-be combatants were separated before any serious blows were struck, but not before the crystal punch bowl shattered into glittering shards, like the rocket's red glare.

Five thousand miles away, another young man was facing a crisis that was precipitated by his own murderous actions. The government of Austria Hungary prosecuted Gavrilo Princip for the assassination of Archduke Franz Ferdinand and his wife Duchess Sophie of

Hohenberg in June 1914. The trial began on October 12, 1914, in Sarajevo, Bosnia-Herzegovina, in a military prison. He was tried along with several of his co-conspirators and many of the underground network that had participated in the crimes. Two weeks later, Princip and fifteen of his co-conspirators were convicted of high treason. According to Austrian law, a defendant like Princip who was nineteen when the crime was committed could not be sentenced to death. He received the maximum, permissible sentence of twenty-years hard labor.

1915 Red Sox at spring training in Hot Springs, Arkansas

1915
Hot Springs, Arkansas

*"A young ballplayer looks on his first spring training trip
as a stage struck young woman regards the theater."*
~ Christy Matthewson

Living with Helen in an apartment with his father on West Conway Street, and working with his father at the Columbia Harness Company that winter, convinced Babe that playing professional baseball was preferable. Although he expressed no dissatisfaction with his new bride, in his heart of hearts, he missed carousing with his teammates after games. Freed from the all-seeing eye of the clergy at St. Mary's, with money burning a hole in his pocket, the young man was in an enviable position. Yet, Babe understood that his future depended on performing on the diamond. He dedicated himself to making the Red Sox and improving on their 1914 second-place finish. Babe dreamed of World Series glory and the monetary bonus that accompanied it. Spring training for the Red Sox 1915 season beckoned and Babe prepared diligently for his opportunity.

"Hon, while you were out doing your roadwork, you got a message from Brother Matthias that no one at the Home is available to catch you today. He said that you will have to make other arrangements," said Helen Ruth.

Still winded from his running, Babe just gave her a disappointed glance. She handed him a glass of water.

"You know, I've been wondering – does Brother Matthias have a last name?"

"I dunno, I never thought about it. I guess his last name is Matthias," said Babe, handing the glass to his wife seeking more water.

"If his last name is Matthias, then what is his first name?"

"What's with all these silly questions? His first name is Brother, of course," said Babe.

"Of course," echoed Helen, wrinkling her nose.

George, Sr. entered the kitchen. When he saw his son's dejected posture, he said, "What's up, champ?"

"Aw, nothing," muttered Babe, eyes downcast.

"He's miserable because there's no one at St. Mary's to catch him today."

"Oh?" said Big George. "Maybe I can help you out."

"Are you sure, Pops?"

"Yeah, I'm sure. What? You think that I'm so old that I can't handle you?" Big George scoffed.

"Alright, if you say so. I'll get my catcher's glove," replied Babe. Helen rolled her eyes. This was not going to end well.

Babe handed his father the catcher's mitt and catcher's mask. The men went to the alley behind the apartment and tossed the ball lightly while warming up. Babe moved back a few steps after each throw until he was about sixty feet away from his father. Big George threw fluidly and soon was embellishing his throws by crow-hopping and slide-stepping like a spry colt. Helen observed from the kitchen window and remarked favorably on her father-in-law's agility.

Babe was loose now and started popping the ball into the catcher's mitt. Big George signaled for his son to halt while the older man donned the mask and assumed a catcher's crouch. After a few pitches, Babe told his father to move the glove around the strike zone so that he could practice his control. Babe's accuracy was perfect. Despite the pounding his hand was taking, Big George grinned at his son's skill.

"Let's see yer high, hard one," shouted Big George.

Shifting the ball to a four-seam grip, Babe reared back and let it fly. As the ball approached Big George, velocity and backspin made it rise. Big George stabbed awkwardly as the ball sailed past his head. Babe's eyes widened as he watched the ball career off the brick wall behind his father, ricochet like a stray bullet, and strike him squarely in the back of the head. Big George wobbled, sank to his knees and tipped over into a fetal position groaning. Babe yelled one word to Helen as he raced in to help his father.

"Ice!"

A few weeks later, Babe boarded a train headed for Hot Springs, Arkansas, the site of Boston's spring training. He would have six weeks to make the team. When in the presence of his wife and father, he acted as if making the team was a foregone conclusion. In private, he feared sabotage by some of the veterans. Professional baseball is a game played by young men under pressure situations and living, eating, and traveling together for upwards of six months. Apart from the perceived glamor of this public occupation, the players were susceptible to petty jealously, prejudice, and all manner of human venality. The Red Sox were a discordant, some might say, dysfunctional group.

While traveling, Babe reflected on the incident with the sawing of his bats. He rued the fact that catcher Ben Egan, his best friend and supporter, had been traded by the Red Sox within weeks after their arrival in Boston the previous summer. Babe hoped that manager Carrigan would control the insidious factions and give him a fair shot. That's all he wanted - a fair shot.

His thoughts turned to his father. This winter was the first time that he had spent any appreciable time with his father since the death of his mother almost three years earlier. Surprisingly, there were no blow-ups. Perhaps the removal of the stress of the deaths of his children and subsequent alcoholism of his mother, had allowed his father to recover emotionally. Babe also thought that his stepmother was a positive influence on Big George. He actually seemed happy. He had even rejoined the men's singing group.

The only blemish in their time in Baltimore was the stray pitch that had struck his father in the back of his skull. Big George could not admit that he just missed it. He insisted that Babe had been wild. When Helen sided with Babe, asserting that the pitch was on target, George flew into a rage. Finally, when Martha, who had been looking out the window, confirmed Helen's view, George changed his story and blamed a reflection off the windshield of a passing truck for his failure to catch the ball. Babe shook his head and declined to discuss it any further. When it was time to leave, Babe was more than ready.

Since earlier in the century, the magnates of several teams had chosen Hot Springs for their preseason training because of the thermal, mineral springs located there. The city was located in southern Arkansas below the western slope of Hot Springs Mountain. For centuries, the area had been prized for its legendary water from superheated areas of the earth's crust that bubbled up into forty-seven springs which flowed to Hot Springs. The water was reputed to have medicinal, healing qualities. What made it unique was the absence of the noxious smell of Sulphur that typically accompanied thermal springs. So prized were the thermal springs that the federal government declared the area a federal reserve in 1832, giving Hot Springs the distinction of being the country's oldest designated reserve.

"Hot Springs! Hot Springs! Spa City, and home of baseball spring training! Next stop, Hot Springs!" shouted the conductor, with a slight southern twang. When Babe stepped off the train at the Hot

Springs, Arkansas spring training grounds, he was hungry for success and adventure.

"Rise and shine, Deac, tee time is in forty minutes. We gonna whup Hoop and East Bend Ernie before lunch," said Babe. He had already raided the dining hall for an early, country ham omelette.

"What? Who?" said Everett Scott, the team's shortstop with a voice murky from sleep. At five-feet-eight inches tall, he was a defensive wizard whose prowess with the leather was much appreciated by Babe. Scott was born in Indiana and broke into the big leagues the prior season. In contrast to his golfing partner, Scott's personality was more subdued, earning him the nickname "Deacon."

"Don't tell me you forgot. We're playing those bums who beat us the other day. Today, we're gonna play the Arlington at the Hot Springs Country Club. I like that course. Those steep, narrow fairways are perfect for my game. Just long, straight drives out of the tee box," said Babe barely able to curb his enthusiasm.

"Who did you say we were playing?"

"East Bend Ernie. I gave him that name when he told me he was raised in East Bend, North Carolina. He calls me Pigtown, Pig for short."

Scott shook his head and couldn't help chuckling. In later years when he was asked about what is was like to be teammates with the Babe, Scott described him with one word – irrepressible.

By the time Harry Hooper and Ernie Shore arrived at the Hot Springs Country Club, Babe had already practiced forty-seven putts on the undulating greens that characterized the course.

"Ha, ha, I'm ready for youse now," chortled Babe.

He grinned at Hooper, the amiable Californian who was a couple of inches shorter than the Babe. Harry Hooper had graduated from St. Mary's College of California with a degree in engineering. He was an outstanding outfielder who used his quick mind to calculate angles for chasing down fly balls hit in his direction. Entering his seventh year as a major leaguer, Hoop, as his teammates called him, was the right-fielder of Boston's "Golden Outfield" along with Tris Speaker and Duffy Lewis. It was one of the strengths of Red Sox teams that was World Series champions in 1912 and looking to return to that summit.

East Bend Ernie was Hoop's partner. The genial North Carolinian was one of the few ballplayers who was taller than the Babe. The Boston press gave him the nickname "Long" when he debuted with the team the previous summer. He, along with Ruth and catcher Ben Egan, were part of Jack Dunn's fire sale to the Red Sox in the summer of 1914. Shore had spent the winter teaching mathematics at Guilford College which gave his twosome a distinct advantage over Babe's team which relied on his helter-skelter method of keeping score on the links. Hoop believed that Ernie's mathematical skill was the equivalent of a two-stroke handicap. In a few years, Shore would join Babe in one of the most memorable, bizarre and astounding games ever played in the major leagues.

With their prodigious drives, the young ballplayers played briskly. The lead see-sawed back and forth, usually as one or the other twosome bogied their way through various traps and roughs. There was a lot of good-natured ribbing among the teammates. Approaching the last hole, the teams were tied. The golf match hung in the balance as Babe stepped up to the tee on the eighteenth hole. Babe was the last to tee off. He turned his flat cap around so that the brim covered his broad neck. His muscular calves stretched the stockings of his knickers to their limits.

The hole stretched over five hundred yards before him. Babe removed his handkerchief from the pocket of his knickers, wiped his brow and then tucked the cloth under his right armpit. He addressed the ball, coiled back, and let fly. The sound of the flat head of the wood was so sharp and loud that Hoop distinctly heard the reverberation off Hot Springs Mountain some three miles away. The ball travelled straight and true, landing seventy-five yards farther than the other balls. Babe easily reached the green on his next shot and one-putted for an eagle. No mathematical prestidigitation by Shore could snatch victory from Babe and Deac.

"Well, kiddoes, it was nice taking your dough," cooed Ruth as he counted the prize.

"Babe, how in heck did you hit that ball so far?" asked Hoop.

"You see, it's all in the connection."

"What?"

"Did you notice how I tucked my hanky under my armpit before I hit?"

"Yeah, so what?" said Hoop, who was not a good loser, even if was only fifty cents a hole each.

"That helps my lead arm stay connected when I unload."

"You know what? I'm going to try it next time. It makes sense."

Hoop and Ernie marveled at the change in the young fellow in one year. When he came to the Sox the previous summer, he was boisterous, but timid when it came to interacting with his teammates. Now, he was one of the best friends a guy could have.

"Excuse me, young man," Babe addressed one of the waiters. He was a muscular, dark-skinned young man wearing the club's livery. "Are you an Injun?"

The waiter nodded.

"What's yer name?"

"Yo-na, it means bear."

"I like that. You kind of look like a bear with strong arms. Do you play baseball?" asked Babe. Yo-na's eyes brightened.

"Yes, sir, very much."

"Do you have a leather mitt?"

"No, sir. It's too costly."

"What time do you finish work?"

"I finish at four, after we prepare the Clubhouse for the dinner shift."

"Well, then, you take this money and buy yourself some baseball equipment and I'll meet you here at five-thirty. You got that?"

"I couldn't do that, sir."

Suddenly, a scowling wait captain walked toward their table with his hands on his hips in a menacing fashion. Yo-na glanced at him without making eye contact and panicked.

"Here, here," he said, throwing the bills toward Babe as he fled. The money fluttered around them. The players snatched for them and caught them all.

"Is that waiter causing a problem, gentlemen?"

"No, sir, we was just talking baseball. Do you play?"

Looking down his nose, he said, "Most certainly not. It's a game for ruffians."

"Too bad," said Babe, looking at his companions. "I guess we's ruffians."

The wait-captain turned bright red and forced a laugh along with the ballplayers. As their party rose to leave, Babe stood over the smaller man and extended his index finger to him, saying, "Pull my finger."

Before the confused man could respond, Deac grabbed Babe by the elbow and dragged him away.

"C'mon, Babe, we want to come back here while we are in Hot Springs, so don't ruin it now."

When the foursome reached the exit doors, they doubled over in raucous laughter.

"Did you see his face? He looked like he had seen a skunk."

"You got that right. He don't know how close he was to an Arkansas barking spider."

"Yeah, I thought he was gonna faint."

Buoyed by a feeling of acceptance, Babe smiled, "I'll see y'all back at the hotel."

Babe started his roadwork back, thinking that a three-mile run back to the Majestic Hotel and the team's baseball facility on Belding Avenue would be a good way to limber up before practice. From behind the garbage containers by the kitchen, Yo-na waved a stealthy goodbye. Babe was wearing a thick, gray sweater, knickers tucked under at the knee, set off by knee-length red sox. To prevent the mountain wind from whisking his flat cap away like an errant skeet, he turned it backwards. Rarely, had Hot Springs Mountain been subjected to such a sight. Soon, he had settled into a rhythm on the trail, negotiating the inclining switchbacks with his short, but powerful, stride.

When Babe first joined the Sox, Hooper in particular had tried to persuade him to lengthen his stride. Babe refused, quoting the wisdom of his mentor Brother Matthias. Babe was dismissive of Hooper's attempts to apply engineering principles like leverage, torque, and thrust to running.

"You see, Hoop, I can run faster this way because I can push off with all five toes. Your way only uses the three main toes," said Babe, demonstrating his point by removing one shoe and sock, while angling his foot and pressing down with all five toes into the turf.

"I have more strength in my pinky toe than most guys have in their thumb toes," said Babe with a wink.

Hoop shook his head, not knowing whether Babe was serious or not. Shortly after this conversation, Hoop became convinced that the issue was academic and resolved never to raise it again. One afternoon, Babe blasted a ball so hard that it went clear out of Whittington Park and crossed the street, finally landing in the Arkansas Alligator Farm. As the team left the dugout to congratulate Babe, Hoop leaned over to Scott and said, "If the big rookie keeps mashing like that, he won't need to revise his running style because he will be doing a lot of trotting around the bases."

Babe's gator shot, as the local papers dubbed it, was memorialized by a photo in the *Hot Springs Sentinel-Record* of Babe accepting a gnarled ball from the farm's owner, Danny Older. The owner quipped that the ball was so tough that one of the gators broke a tooth on it and was last seen in the waiting room of a local gator dentist. The two men posed before the Farm's most-visited attraction, a life-sized merman. The headline read:

"Rookie Ruth Clubs Ball Out Of Whittington Park Into Feeding Pool At Alligator Farm!"

Later that week, Babe carefully folded the news article and sent it along with a letter to his wife Helen. 'I'm having the best time here. Living in a hotel sure is great. A maid cleans the room every day and the dining room serves as much food as I want three times a day. This morning I ate four omelettes. Don't worry though, I'm not gaining any weight because of all the physical activity – golf, mountain climbing, and baseball. I think the chef likes me because every time I order another dish he comes out of the kitchen to check on me.

Yesterday, he asked me to stand up because he thought that I might be putting the food into my pockets. I thought about it, but my pockets are too full of money that I won at the race track.

'Me and the guys went to Oaklawn Park. It's a neat place that they built around a track where the farm boys used to race their ponies. Anyway, I bet on a nag named Wopper who went off at 19 – 1. I can't explain it, but there was something about the name of that horse that reminded me of my favorite thing, the sound of a bat hitting a baseball. The guys ragged on me for that bet. They called me a babe-in-the-woods and worse. But, don't you know it, that sonuvagun won the race! I sure had fun stuffing that dough into my pockets.

'I'm sending you a news article for your scrapbook. I hit another circuit drive; it cleared the fence and landed in an alligator farm. Who knew that farmers can grow alligators? After the game, one of the reporters took me to meet the head gator farmer. We had a good time joking about the home run and the gators. I thought you would get a kick out of this picture. The funny-looking guy in the middle is supposed to be a merman, you know, a creature with the body of a man and a tail like a fish. To me it looked like somebody made a statue of the owner and slapped a fish tail on his butt.

'I miss you, Hon. I'll be back in four more weeks for the home opener at Fenway. Until then, take care, Love, Hon 2'

"Hey, Babe, do you want to go take the waters with us before we have dinner," asked the Deacon.

103

"You sure deserve it after the way you pitched and mashed the ball today," said Hoop.

"Ok, but I gotta meet a friend after dinner."

"What's her name, Babe?" teased Ernie.

"C'mon, guys, It's not like that," protested Babe.

"I know better than that; I'm your roomie."

They headed over to the Maurice Bathhouse on Bathhouse Row, a series of spas, shops, and gardens off the main drag in Hot Springs. The entrance was filled with marble columns, stained glass windows depicting mythical sea creatures, and sparkling, decorative tiles - all designed to create an aura of a hygienic, sumptuous, healthy pleasure palace. While the other players luxuriated in the thermal baths and discussed their plans for the evening, Babe wandered off to a new annex that bore the sign, Nauheim bath.

He discarded his towel and stepped into the rectangular marble tub. His eyes closed as the attendant filled the tub with warm, mineral water. He was drowsy from the day's activity and a deep Swedish massage. The lights dimmed and he fell into a somnolent state. Alone and totally relaxed, he mused about his reluctance to sign with Jack Dunn a little more than one year ago. Brother Matthias had been right and the man who was no longer Jidgie said a prayer of gratitude for his good fortune.

Babe was so relaxed that a pulse of flatulence escaped and bubbled to the surface. He giggled. He was interrupted by the sound of air rushing through pipes, followed by the strange sensation of bubbles surging all around his body. The water foamed under the pressure of the forced air. Babe felt like a cork propelled and lifted by a stream of beer escaping from a keg. Only, he wasn't floating on beer suds; he was buoyed by jets of carbon dioxide emanating from holes in the bottom of the tub.

"Hey, what the hell's going on here," he screamed.

The attendant, a middle-aged black man, bolted into the room. He flipped on the lights. The man suppressed a grin at the sight of Babe in the tub, squinting and breathing rapidly, eyes ablaze.

"It's alright, Mr. Babe. It's the Nauheim bath; it's supposed to send the bubbles through the water like that. It's relaxin'."

"To hell it is! Get me outta here!"

Babe left the hotel slightly agitated, but, refreshed. He headed for the trail out of town following the directions of his friend. It wasn't long before he spied a low structure through the trees. The rudimentary structure housed a small, general store that sold everything a mountain man or a tourist could need. The exterior was speckled with faded metal signs, advertising everything imaginable. There was a circular sign for Tom Moore's cigars 10¢. An R.C. Cola and moon pie sign reminded him that he had to hustle in order to be back in time for dinner with the fellas. He laughed out loud at a sign touting Whazoo River excursions with the tagline that, "You haven't been anywhere until you've been up the Whazoo!"

"Mr. Babe, what are you doing here?" said a surprised voice. It was Yo-na, the Cherokee waiter from the Hot Springs Country Club who had just emerged from the back of the building carrying several logs for the fireplace. A tentative smile emerged amid his handsome dark features.

"I brought you something," said Babe, a little embarrassed by the formality of the boy who was only a couple of years younger than him.

"Here," said Babe, handing Yo-na a worn baseball mitt holding a ball.

Yo-na was so overwhelmed that he dropped the logs, narrowly missing his foot. No white man had ever done him such a kindness. When Babe flipped the items to him, Yo-na was so excited that he fairly juggled them before securing them to his chest.

"Listen, kid, I'd like to stay and have a catch with you, but, my teammates are waiting for me. Maybe next time."

"OK, sure, . . . next time. Oh, wait Mr. Babe, I have something for you," said Yo-na, running toward the back before Babe could decline.

While he was waiting, Babe decided to examine the stuffed horse that stood by the entrance to the store. It was a palomino with a striking white mane and tail. The horse was reared up on its back legs in a kind of permanent salute to visitors. A weathered bridle and saddle adorned the beautiful creature, captured so vividly by the taxidermist.

"That there palomino was one of the great, great grandsons of the first Isabella horses that came here from Spain. Queen Isabella loved these beautiful creatures and wanted them to populate the Spanish colonies. The Cherokee people learned to breed the palomino from the Spanish missionaries who settled the American southeast," said Lone Bear, who emerged from the shadows.

He was an outcast of the tribe who lived alone in the forest. His solo existence stemmed from his cruel and erratic behavior. Scars from an unfortunate encounter with a turkey vulture over a carcass they both wanted to eat crisscrossed his face. His upper lip had been rearranged in a perpetual sneer. A long, gray mane of unruly hair ran down his back. In his right hand, he grasped a spear adorned with hawk feathers. His other hand was out of sight behind his back. Muscular, with thick limbs, he limped noticeably on his left leg.

Ruth regarded the man who was dressed in buckskin pants replete with Bowie knife at the waistband. Babe was incredulous to be standing eye-to-eye with an honest to goodness savage. He leaned the spear against his shoulder and presented a small pottery jug. It was clay red and emitted a foul odor.

"Mister, have you ever heard of the elixir developed by Chief Kahnungdatlageh, 'the man who walks the mountain top'? It is a mixture of Ozark Mountain oysters and Indian herbs and spices. Drink this and you will have superhuman strength and stamina. Just look at me!"

Babe gave him an astonished look.

"Only two American dollars for you; it will last for four moons. What do you say?"

"No thanks, Doc, I'm already super strong," chuckled Babe, striking a circus strongman's pose.

Suddenly, Babe saw Lone Bear's left hand flash toward him. Before he could strike Babe with a long, thin knife, there was a loud crack and the man wobbled and fell. A baseball rolled to a stop next to the savage's head. Yo-na raced over and stood between Babe and the stunned man who was stirring. Lonely Bear rubbed the side of his ear; it was bloody from the blow administered by a wicked fastball from the arm of Yo-na.

"Yiiihee, vamoose, *nu-da-nv-dv-na watali*, you insane prick," screamed Yo-na.

Scrambling like a crab, Lonely Bear scuffled away on his back, up a dusty path. When he reached the woods, he hobbled to avoid a hail of stones hurled by Yo-na and Babe, who joined in for the fun of it. Lone Bear winced under the impact of the fusillade and hurled curses down on the young men.

"I'm so sorry, Mr. Babe. That madman has been skulking in the woods over the last few weeks. He belongs in an asylum for crazy people."

"I gotta say, your fastball saved my butt. Did he really intend to stab me?" asked Babe.

"Sure thing, he's insane and probably wanted to steal your wallet. It's a good thing I returned when I did."

"You know, Yo-na, you should get on a team and work hard. With that arm, you just might be able to turn pro."

"You are kind, Mr. Babe, but I am the only man to support my family."

"All I can say is look at me. I'm living proof that an ordinary guy can earn a living playing baseball, if you have talent and you work hard enough. Ya gotta keep your hope."

"Thanks, Mr. Babe," replied Yo-na. "Oh, . . . I almost forgot. Here, I have a special drink for you," said Yo-na.

Babe accepted a large bottle and sniffed. The clear liquid had a pleasant smell. Tiny bubbles tinkled his nose. Tilting back, he gulped a long swig of the cold mineral water.

"This water is from the sacred well. It is the healing water of the Cherokee. Our legend says that the Under World, Elohi, is a place of water and chaos that is a source of creative power. We draw this water from a secret place. I want to share this power with you."

"Thanks, I am humbled and grateful."

"Hey, Babe, where've you been? We're waiting to go to dinner!" shouted Harry Hooper. The lanky outfielder and the Deacon were walking up the path to the store.

"Come on, man, we're starving," said the shortstop.

"OK, there's just one more thing I have to do before we head back," said Babe. "I want a picture of me on that horse."

"That stuffed horse?" said Deac. "You're in luck. I brought my Kodak Vest Pocket camera with me to shoot the sunset. I'm sure I can spare a shot for you."

Babe grinned and lifted his left leg into the stirrup and hoisted himself into the saddle. He grabbed the reins and waved his hat over his head in his best imitation of Buffalo Bill Cody. The Deacon extended the lens and stepped back. He had snapped a photo and was fiddling with the camera when he heard a sharp crack. He clicked the shutter just in time to capture the Babe falling backwards as the ancient saddle split apart under his weight.

Deac snapped numerous pictures of the Babe dangling nearly upside-down while hanging on to the saddle-horn for dear life. Hopp was doubled over laughing hysterically, while Yo-na desperately tried to lever Babe back into position.

The sequence of images featuring Babe triumphantly waving his hat, to the astonished look on his face when the saddle snapped, to the Babe hanging helpless over the horse's rear end was priceless. The snapshots earned the Deacon a pretty penny and Babe a temporary nickname as the Horse's Ass.

1915 – Babe doing roadwork, Hot Springs, Arkansas

May 1915
New York City, New York

"I never heard a crowd boo a homer, but I've heard plenty of boos after a strikeout."
~ Babe Ruth

By any metric, George Herman Ruth, Jr. was a large person. Although he was tall, he had the proportions of Michaelangelo's *David*. His musculature was impressive, with bulk through his torso atop powerful legs. He presented a formidable figure. The most amazing aspect of his persona was the grace of his movements. When in motion, he seemed to glide through space and had a superior athlete's gift of acceleration and economy of effort that was the envy of opponents. These traits made him graceful and powerful at once. His hands were wide and muscled with long, nimble fingers. No doubt his physique was the result of his heritage and countless hours on ballfields that gave his face a ruddy outdoor glow.

Despite the difficulties of his younger days, he blossomed after becoming a professional ballplayer. He had a round, almost cherubic face that was notable for its sparkling, brown eyes highlighted by crow's feet. There was a mischievous glint in his eyes, like he was sharing some secret with you alone. Babe had a ready smile that erupted into a contagious guffaw at the slightest provocation. He was a man's man, who was comfortable in his virility and physical in his emotions. Both men and women enjoyed being near him and his incessant pokes and touches.

During spring training, manager Carrigan and his right-hand man, Heinie Wagner discussed changes they saw in the young man. Lord knows it was not quite maturity. Babe often acted like a street urchin in search of adventure. On one occasion when Babe was scheduled as the starting pitcher of an afternoon game he headed to the clubhouse while the rest of the team participated in a morning workout. Since the club provided lunch before the game, Babe decided to have some fun. He inserted a piece of paper into one of the sandwiches. Then, he watched with glee as one of his unfortunate teammates chewed and chewed until he realized he was chewing on paper. Babe laughed so hard at the facial expressions of his victim that he gave himself away.

When Carrigan and Wagner learned of the prank they realized that it was a good sign for the team. Any time a couple of dozen men are required to eat, drink, sleep together, and perform daily in a highly competitive environment like a major league baseball season, it can become like living in a pressure cooker. Practical jokes helped release the built-up steam that can destroy ball teams. Carrigan had seen more than one good team self-destruct without a release valve. Babe just might perform that role on this team. In addition, Carrigan sensed a renewed dedication to his craft in the youngster. Last summer, the manager watched a distracted player go through the motions. Now, he watched an invigorated player let his talent shine.

Based on his performance during spring training, Babe made the big club and returned east to open the season. Due to his enthusiasm and prodigious talent, his teammates tolerated his quirks and frequent lapses of couth. There was one exception. Catcher Hick Cady, a nativist, immediately disliked the young German-American. Cady was a nervous, angry man who was fighting to survive in the big leagues. Throughout the spring, he taunted the big rookie mercilessly, calling him Baboon or Kraut.

The Red Sox muddled through April and were one game above mediocrity when they pulled into New York City for a series with the Yankees. Babe drew the first game start. On May 6th, Babe entered the Polo Grounds, in what would prove to be a momentous occasion. After his pre-game stretch with Doc in the trainer's room, Babe returned to his locker to get dressed. Because of his garrulous nature, Babe liked to chat with his buddies, asking how they spent the previous evening, or what they planned to do after the game. As a result, he had a tendency to dress at the last minute.

"Hey, where's my uni? It was here when I went to see Doc," said Babe wearing only his jock strap, as he fumbled through the clothes in his locker.

"Hey Ruth, Rough's waiting for you in the bullpen. He said that you'd better get a move on!" yelled one of the batboys. A look of panic crossed Babe's face.

Just then Heinie Wagner emerged from the toilet. As he adjusted his pants, he assessed the situation. He scanned the locker room. His attention settled on Cady who was working a little too hard on the laces of his catcher's mitt. Although Wagner was five inches shorter than Cady, he outweighed him. Wagner walked over to Cady and growled, "I will knock you from here to the Statue of Liberty, if you don't give the boy his uniform immediately!"

The only sound that could be heard was low tumbling of the washing machine in the adjacent room. The banter among the players stopped. The room was tense. All eyes were on Heinie who stood over Cady, daring him to stand. Cady nervously searched the room for an ally. No one met his pleading gaze. Seeing that no one was coming to his aid, Cady mumbled, "Ok, ok, no reason to get huffy. I'll get it. Let me up."

Heinie inched back, still maintaining his threatening presence. Cady slid past him and produced the uniform from a utility closet in the corner. Without contrition, he tossed the uniform to Ruth. Babe dressed in a flash and nodded appreciatively to Heinie.

"Give 'em hell, kid," murmured someone from the back of the room.

After an uneventful couple of innings, the crowd was listless. Many of the cranks were preoccupied with eating the unique-named delicacy known as the hot dog. In the early 1900s, the Polo Grounds was known for serving red hot dachshund sausages. Reporting on this savory delight, New York sports cartoonist Tad Dorgan invented the term 'hot dog' because he could not spell dachshund. It did not take long for the phrase to catch on with the vendors selling the product to patrons in the stands. Leo the Lung, a vendor in the Chicago ballpark, endeared himself to the cranks with his sales pitch, "Hey, hot dogs, getcha hot dogs! You're gonna love my buns!"

During his legendary career, Babe would develop quite a reputation for gorging himself on hot dogs. On this day, his reputation as a power hitter would begin. The game was scoreless when Babe approached the plate in the third inning. Without warning, Babe shattered the calm of the afternoon when he launched his first major league home run deep into the right field stands. The crack of the bat on the ball was so vicious that some fans recalled hearing a thunder bolt and wondering why there was thunder on a sunny day. As chronicled by the inveterate sports writer Damon Runyon, "In the third inning, Ruth knocked the slant out of one of Jack Warhop's underhanded subterfuges, and put the baseball in the right field stands for a home run."[x]

Babe pitched well and gathered two more hits in his five turns at bat. He pitched into the thirteenth inning only to watch his Sox lose 4-3 in fifteen innings.

In the locker room after the game, Wagner mocked Cady's disdain for Babe by imitating the sound of the ball striking the bat on Babe's homer.

"Man, that big ole bat went WOP when it hit the ball. I mean, you could hear that WOP all the way out to Coogan's Bluff, WOP!"

The genial infielder walked over to Babe and patted the big rookie on the back and said, "Good job, Wopper." The locker room erupted in raucous laughter.

Off in the corner, Lemuel Jefferson, the beat writer for the Red Sox from the *Boston Gazette*, furiously scribbled down the nickname and used it to describe Babe in his story. That, and a torrid start to his career, helped propel Babe into a household name in baseball-loving Boston. Babe took it all in stride, smiling at the persistent chants of "Wop-per, Wop-per" when he approached the plate at an important time in the game.

The unseen web of life continued to play a role in Babe's life.

Now, in New York on this early May evening, Babe was delighted to be in Gotham again. Even though his team had lost a heart-breaker, Babe had smashed his first major league home run. The night was still young and he was looking to enjoy what New York City had to offer. His wife Helen was back in Boston and Colina was fading into a painful memory of someone that he used to know.

He strolled into the Ansonia Hotel where the Red Sox were staying with a feeling of ambivalence that he always felt when he was in New York. Since he had spent several furloughs from St. Mary's in the City, he was comfortable there. Yet, there were so many places in the City that reminded him of Colina. Just crossing an intersection, or descending into the subway might trigger a memory of her. His life had changed dramatically since he betrayed Colina. Babe wondered if anyone ever truly forgets their first love.

The Ansonia Hotel was located on Broadway, north of Times Square, at the intersection of Amsterdam Avenue at 73rd Street. The hotel was the brainchild of the eccentric heir to the Phelps-Dodge copper fortune, William Earl Dodge "Weddie" Stokes who named it after his grandfather, Anson Greene Phelps. The Ansonia was a residential hotel with three hundred suites that Stokes built to define what was to become the Upper West Side of Manhattan. After five years of construction, the Ansonia opened in 1904.

In little more than a decade, the hotel had become a grand New York landmark. It was built in the Beaux-Art style and crowned with a three-story mansard roof comprised of steep sides and a double pitch allowing more effective use of the attic space. The corner towers of the eighteen-story structure rounded into majestic turrets. The roof had several interesting features. There was a huge domed skylight that sent light through the entire building, illuminating a massive interior staircase that wound from the ground floor to the skylight. It was ornamented with delicate ironwork and terra cotta panels that were fabricated in a factory located across the river in Perth Amboy that was owned by Stokes. Similarly, the oversized elevators and huge service elevators were manufactured in a plant Stokes owned in Worcester, Massachusetts.

Always a bit eccentric, Weddie wanted the building to be self-sufficient, so he maintained a "farm on the roof," featuring hundreds of chickens, ducks, dairy cows, and even a small bear. The roof was serviced by a livestock elevator that delivered the suppliers of milk and eggs to their lofty perches. Another innovation that the Ansonia implemented was that the temperature in the hotel was maintained at seventy degrees in the warm weather by dint of flues in the walls through which an intensely cold, brine slurry was pumped. This system provided climate control that was unique in the City.

Babe sat in the lobby waiting for his teammate and fellow pitcher, Herb Pennock who had been designated by Wagner as Babe's sitter, or, guardian if you will. Although Pennock was only one year older than Babe, he was a veteran of three major league seasons. He was a tall, string bean of a man from around Philadelphia. He hailed from Kennett Square, known as the mushroom capital of the world. Pennock worked in his family's farm equipment business until he signed with Connie Mack's Athletics.

The legendary Mack was perplexed by the young pitcher's languid temperament and mistook it for lack of competitive fire. So, the magnate gave up on Pennock, a left-handed pitcher, and later regretted it, as Pennock would develop into a reliable winner who thrived in pressure situations.

Known as "Penny," Pennock was a quiet, humble man of Quaker background. He was clean shaven with an angular, open face. Although he was slight of build, he was wiry-strong. Pennock was devoted to his high school sweetheart and never caroused like many of the other players did. He was the ideal person to temper the antics of the rambunctious Babe as he became indoctrinated in the vagaries and temptations of life as a celebrity.

One of the novelties of the Ansonia was a lobby fountain that featured live seals to entertain the guests. The Ansonia was also known for its Turkish baths and the world's largest swimming pool in the basement. Babe was wearing his new tan linen suit, white shirt and a tie in Boston Red Sox colors, red with blue trim. He was sitting in the lobby on a plump armchair upholstered with a tasteful, silver and burgundy striped fabric. He was watching the seals frolic in the fountain, when Penny approached.

"Sorry to keep you waiting. I was on the phone with my gal, Esther. She always worries when we travel. I like to let her know that we made it safely. Come, I'll take you to the Colonial Club for some good eats."

The two athletes left the lobby and ambled down Broadway toward the Colonial Club. The wide avenue tracked an old Indian trail and had become the primary route north through New York City. When it was New Amsterdam, the street was called Bloomingdale Road in honor of the flower growing district, *Bloemendaal,* in Holland. As they approached the handsome front porch, Penny explained that they were entering through the men's entrance to the Colonial Club. He further advised that the Club was revolutionary in that it accepted women who entered through a separate women's entrance around the corner.

After a light dinner, they played a game of billiards and returned to the Ansonia for the night. Babe arose early the next morning and headed to the large subterranean swimming pool for some exercise. He enjoyed swimming because it reminded him of his youth in Baltimore where he swam in the Inner Harbor despite his mother's admonitions. Babe pushed himself through the water as he contemplated how his extraordinary life was unfolding. Finally, he had had enough so he emerged from the pool and headed for the Turkish baths.

Babe crossed the men's locker room and pushed open the wooden door into the baths. Peering through the steamy interior he found a spot on a tiled bench and settled down for a rest before his scheduled massage. Babe enjoyed the coolness on the marble on his bare skin. He noticed a handsome man to his left, sitting with a plush, white bath towel wrapped around his waist. He looked familiar, but, between the steam and the sweat, Babe could not place the face.

"Butt fungus."

"Excuse me. Did you say something to me?" asked Babe.

"Yes. Butt fungus."

"What?"

"If your skin touches the marble, you might get butt fungus. Sit on a towel and no butt fungus."

Babe went to the rack and took a towel for his butt. He smiled and nodded to the gentleman. Then, like watching a fastball float into his wheelhouse, Babe recognized him as the great tenor Enrico Caruso. Babe's mind dialed back to a summer nine years earlier.

"*Pardone mi, Signore*, You may not remember me, but I met you at the Central Park Zoo back in 1906," said Babe.

As soon as the words left his lips, Babe felt stupid and ridiculous. Why would the great Caruso remember the presence of a young boy at the scene of his arrest? In the ensuing silence, Babe sort of wished that Enrico would choose to ignore his statement.

The famous tenor sat Sphinx-like in the haze. Slowly, he turned toward Babe and stared without speaking. With the compulsion of someone who cannot abide silence, Babe forged ahead.

"I was the young boy that was posing for the photographers with you and your girlfriend in the Monkey House."

"I remember that day well," Caruso laughed. He could picture the startled showgirl and the ensuing news furor over the bottom-pinching scandal. Enrico stared intently into the young man's face.

"Yes, I can see the boy in your face. How are you, my friend?"

"I was so sorry to read about your court case afterwards. It must have been dreadful. *Disgraziata.*"

Caruso regarded the younger man paternally. Then, the great singer broke out into a belly laugh so forceful that his eyes bulged with mirth.

"Did I say something funny?" asked Babe.

"No, no, *escusi mi.* I'm laughing because you reminded me of the crazy scheme concocted by my agent. I was using a publicist named Edward Bernays to handle my career back then. He's very good by the way, you should consider engaging him. Anyway, I was seeing this young showgirl, her name is Lillian Lorraine, you may have heard of her. She's the star of the Ziegfeld Follies. Well, back then, she was very young and needed a boost to her career. So, we staged the whole thing with the chimp and all.

"You were the perfect trigger for the plot. The cop was her cousin who we knew would be on duty that afternoon. When this beautiful *bambino,* arrived like clockwork," he said, grabbing Babe by the cheek with his fleshy thumb and index finger, squeezing affectionately.

"The scene unfolded better than we could ever have planned. I'm truly sorry if it caused you any distress. It was just a harmless publicity stunt. The 'complaining' witness never even showed up in court. It was all a mockery."

They both laughed. There was a natural affinity between them. Both were noisy and lively and loved a good story.

"You know, *Signore,* I was only eleven at the time, but I was so thrilled to meet you that I told all my friends about it."

He feigned a cough to disguise the sudden emotion he felt when he remembered how he had first experienced the heavenly voice of his new friend. He wondered what Colina might be doing at this moment.

Enrico sensed Babe's emotion and asked, "Are you missing someone?"

Hoping to banish the thought, he lied, "This Sunday is Mother's Day and I miss my Mom. She died almost three years ago. Do you have anything planned for Mother's Day?"

Enrico gave him a confused look.

"Oh, I'm sorry. Mother's Day is an annual holiday that President Wilson declared last year to be celebrated on the second Sunday in May to honor mothers for all their sacrifices. Do they have a similar holiday in Italy?"

"The Church celebrates the mother of Jesus, but we don't have a separate day for Mothers. Perhaps we should. My mother, God rest her soul, is no longer with us. She is with the saints," said Enrico, making a discreet sign of the Cross that ended with him kissing his thumb and raising it toward heaven.

"I'm sorry," said Babe.

"Don't be," said Caruso. "What about your father? Is he still alive?"

"Yes, he runs a saloon in Baltimore. I haven't seen him much since he deposited me at the reform school when I was seven. He never visited – never cared whether I was dead or alive. Well, that is, until now. Since I got my first professional baseball contract, he has meddled in my affairs. I just wish he would go away."

"Don't say that, *Bambino*. There is much to learn from your father. Even if your father is a crude bully, you can learn from him. Sometimes the lessons come from positive experiences, as when the father supports and nurtures the family and sets a shining example. Other times, you can learn what not to do by watching your father and deciding that you do not want to repeat his mistakes. In my case my father was an example of what I did not want in life."

"How did you know what you wanted?" asked Babe.

"My father, Marcellino, was a proud man, a hard-working man. He was a mechanic and wanted me to be a mechanic like him. When I was eleven years old, my father apprenticed me to an engineering company that built public fountains. As you can imagine, building fountains is a big deal in *Italia*. We have the world's most beautiful fountains," said Enrico with a twinkle in his eye.

"Then, what happened?" asked Babe.

"My mother, God bless her soul, made sure that I sang in the church choir. I loved singing in the choir so much that I dreamed of becoming an opera singer. I was fifteen when my mother died. After my mother's funeral, my father dragged me to work in the Meuricoffre factory where he tended the industrial machines. I hated it. I hated the acid smell of oil pulsing through high speed machines. I hated the indelible stain of grease on my hands and nails. I hated the physical exhaustion at the end of the day.

"My father grieved, I grieved. Our lives were miserable. My only comfort was singing. When I sang on the streets, or in the cafes, my pain rushed out of me in the way that smoke escapes up the chimney."

"You know, I never thought of it that way, but, when I smash a baseball out of sight, I feel like I've cleared my shoulders," said Babe. Enrico looked side-wise at the young man.

"The day of my mother's funeral was when I dedicated my life to singing to honor my mother and her belief in me," said Enrico wistfully.

They conversed for a long time. Caruso was fascinated by Babe's nascent career in baseball. Babe offered to leave tickets for the great tenor at the 'will call' window at Polo Grounds when the Red Sox were in town in again. Caruso smiled and accepted, but, only on the condition that Babe attend the opera, *Tristan and Isolde*, the next day as his guest.

An attendant interrupted them and advised the tenor that his masseuse was ready.

"*Ciao, mi amici*, I look forward to seeing you tomorrow," said Enrico, patting Babe on the knee.

By the time Babe got to his luxurious suite and entered through the double-width mahogany doors, there was a canister in the message tube. Babe excitedly opened the cover to the pneumatic tube that was a unique system of tubes that carried messages to designated suites throughout the Ansonia. Inside the canister was a pair of opera tickets and a note from Enrico inviting him to dinner after the performance. Babe crossed the Persian-carpeted room and flopped onto the bed, beaming with astonishment at the good fortune of his new life.

July 1915
Boston, MA

"Never underestimate the mayhem Babe is capable of."
~ Heinie Wagner

Heading into the summer of 1915, the war in Europe was in its full barbarity. In the United States, there was considerable activity in reaction to the events in Europe. With the cooperation of the press, the government began to orchestrate support for Britain and France. The media voiced a steady stream of pro-British, anti-German propaganda.

To the young Babe Ruth, the war was distant and faint. He was more interested in exploring the limits of his new-found freedom, both economic and social. Babe and Helen rented an apartment in the West Fens neighborhood not far from the ballpark.

When Babe opened the mail box he was surprised to see a gilt-edged envelope addressed to him in elaborate calligraphy. He and Helen were so entranced by the elegance of the missive that they did not want to spoil its beauty by tearing it open. It lay on the kitchen table for a day and a half before their curiosity overcame their timidity.

Dr. and Mrs. Karl Muck
cordially invite you to a soiree at their home
50 Fenway, Boston
On the evening of May 5 ,1915 at 7 P.M.
R.S.V.P.
Black tie

"This must be a mistake. Hon, did one of your cronies send this as a joke? Do they think that we would actually fall for this?"

Babe examined the gold-lined envelope and a response card flipped onto the linoleum floor. He picked it up.

"No, Hon, this is real. The guys are too cheap to do something this fancy. See here, it says black tie. I guess I have to go and buy a new tie."

"No, silly, that means you have to wear a tuxedo."

"Where am I going to get one of those monkey suits to wear?"

"Ask, Rough. He's a college man. He'll know."

When the appointed day came, the Ruths checked themselves in the mirror for the hundredth time. Helen was wearing a stylish new, green chiffon dress. Her lips pressed and smoothed her ruby-red lipstick until they hurt. Babe gazed into the mirror and saw a surprisingly attractive man wearing a tuxedo borrowed from Heinie Wagner. The suit fit snugly and there was a sizeable gap between the edge of his trousers and the tops of his shoes. He grinned, just like the old days in Pigtown where the length of his pantlegs never kept up with his growing limbs. Anyway, he hoped that the party would be so crowded that in the crush of guests no one would be able to see the shortness of his pants.

The following day, Babe strode along the warning track at Fenway carrying the tuxedo on his arm with a careless grip. Babe was oblivious to the pant leg and jacket sleeve that dragged along beside him. Wisps of dust followed Babe as the tuxedo trailed him like a forlorn kite tail on a windless day. Heinie winced inwardly and held out his hands to receive his dusty garment.

"So, how was your fancy party?"

"It was great, the music was real fine," said Babe. "Dr. Muck is an excellent piano player. He and his wife, Anita, spent a lot of time with me and Helen. He reminded me of an exhibition game on Long Island that I pitched against the Boston Symphony team back when I was seventeen. When he told me how much money he lost betting against my team, I felt embarrassed and offered to repay him. He just laughed and said that he would make it all back when the Sox win the pennant this year. He had a strange look in his eyes."

Heinie scrambled for a different topic. "So, how were the dames? Were there a lot of show business types?"

"Yessir, there was lots of pretty young women there. They were real friendly to me and Helen. They seemed to like this here tuxedo; they couldn't keep their hands off it. They kept coming over and patting and stroking it. The food – now that was another story."

"What do you mean?"

"I mean it tasted fine. They had these waiter fellas offering food on trays to the guests."

"So? What's wrong with that?"

"I don't know. It looked like regular food, but they kept asking me if I wanted a can of peas. I ate 'em, but they did not look like a can of peas to me."

Heinie laughed out loud. In his mind's eye, he pictured a waiter carrying a tray of tin cans of peas, rather than a tray covered with fancy French canapes.

Ballplayers emerging from the clubhouse reminded Babe that he'd better get ready for pre-game practice. He and Heinie walked through the dugout into the clubhouse. The manager beckoned for Heinie to join him in his office.

"We need to go over our plans for the upcoming road trip," said Rough.

"Sure thing, Skip," replied Heinie.

Heinie sat in the manager's office. As he draped the tuxedo over a chair a flurry of cards and paper fell out of a pocket and fluttered to the floor like confetti. Heinie picked up a few and whistled.

"You're not going to believe this, Skip. These are notes from women imploring Babe to call them for a good time. That kid has no idea just how magnetic he is."

"Right, and if he ever finds out, we'll never be able to put that genie back in the bottle."

The veteran manager sighed, recalling more than one promising young ballplayer who dissipated his talent while succumbing to the temptations of carnal pleasure. He hoped that this Ruth kid would be different.

During the 1915 season, his performance on the field was consistent, if not spectacular. The manager, Bill Carrigan enjoyed nurturing the youngster's development on the field. Off the field was another matter. Every time the manager tasked Heinie Wagner with shadowing the young man, the veteran invariably returned bleary-eyed from Babe's late night gallivanting. It would not be long before Babe tested the manager's resolve.

In mid-June the Sox went on a tear, closing within two and one half games of the league-leading Chicago White Sox. The team from Beantown was on a seven-game winning streak as they faced a getaway game in St. Louis against the hapless Browns. The Sox were concluding a thirteen-game home stand where they would only lose three games. They would have a short road trip to Washington for five games with the Nationals before another extended home stand. Even though the last game against the Browns ended in a tie, the team boarded the train that Saturday evening in good spirits.

Babe poked his head into the manager's compartment where he sat playing cards with Heinie Wagner, the trainer, Charlie Green, and Duffy Lewis.

"Hey, Skip, we have a couple of off-days. Would it be ok if I jumped off when the train stops in Baltimore to see my people?"

The manager was in a good mood. That's what a winning streak will do for a man's disposition. He was glad to see that Babe was dressed appropriately in a suit and tie. He sported a white straw skimmer, trimmed with a wide red hat ribbon that proclaimed Boston Red Sox in white script around the circumference. The skimmer was tilted at a rakish angle. Rough had to hand it to the kid; he certainly had learned how to look stylish.

"Sure. Give your Dad my regards," said Carrigan in a jovial tone. He thought what the heck, how much trouble can he get into on a Sunday with his family. As Heinie Wagner would later remind him, "Never underestimate the mayhem Babe is capable of."

Babe's first stop when he arrived in Baltimore was the Dregs, a marginal establishment that served alcohol to the maritime crowd of longshoremen and sailors who rotated through the port of Baltimore. It was there that he met up with Stash, Noodles, and a couple of other Bunnies. They were in the midst of a billiards marathon and welcomed Babe with open arms. They laughed, caroused, and drank until they were thrown out when the bar closed at dawn.

Babe ambled from the Dregs to the home of Gunny. Over the course of Babe's short professional baseball career, he and Gunny had regularly written letters to each other. As Babe approached the front door, he smelled breakfast links and hash on the stove. Babe knocked firmly. When Gunny opened the door, he gasped in surprise.

"Oh my *Gott*, look who's here? Come in, come in," said Gunny who shouted over his shoulder, "Ma, set another plate. We have a guest."

Babe swept through the house like a tornado honing in on Mrs. Gunther. He gave her a big hug and twirled her in an aerial circle so vigorously that she fumbled to maintain her spectacles on her nose. Mrs. Gunther giggled and feigned protestation.

"George, you are such a *kinder*. Put me down so that I can fix you some *frühstück*, breakfast. Here, have some *brötchen*, bread rolls while I prepare an omelette."

While she puttered, and fussed around the kitchen, Babe and Gunny chatted.

"I know that it's not as glamorous as your career, Jidgie, but I got a promotion at the bank. I am now a junior supervisor of tellers at the downtown branch. My boss told me that if I keep working hard I could become a bank officer within ten years."

"Golly, that's great."

"My biggest concern is that there is a growing anti-German sentiment that is seeping into our daily lives. Things have changed since the war in Europe erupted."

"I've seen some of that myself," said Babe. "At the ballpark, the cranks yell some vile insults about my German background. I try not to listen."

"President Wilson claims that he will keep us out of war, but I don't believe him. He is sending munitions to England and France while claiming neutrality. The Kaiser isn't that dumb. That's why the German Navy declared unrestricted submarine warfare against merchant vessels."

"I know. When the U-boats sank the *Lusitania* last month, the insults hurled at us players with German backgrounds were brutal. We were in Chicago a few weeks ago and I almost got beaned with a soda bottle in the outfield. It missed me by a foot. When I turned to see who threw it, I saw some crazy woman yelling at me. When she called me *Deutsch pavian*, German baboon, I decided to face our flag and salute. That got them laughing. After that, the cranks backed off."

After a sumptuous meal, Babe and Gunny walked around Baltimore, stopping in arcades and bowling alleys. Gunny wanted to go see a flick on the silver screen, but Babe refused, saying that he did not want to risk his eyes watching a movie. He told Gunny to go see the movie and Babe went next door to a new roller-skating rink. The next few days were a marathon of roller-skating, billiards, and drinking with his buddies.

The following Tuesday Babe strolled into the Red Sox' clubhouse only one hour before game time. Acting like he was attending a church social, Babe bantered with his teammates. He was still wearing the same suit. Considering that he had spent his visit to Baltimore playing billiards and then roller-skating until dawn, his clothes had held up fairly well.

Only a skid mark on his right knee from a failed pirouette marred his appearance.

From his office in the corner, Carrigan glowered at his young pitcher. There was no written rule about how early to arrive before a game. However, it was customary for that day's starting pitcher to be in the clubhouse preparing at least several hours before game time. Carrigan fumed while Babe dallied.

"I'll be waiting to warm you up in the bullpen. Be there in five minutes," growled Rough as he walked past Babe who was regaling a small group of players about the new roller-skating rink in his home town. The group scuffled away in Carrigan's wake.

"What's got his goat?" muttered Babe to no one.

In the bullpen, the manager put Babe through his paces and was pleased with the sharpness of his pitcher's stuff. Babe blazed in slant after slant to his catcher whose glove never moved. By the time Babe had completed his warm-ups, Carrigan's mood had brightened considerably. With this kind of movement on his pitches the kid should dominate today.

With warm-up completed, the two men walked toward the dugout with Carrigan briefing the pitcher on the strategy they would employ to offset the strengths of each batter. Babe was concentrating so attentively that he never saw it coming. A man was standing at his seat behind the Red Sox dugout. He bellowed to Babe.

"Nice going George. You're down here and never come out to see us."[xi]

Carrigan looked at Babe's father and turned crimson. He gave Babe an expletive-filled tongue-lashing that was audible in the visiting team's clubhouse. The tirade continued until the home plate ump Bill Dineen exhorted Carrigan to get his team on the field. Sheepish and contrite, Babe channeled Carrigan's anger at the Nationals and defeated them 8 – 3, with a complete game, allowing just six hits. Babe recorded the final out by retiring the great pitcher, Walter "Big Train" Johnson who was pinch-hitting.

By the end of July, the Red Sox moved into first place where they would remain except for two days in August for the rest of the season. They would win 101 games and the American League pennant. Babe enjoyed his first full season in the big leagues. He saw his father occasionally when the team played in Washington or Philadelphia. He ended the season with an 18 – 8 record. Although he would have fewer than one hundred at bats, Babe would lead the team with four home runs, twice as many as the next batter. With his antics on and off the field he soon became a fan favorite.

The Red Sox breezed through the World Series, defeating the Phillies in five games. Except for one pinch-hitting appearance, Babe was a spectator at his first championship. The final victory took place at the Baker Bowl in Philadelphia. In the locker room after the final victory, Heinie walked over to Babe with a trademark yellow envelope. Acting on his phobia, Babe held up his hands in a gesture of avoidance. Heinie knew about Babe's aversion to telegrams and sat down next to the big fellow. Opening the wire, he cleared his throat.

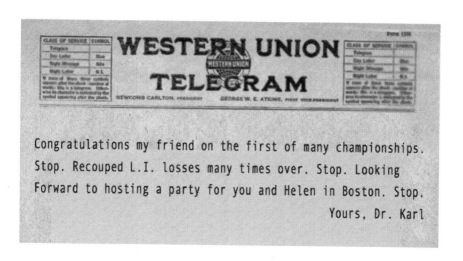

Congratulations my friend on the first of many championships. Stop. Recouped L.I. losses many times over. Stop. Looking Forward to hosting a party for you and Helen in Boston. Stop.

Yours, Dr. Karl

After Babe made a perfunctory appearance at the team celebration, he took a late train to New York City to enjoy a dinner with several of his old friends at a social club in Little Italy. He walked up to a plain, nondescript building on Mulberry Street and knocked on a weathered door. While he waited in the street, he inhaled the air redolent with delicious food being cooked to perfection. His salivary glands began sending signals to his stomach that succulent treats were imminent. The noise of a peep window sliding drew his attention. Two dark eyes scanned his personage. He heard some exaggerated whispers behind the door. Then it opened, creaking on rusty hinges. Babe entered a dark entryway.

"I told you it was him. I told you – just look at that mug," said the taller of two men who stood as guardians of the inner sanctum. The other man's eyes pleaded with the first man to stifle his enthusiasm in deference to their guest. A look of amusement spread across Babe's face.

"Hey, fellas, I'm meeting Rico here. Is he here yet?" said Babe who reached into his pocket.

"*Si, signore. Signore* Caruso is in the room straight back." said the shorter man. Babe nodded and stepped forward, flipping an autographed baseball that he had withdrawn from his coat. He chuckled as the men scrambled for the ball that bounced erratically down the hall.

Caruso sat across the room. His expensive suit and silk tie were covered with a white napkin stuffed under his chin. He raised his wine glass in a welcoming gesture.

"*Complimenti per campionato del mondo!* Congratulations on your World Championship!"

Enrico beamed with approval at his friend's success.

"Ah, *Bambino*, you arrive just in time a *mangiare*. Come, sit here." said the singer, patting the chair next to him.

As soon as Babe sat, another gentleman entered. He was dressed in full opera regalia – silk top hat, opera cape, a black cane, matching gloves, and spats over patent leather shoes. With the grace of a continental noble, Otto Kahn bowed deeply from the waist and greeted the two men.

"*Glückwünsche für Weltmeisterschaft!* Hail, World Champion!" said Otto.

"Enrico, Mr. Babe, it's so good to see you again. It's a shame that you were not at the Met this evening. *Il Signore* was an absolute genius. His performance of *Pagliacci* was astounding. The depth and range of emotion that he portrays is beyond sublime."

"I know," said Babe. "The first time I heard that voice, I thought that it was the voice of God. I don't know much about opera, but I know genius when I hear it. You're right, this man is a genius."

"Babe, I am touched by your words. However, it is I who is in the presence of genius. I have been enjoying the stories of your prodigious exploits on the ball field. I have witnessed your excellence first hand. That is genius," said Enrico.

"You are both geniuses," said Otto. "I wish that God had given me such talent."

"Otto, you are mistaken," said Enrico. "The talent, yes, it comes from God; but, it does not become genius without countless hours of practice and refinement. Am I right, *Bambino?*"

"I never thought of it that way, but I think you are right. I spent thousands of hours working on my swing before I could hit the ball a mile," said Babe, chuckling.

"*Ecco*, the food is here. It is time to feast," said Enrico, smacking his lips in anticipation of enjoying the culinary delights before them.

A waiter wheeled in a cart covered with plates of *anti-pasti – polpo alla griglia, involtini di melanzane* and *cozze e vongole posillipo*. He deftly plated three servings of grilled octopus, eggplant rollatini, and mussels and clams in red sauce. Before digging in, Caruso fanned the luscious aromas rising from his plate toward his face. He broke into a wide smile and sighed with contentment.

"*Mangia tutti*, let's all eat!"

The trio lapsed into silence as they gorged themselves on the *prima piatti*, first course. While they waited for the next course, Rico asked Babe how things were now that he was a champion. Rico nodded when Babe told him it was not all it was cracked up to be. Babe recounted some of the ugly incidents of anti-German venom in Chicago and worse, heckling from players on other teams. Enrico expressed relief that his opera schedule did not include any German operas this season. Babe told of rumors accusing his friend who was the conductor of the Boston Symphony of being a German agent.

"I know Dr. Muck. He may have strong opinions favoring the Fatherland, but he is not a German agent," said Otto.

When Rico asked Otto whether he had experienced anti-German prejudice, Otto weighed how to respond. He concluded that he was among friends.

"Sadly, I must answer yes, particularly after the events of last July third."

"What happened then?" asked Babe.

"It was shocking. It happened not far from the place where I'm going to build my new home," said Otto.

Rico and Babe looked toward the kitchen door in hopes that the second plate might rescue them from Otto's dramatics. The door was motionless. Their gaze returned to Otto.

"OK, since you don't know, I'll tell you. A deranged German sympathizer named Eric Muenter planted a time bomb in the reception area of the United States Senate. After the explosion, he took a train to New York and appeared at the home of J.P. Morgan on Long Island the following morning. Muenter forced his way into the home and shot Mr. Morgan twice before he was subdued. Muenter who several years earlier had been a professor of German at an Ivy League university told the police that he decided to assassinate Mr. Morgan because the immoral, rich bankers were responsible for arms shipments to the Allied countries."

"That's quite a story," remarked Babe.

"That's not all; prior to his arrest he planted pencil bombs on a merchant ship carrying cordite and ordnance to Britain. The ship caught fire. Fortunately, the ship made it to port before it was destroyed."

"This man was truly *pazzo*, insane," said Enrico.

"That's not the whole of it. Before he went on this crime spree he murdered his pregnant wife by giving her small doses of arsenic."

Babe whistled in amazement.

"Insane crimes like this by German-Americans fuel the anti-German hysteria that is taking hold in this country. The best way to avoid being tarred with the brush of Kaiserism is to stand tall for America," said Otto.

"That's good advice, *mi Bambino*," said Rico.

As Babe nodded, the kitchen door swung open filling the room with aromas befitting a dinner of champions.

1915 – Babe with father tending bar in Ruth's Café

March 1916
Hot Springs, AK

"Luck Is the Great Stabilizer in Baseball"
~ Tris Speaker

"**C**ongratulations!" yelled the excited crowd as George senior cut the ceremonial ribbon that draped across the front doors of Ruth's Café. With his arm around his son, George Ruth stood at the corner of Lombard and Eutaw streets facing the revelers who had gathered for the grand opening of his new establishment. Babe had used his $3780 World Series bonus to fund his father's latest business venture. The bonus was more than his annual salary of $3500 in 1915.

"It's New Year's Eve and Babe and I welcome you to Ruth's Café. We owe our good fortune to the cranks in Boston and Philly who contributed so generously to my son's World Series bonus. We used this money to transform this old saloon into the swankiest place in town," said Big George who was slightly inebriated.

"Now, we are going to party like there's no tomorrow!"

With that, he flung open the doors and beckoned the crowd to follow him. A handful of newspaper people had come to cover a story of the young, successful Red Sox pitcher and World Series champion. They loved Babe because he always managed to provide them with good copy. However, if pressed, most of the reporters would have admitted that they were drawn just as much by the prospect of free food and booze. Others were drawn by the likely presence of attractive young women who flocked to the charismatic Babe.

Flashbulbs reflected off the shiny brass surfaces and mirrors that adorned the spacious tavern. The crowd gasped at the tasteful décor. Tinsel garlands and colored lights hung from mirrors behind the bar. A Christmas tree covered with Red Sox red and blue decorations graced the far corner. A fieldstone fireplace glowed and crackled with a roaring blaze.

The Ruth men donned aprons and went to work behind the bar. Big George held champagne in one hand and a pitcher of beer in the other while shouting, "Bubbly or brew?" to the thirsty throng. Helen along with several other women trafficked in and out of the kitchen with platters piled high with brats, *sauerbraten* and roasted chicken.

As the clock passed eleven, George and several members of his lodge formed a barbershop quartet. They entertained the crowd with traditional German Christmas songs. As midnight approached, Babe sensed that some of the partiers were becoming agitated with the selection of music. He gestured to Helen to take his place behind the bar. Babe sidled over to his father as the quartet was conferring on their next selection. Babe whispered in his father's ear. George's face turned solemn.

"Ladies and gentlemen," shouted George. A hush settled over the crowd. "My son (a smattering of cheers rippled through the crowd) has reminded me that there are many tonight who are suffering in Europe from the ravages of the war. Our hearts go out to them. We are thankful that we are not at war. We will now honor our country with a song that was written right here in the Baltimore harbor over a century ago."

The quartet was quickly joined by the entire assemblage in an emotional rendition of the Star-Spangled Banner. While the last note reverberated, someone shouted that there were only two minutes left to 1915. Hats and noisemakers were distributed just in in time for the countdown to the New Year. With church bells ringing the twelfth hour, the group sang *Auld Lang Syne*. With tears in his eyes, Big George hugged Babe and Helen. A photo taken a moment later captured a father and son behind the bar looking almost like brothers, albeit a generation apart.

With local celebrity Babe Ruth tending bar and regaling patrons with stories of his big-league exploits, Ruth's Café was successful. In his first full season with the Red Sox, Babe had recorded eighteen wins against eight losses, with an earned run average of 2.44 runs per nine innings. Even though he batted only one-hundred and three times, he led the team in homers with four. The young man was now an established and important member of the Red Sox.

As spring training approached, Babe felt baseball drawing him toward his real vocation. He loved everything about the game and was anxious to begin defending the Red Sox championship. Babe couldn't wait for the upcoming six weeks in Hot Springs training for the 1916 campaign. This was his opportunity to convince manager Carrigan that he was valuable as a hitter. Since New Year's Day, he had devoted an hour a day to strengthening his hands and wrists by swinging a weighted bat in the alley behind the bar.

His March getaway day arrived and he made his way to St. Louis where he met with Penny and Pinch on their way to Hot Springs. Herb Pennock, the left-handed pitcher, and Pinch Thomas, the catcher, were Babe's best friends on the returning squad. When they checked into the hotel, Babe wondered how his friend Yo-na was. Babe made his way to the kitchen in search of his friend and, of course, a snack. To his dismay, he could not find his young Indian friend.

After a successful rookie season in 1915, Babe was confident that he belonged. With this state of mind, he worked diligently on preparing for the season without the anxiety of impressing the coaches. His pitching was sharp and strong. It was a foregone conclusion that he would be a mainstay of the starting rotation. Influenced by the belief that it was harder to repeat as champions than it was to win the title in the first place, Carrigan worked the players hard to prepare them for the campaign. As spring training progressed, one thing became glaringly obvious. The Red Sox had a weapon in Babe unlike anything ever seen in professional baseball. Babe consistently hit the ball so high and far that as one wag quipped Babe's blasts would go out of any park in the country, including Yellowstone.

In Europe, another type of campaign was underway. French and German forces engaged in a ten-month battle over the city of Verdun. Both sides would suffer over one million casualties in Germany's failed attempt to capture Verdun. The five-month long Battle of the Somme ended inconclusively with both sides suffering 600,000 casualties. Among the German wounded was a corporal named Adolph Hitler. At the same time this carnage was occurring, Woodrow Wilson was re-elected President of the United States on the platform that: "He kept us out of war."

The battle for the sympathy of the American public continued to rage. When the British cut the transatlantic cable between Germany and the United States, the tide of opinion shifted toward the virtual monopoly of information held by British interests. In counter-balance, the National German-American Alliance, a federation of German organizations dedicated to promoting all things German, stepped up its efforts advocating for neutrality so that the United States would not enter the war. In cities like Chicago and Baltimore where there were significant German-American populations, a simmering tension grew.

Babe was more concerned with improving his baseball skills and after-hours mischief than he was interested in world news. Babe picked up bits and pieces of news from beat reporters and older players like Heinie Wagner, but he rarely pondered the implications of international events.

In contrast, Babe was extremely engaged with any news about the status of the Federal League. His reason was based on the simple fact that the existence of the renegade league helped to drive salaries higher. Now that it appeared that the Federal League was doomed, the magnates were cracking down on the salaries paid to their veteran ballplayers who had received inflated pay over the last few years to ensure their loyalty.

The prime example of this regressive practice was the negotiations between Red Sox magnate Lannin and his star player, centerfielder Tris Speaker. In 1915, Speaker's salary was $18,000. During the winter after the World Series championship, the club offered Speaker $9,000 and made it clear that he could take it or leave it. The message was not lost on the rest of the players. If the club could mercilessly cut the salary of Speaker, the Grey Eagle of the sport's greatest outfield, then, it was hopeless for the others. At first, Speaker refused to report to spring training. After a few weeks, he relented, stating that he wanted it understood that he was not a holdout.

In light of these developments, Babe still harbored resentment over the fact that in 1914 he had turned down tens of thousands of dollars from the Terrapins, bowing to admonitions that defecting players would be barred from major league baseball for life. To his chagrin, players who had jumped to the Federal League were being welcomed back to the major leagues without any consequences for their defection. Whenever his frustration rose, he reached out by phone to his father who counselled him to worry only about things he could control. Invariably, Babe took his big wooden club and vented his frustrations out on the ball. The result was dented fences wherever he played.

After two weeks of balmy weather, a storm front hit the region and Carrigan reluctantly cancelled practice. This respite gave Babe enough free time to climb up to the small general store outside of town that was operated by Yo-na's family. As Babe approached the low wooden structure, he was overtaken by forlornness. Shabbiness permeated the area. The R.C. Cola sign pivoted in the breeze on a single nail and the once-proud stallion now reared with only the base of a saddle. Babe felt a pang of remorse at the careless damage he caused to the saddle last year. Surely, by now, Yo-na would have repaired it.

"Can I help you?" asked a feminine voice from the shadows of the front porch.

"Yes, my name is Babe and I'm looking for my friend Yo-na."

"Were you here last spring with the Red Sox?"

"Yes, Ma'am. I'm the one who gave him the baseball glove."

"I remember you. Yo-na was inspired by you."

"Can you tell me where he is? I have more equipment for him."

As Babe climbed onto the porch, he saw a frail woman sitting on a rocker. Tears slid down her face. Her skin was dark, weathered, and bore the wrinkles of a harsh life. She was wrapped in a coarse horse blanket. Her mostly silver hair was held in place by a beaded headband.

"Can I help you?" said Babe.

"No," she replied. "My Yo-na is gone."

Seeing a facial resemblance, Babe realized that he was talking to Yo-na's mother.

"Last fall, a man from the north came here and recruited many of the Indian boys for the Canadian Expeditionary Force. He said that the people of the First Nation were obligated to fight the evil Huns. He appealed to the boys' lust for glory and a chance to get away from this godforsaken place. Yo-na was seduced by the man's words."

"Where did he go? Where can I write to him?"

She reached under her blanket and withdrew a crinkled envelope. She withdrew a letter that bore evidence of numerous tearstained readings. Babe accepted the letter. It was on official C.E.F. stationery. It read:

Dear Mrs. Brighthorse,

We regret to inform you that your son, Yo-na Brighthorse made the ultimate sacrifice in the Battle of Loos during the Loos-Artois Offensive. He perished on September 25, 1915. You will be contacted by officials of the Canadian Expeditionary Force with respect to burial arrangements for the remains of Private Brighthorse. As the next-of-kin you will receive a monetary stipend. We are sorry for your loss.

Sincere Condolences

Lt. Colonel Wilkerson Jones

Tears welled up in Babe's eyes. He handed the letter back to Yo-na's mother. They sat in silence.

October 1916
Boston, MA

"I told you a year ago I could take care of those National League bums, and you never gave me a chance."
~ Babe Ruth to his manager Bill Carrigan

It was the last week of spring training in Hot Springs. Babe was glad that the season was finally here. He settled into the Nauheim tub at the Maurice Bathhouse and closed his eyes. He chuckled to himself as he recalled his first experience with the Nautheim. He nearly jumped out of his skin when he thought that his butt was under attack by surging bubbles. Now, it was one of his most favorite and relaxing activities. He closed his eyes and focused on the untangling of his muscles. If only the Nauheim could have the same effect on his mind.

News of the death of his friend Yo-na in France while fighting for the Canadian Expeditionary Force weighed heavily on Babe. He recalled the boy's gentle smile and vibrant spirit. Babe had never been much of a student at St. Mary's and he could not articulate in detail the causes of the hostilities in Europe. Babe surely could not find Loos-Artois on a map. One thing he knew for certain was that the Kaiser's army had taken his friend's life. The steamy bath caused beads of sweat to run down his face. The sweat mingled with his tears. With his jaw firmly set, Babe resolved to dedicate the upcoming season to the memory of Yo-na.

When Babe emerged from the bathhouse relaxed and ready for a night of drinking, he never expected what happened next. Penny, his fellow southpaw approached him with a worried look.

"What's up, Penny?"

"Babe, you are not going to believe it. Let's go to the lounge in the Majestic Hotel," said Pennock, hooking Babe's elbow and steering him to the hotel lobby.

"Boy, this must be serious. Hey, Kid," said Babe hollering to an attendant, "Get us a couple of brews."

Penny sat down and splayed the Boston Globe on the worn table. Babe stared at the headline in disbelief.

RED SOX TRADE TRIS SPEAKER TO CLEVELAND

"Ok, you got me. This is an April Fool's joke, right?"

"I wish it was," said Penny. "Look at the dateline. It's April 8th. This is real."

"I know that management is a bunch of knuckleheads, but, no one would trade the best centerfielder in baseball," said Babe, his voice reflecting false confidence.

"They are and they did. He's already gone. He left on the first train this morning."

They sipped their beers in silence, staring without focus out the window.

In the early season defense of their championship, the Red Sox scuffled due to offensive deficiencies and inconsistent pitching. In May, the team reached its nadir when Speaker and the Cleveland Indians visited Boston. The Indians were in first place and the Red Sox languished in fifth place, their record below .500. Tilly Walker, whose contract had been purchased with the hope that his bat could replace Speaker's, was in a miserable slump. Yet, the team was too talented and too proud to succumb to a poor start.

The resurgence began with pitching. Near the end of May, Babe kalsomined the Tigers, whitewashing them, 4 – 0. One week later, Babe hooked up against Walter "Big Train" Johnson and the Washington team. Behind Ruth's three-hitter, the Red Sox prevailed 1 – 0.

At mid-season, the Sox were in sole possession of first place. Babe entered the clubhouse on July 31st to prepare for his start versus the Detroit Tigers.

"How's it going, big fella?" asked Heinie Wagner.

The veteran was seated in his locker, leaning back on a folding chair. He had just finished reading the morning paper and threw it onto a nearby bench. Babe's jaw dropped when he saw the lead story. The headlines trumpeted a major explosion at a munitions depot on Black Tom Island in New York City harbor. As authorities struggled overnight to quell the ensuing fires, witnesses reported seeing fiery shards of shrapnel strike the Statue of Liberty. Early estimates pegged the death toll at fifty. There was speculation that the explosion was the result of sabotage by German agents.

Babe sat, stunned and turned the paper to the jump page where the story continued. There he found something that enraged him. A large ad in the lower quadrant of the page called for Americans to purchase German war bonds. The bonds were under-written by Zimmermann & Forshay, members of the New York Stock Exchange. The effrontery of this ad on the same page as the reportage of German agent sabotage and American deaths sent Ruth into a rage. His thoughts turned to his fallen friend from Hot Springs. He ripped the paper into pieces and threw the chair into lockers across the room where it slammed with a loud crash.

That afternoon Babe brought his emotions to the mound. With blazing slants and knee-buckling breakers, he dominated the contending Tigers in their home stadium with a two-hit shutout. It was his fifteen victory of the season in which he would win twenty-three games, lead the league with a 1.75 earned run average and set a record for nine shutouts by a southpaw.

Before he knew it the season was over. Led by pitching and fielding prowess, the Red Sox won ninety-one games and repeated as American League pennant winners. In the rival National League, the Brooklyn Robins surprised everyone by winning ninety-four games, streaking to their first ever pennant. Heading into the World Series, the odds-makers favored the Red Sox by a 10 – 7 margin. Carrigan started Ernie Shore in the series opener. The North Carolinian won the first game.

In game two, Carrigan decided to give the ball to the pitcher who had won forty-one games over his first two seasons with the Red Sox. With a chip on his shoulder, Babe took the ball. He still felt the sting of not playing in the 1915 World Series. Except for a lone pinch-hitting appearance, Rough had kept Babe on the pines throughout the series. To Babe, the reasons were unfathomable. This would be his World Series debut and his performance would be beyond memorable.

In the 1916 World Series, the Red Sox abandoned Fenway Park for Braves Field which had several thousand more seats. Over forty-seven thousand cranks crammed into the ballpark, making the magnates swell with pride and lucre. Boston magnate Joseph Lannin gave an enthusiastic thumbs-up to his counterpart Charles Ebbets. The National League was represented by the Brooklyn Robins, led by twenty-five game winner Jeff Pfeffer on the mound and the flamboyant outfielder Casey Stengel on the field and at the plate.

"How ya feelin', Babe," said Pinch Thomas, the Boston catcher that had the best rapport with the young pitcher.

"I'm good. Let's whip these National League bums."

Before climbing the hill, Babe surveyed the scene. The cavernous dimensions of Braves Field appealed to Babe's pitcher's sensibilities. The fences were over 400' in left and right and 550' in center. It was built of concrete and steel on the site of the former Allston Gulf Club on Commonwealth Avenue, one mile west of Fenway Park. Opened in August 1915, the new stadium featured a single deck covering the home plate area and extending down the lines. Sixty rows of seating sloped gently up and away from the field. There were uncovered pavilions surrounding the outfield for the cranks of lesser means. The scoreboard loomed over the bleachers in right field. The flag on a tall, white pole in right-centerfield snapped in the crisp air. The horn of a train chugging through the railyards behind the left field stands echoed off the roof. It was followed by a cloud of dense black smoke that drifted over the bleachers.

Clouds hung low over the stadium on this early October afternoon. The forecast predicted possibility of rain. Babe located Helen, her brother Will, and Big George in reserved seats behind the Red Sox bench. For a fleeting moment, he wondered whether the fourth seat in the box would be occupied. After tipping his cap, he went to work.

He retired the first two batters with no problem. The third hitter was Hy Myers, a speedy centerfielder with a unique running style. According to sports writer Murray Robinson, "Myers galloped with his long arms held straight down by his sides, like a man running for a train with a heavy suitcase in each hand, or an authentic Irish dancer doing his stuff." [xii]

The cranks were still filing into their seats when Myers launched an offering from Babe into deep right-centerfield. Tillie Walker in center got a late start. Right fielder Harry Hooper never had a chance. By the time Hoop caught up with the ball, Babe was backing up home plate. He watched in frustration as Myers raced in from third to plate the first run of the game.

Manager Wilbert Robinson elected to send his young lefty, Sherry Smith, to the hill for the Robins. Although he had won fourteen games that year, he was a surprise starter. After a few innings, it was apparent that Ruth and Smith were locked in a game for the ages.

Down 1 – 0, Babe battled the Robins. In the top of the third inning, Sherry Smith, hitting right-handed, drove a one-out shot to right field.

While Hooper was chasing the ball in the immense outfield, Smith raced around the bases. Smith was at second base when Hoop tracked down the ball in the corner. The baserunner never hesitated. He cut the bag and headed for third. Hoop threw a perfect relay throw to his centerfielder who whipped the ball to third baseman Larry Gardner who tagged the winded pitcher. Babe retired the next batter and headed to the dugout where he was scheduled to be the third batter.

Although the batters returning to the dugout after facing Smith tried to explain the movement on his ball, they were at a loss to solve the lefty who had everything working. It was going to be a long afternoon. Little did Babe know how important each run would be. Everett Scott led off the inning with a long fly to deep left-center. It fell between left-fielder Zack Wheat and centerfielder Myers. Scott legged it out for a triple. After the eighth batter grounded out, Babe strode to the plate. His eyes narrowed in concentration. He waited for the third-base coacher Wagner to give instructions to Scott. Ruth stepped into the box and took a few practice swings. As he took his stance, his bat was nearly vertical.

Ahead in the count, Smith dealt a pitch that tailed in and faded just as Babe swung. The pitch was too low for Babe to lift, but he connected solidly. As the ball bounded toward right field, George Cutshaw the second sacker appeared out of nowhere to snag it. Scott read the ball perfectly and broke for home. In his haste to set his feet for a strong throw home, Cutshaw failed to field the grounder cleanly. He had no choice but to throw Babe out at first. Babe knew from the crowd noise that Scott had scored to tie the game. Babe vowed that the Robins would not dent the plate again that day.

With the score tied at one, both pitchers settled into a pitching duel that was later dubbed the "double masterpiece." For each goose egg that Babe recorded for the home team, Smith matched it. At the beginning of each inning, Pinch asked Babe the same question and invariably got the same answer.

"How ya feelin', Babe," asked Pinch Thomas.

"I'm good. Let's whip these National League bums."

As Babe was ready to toe the slab in the top of the fourth inning, he heard a buzz go through the crowd. Glancing toward the box with his family he saw a majestic figure settling into the seat next to his father. The one and only Enrico Caruso, resplendent in a silk mohair suit under a camel hair coat draped over his shoulders in the European fashion and matching tan bowler, waved to Babe with his leather gloves clinched in his right hand. He turned and waved to the crowd. Babe smiled in awe at the natural magnetism of his friend. His inattention was broken by the gruff voice of home plate ump Bill Dineen.

"We got a ballgame here, kid. Let's play!"

Distracted, Babe committed a cardinal sin of pitching; he walked Jake Daubert, the first batter in the fourth inning. A confident Hy Myers approached the plate. He tapped his bat a few times and gave Ruth a malicious smile. Babe stood tall on the mound, twirling the ball behind his left leg until he found the proper seams. He came set and unleashed a blazing fastball that dipped and faded. Myers swung and hit a two-bouncer to Everett at short who promptly flipped to second, relay to first, double play. Babe and Sherry continued their excellence.

Baseball history is littered with the exploits of minor characters who influenced important games. One such character was Ivan "Ivy" Olson the journeyman shortstop of the Brooklyn team. Baseball writer Murray Robinson gave this colorful description of Olson in an article written when Olson passed away: "...there was a special niche for Ivan Olson, the club's swaggering bow-legged shortstop; a spike-scarred, swarthy veteran with a barrel chest, high shoulders, a sharp nose and chin, and piercing black eyes. All Ivy Olson needed to make him look like a pirate of old was a bandana on his head, a patch over one eye, and a cutlass instead of a bat. Maybe that's why we kids in the left-field bleachers were so enamored of him." [xiii]

With two out in the home fifth, the Red Sox threatened. Pinch Thomas was at bat with Babe on deck. Pinch inside-outed a pitch and blasted a liner over the leftfielder's head. Pinch motored around the bases. He was on his way to third when he was tripped by Brooklyn's shortstop, Ivy Olson who tagged out the sprawled runner and started to run off the field.

When Olson reached the third baseline, Boston coacher Heinie Wagner confronted him and called him a dirty cheat. Olson cursed Wagner and the two men squared off and began throwing punches. The crowd roared as peacemakers tried to separate the combatants. While this was occurring, Rough Carrigan was seen talking with the home plate ump. When the melee abated, Bill Dineen ordered the Robins back onto the field and awarded Thomas third base.

With the lead run ninety feet away, Babe stepped up to the plate. Above the roar of the home crowd, Babe thought he heard the powerful voice of Caruso exhorting *il Bambino* to succeed. Sherry Smith had a different idea. There was no joy in Boston when the mighty Babe struck out. Despite this setback, the Red Sox were energized by Wagner's feistiness in standing up for Pinch. The team was determined to prevail; all they needed to do was to figure a way to solve the Brooklyn lefty.

As each pitcher worked his magic tossing up zero after zero, the tension built. In the eighth inning, Robins' third baseman lashed a single to left. Olson executed a perfect sacrifice bunt, moving Mowrey into scoring position. It was now up to the burly veteran catcher Otto Miller to break the tie. He roped a hard single to center field. The crowd tensed as Walker charged and fielded the hit. As Walker poised to throw home, all eyes shifted to Mowrey who was rounding third. He came to a screeching halt and retreated to third. Once again behind the plate, Babe realized that he had dodged a bullet as Walker's throw veered wide of its target.

Babe was now confronted with the task of retiring his opposite number, Sherry Smith, who had ripped a hard double to right earlier in the game. Babe assessed the right-handed batter and dealt a pitch on the inside corner. Smith swung and rapped a grounder to Scott at short. Mowrey was off on the crack of the bat. Scott never hesitated and rifled a strike to Thomas at home. Mowrey screeched to a halt and reversed toward third. Thomas followed his throw to Gardner. That left the plate exposed. Mowrey seized the opportunity and raced toward home. Gardner fired home to Babe. His experience behind the plate came in handy as he deftly took the throw and swipe-tagged the sliding Robin. The crowd held its collective breath as umpire Dineen waited for Babe to show him the ball. Babe popped up with the ball in his left hand ready to throw. Smith breezed into second base. Upset that Smith was now in scoring position, Babe slapped his hands in disappointment. He was snapped back to reality when Dineen bellowed, "You're out!" over a prostrate Mowrey. The crowd was ecstatic.

Both pitchers refused to yield. In the bottom of the ninth inning, it appeared that the Red Sox would break through. Boston Red Sox Hal Janvrin led off with a double to left. Pinch-hitter Jimmy Walker placed a bunt toward third in an effort to move Janvrin over. Sherry Smith was equal to the challenge. He sprinted to the ball and pegged a strike to third baseman Mowrey who tagged out the sliding Janvrin. When the ball trickled out of Mowrey's glove, umpire O'Day reversed his out call.

The crowd rose to their feet, screaming in anticipation. Hobby Hobitzell who had reached safely in each of his previous at bats was the batter. He smoked Smith's slant hitting a frozen rope to center. Unfortunately for the Sox, Hy Myers caught the ball on the run and fired a strike home to nail Janvrin. The mood of the crowd went from joyous when the ball left the bat, to deflated like a flat tire when Brooklyn's catcher applied the tag on Janvrin.

Emotions see-sawed as the game continued for five more innings. Babe held the Robins hitless for the final seven innings. In the fourteenth inning, Sherry Smith surrendered a walk to Hobby, his fourth of the day. After a sacrifice bunt moved Hobby into scoring position, manager Carrigan replaced Hobby with Mike McNally, a fleeter runner. Carrigan pulled out all the stops by pinch-hitting for the lefty-batting Gardner with righty-batting Del Gainor. In the dimming light, Gainor stroked a single into the leftfield corner. While future Hall-of-Famer Zack Wheat desperately chased the ball, McNally sprinted home with the walk-off winner.

Babe was the first one out of the dugout to hug McNally. After hurling thirteen consecutive scoreless innings, Babe was victorious and exhausted. Carrigan reached for his neck and whispered to Babe, "I know that you were disappointed during the World Series last year. Forget it Babe. You made monkeys out of them today!"xiv

With a two game-to-none lead, the Red Sox traveled to Brooklyn. The Robins won the next game, but fell to the Red Sox in the following two games. The Red Sox went home for the winter with their second consecutive World Series title.

1916 – Babe Ruth pitching for Red Sox

1917

> "I am too much of a fan to run a baseball club
> and found that it was interfering with my health."
> ~Joseph Lannin, Boston Red Sox magnate

Babe would always call the month following the 1916 World Series victory as the November from hell. He had always heard that bad things tended to happen in clusters of three, but he never paid it much attention until now. Ripples from the events of that November would affect him in large and small ways.

The first blow came when he learned that manager Bill Carrigan was following through on his pledge to retire after the 1916 season. With a wife and infant daughter at home in Maine, Carrigan could no longer stand being away from them each year from February to October. In later years, Babe would say unequivocally that Rough Carrigan was the best manager he ever had. Carrigan's no-nonsense approach to the game and his deft handling of Babe's shenanigans off the field would be sorely missed.

The second shoe to drop occurred when Joseph Lannin sold the

Red Sox to Harry Frazee, a New York theater impresario. Lannin claimed that he was too much of a fan to run a ball club. That may have been true, but he also capitalized on the World Series triumph by getting top dollar for the franchise. He received a cool one million dollars. The terms of the sale included a note that was payable in November 1919. As will be seen later, this note was to have a profound influence on the future of two storied franchises.

In contrast to Lannin's love of the game, Frazee considered baseball to be just another show. He summed up his philosophy in an interview with *Baseball Magazine* saying, "If you have any kind of a production, be it a music show, a wrestling match, or a baseball game that people want to see enough to pay good money for the privilege, it's a show business and don't let anyone tell you different."[xv] Frazee's attitude filtered down to every aspect of baseball operations, resulting in increasing resentment by the ball players.

The third component of the month from hell was the election of Woodrow Wilson on November 7th. Despite winning on a platform of 'He kept us out of war,' Wilson quickly adopted a much different approach to the European conflict and, in particular, the status of Germany and German-Americans in American policy. Wilson adhered to the derogatory sentiments expressed by Theodore Roosevelt in a famous diatribe about so-called hyphenated Americans, like German-Americans. According to Roosevelt, "There is no room in this country for hyphenated Americanism .... The only man who is a good American is the man who is an American and nothing else."[xvi]

Waves of immigration from Germany in the 18th and 19th centuries had resulted in robust German-American communities. The Germans were proud of their heritage and established social, intellectual, and cultural networks to preserve their *Kultur*. At the height of German-American organizations, there were 800 German-language newspapers. As the United States came closer to war with the Kaiser's Germany, there was a rise of anti-German hysteria. Roosevelt's derision of hyphenated Americans hit German-Americans hard.

1917 was so eventful that major league baseball quickly was relegated to the back burner. During the years between the initiation of hostilities in 1914 in what was called the War to End All Wars, and 1917, there was a vigorous debate in the United States between those in favor of Great Britain versus those in favor of Germany. The public was subjected to an unprecedented barrage of propaganda from both sides. With the sinking of the British liner, the *Lusitania* in 1915, the Black Tom Island explosions in 1916, Germany's declaration of unlimited submarine warfare and the release in January 1917 of the Zimmerman telegram promising Mexico sections of the United States in return for its allegiance, the tide of public opinion turned against Germany.

Throughout the winter, the President used incendiary rhetoric and oppressive policies to put targets on the backs of all German-Americans. Wilson propagated the idea that the Kaiser had established a nefarious organization of German and German-American spies in America to foment sedition and sabotage.

"They filled our unsuspecting communities with vicious spies and conspirators and sought to corrupt the opinion of our people in their own behalf."[xvii] The President believed that many German-Americans had been corrupted and were engaging in hostile intrigue.

The President and his Attorney General Thomas Gregory had repeatedly tried to no avail to enact alien and sedition legislation in previous years. He voiced the view that it was essential to crush out those ". . . who have poured the poison of disloyalty into the very arteries of our national life."[xviii] After relations between Germany and the United States degenerated into war, Wilson pushed through espionage and sedition legislation. The result was that a climate of distrust, suspicion, and fear began to permeate the country that did not portend well for citizens of German heritage.

For much of the winter, Babe lived under a protective veneer of isolation. Babe and Helen rented a cabin on Willis Pond in the Pine Lakes area at Sudbury, Massachusetts. One of their neighbors was Babe's catcher Pinch Thomas. Ruth, the street urchin from the inner city, threw himself into the rustic life – chopping wood, hunting, and fishing. When Babe got cabin fever, he would get Pinch and drive a couple of miles on Route 27 to nearby Maynard. They would go for beer and billiards at the Bughouse Corner, at the intersection of Waltham and Parker Streets.

The Bughouse Corner was a neighborhood bar frequented by workers from the nearby woolen mill. It reminded Babe of the saloons his father had operated throughout Babe's childhood. He recalled the conversation he had with his father when he told his father that he and Helen were not returning to Baltimore for the winter, that they had decided to stay near Boston. The look of disappointment on Big

George's face nearly made Babe change his plans. But, Helen was adamant that Babe needed to get away from Baltimore before his father and his new wife sucked him dry. She even quoted scripture, something about a man must leave his parents and cling to his wife. Helen hoped that life in a secluded area away from the temptations of the city would temper Babe's carousing. She was mostly right.

One night after the boys had been doing some serious drinking at the Bughouse Corner, Babe asked the owner, a fellow by the name of Niilo, why there was a tire iron hanging behind the bar. The owner was all too ready to tell the tale.

"It is a memorial to how this place got its name. As you know, Babe, bughouse is slang for insane asylum. When we moved to Maynard from Providence years ago, I was driving here in my truck with a load of furniture. I got lost and ended up in Medfield. To make matters worse, the truck started going thumpa-da, thumpa-da, thumpa-da. Wouldn't you know it, I had a flat tire.

"As I was changing the tire, I noticed that I had stopped right by a sign that said Medfield Insane Asylum. I jacked up the truck, removed the lug nuts and placed them in the hub cap. While I was changing the tire, a fellow came over to the fence and stared at me. His maniacal stare gave me the creeps," said Niilo, mimicking a distorted countenance.

"I couldn't wait to get the heck away from this guy. I got so nervous that I fumbled with the hub cap. It tipped over and all of the lug nuts rolled into the sewer. It was getting dark and this guy is still staring at me. I started to panic. I searched for help, but the street was deserted. Finally, the guy says, 'Why don't you take one lug nut from each of the other wheels and use them on this wheel?' I was astounded at this simple, yet brilliant solution. I just looked at him in amazement. Get this. He shrugs and says, 'I may be crazy, but I'm not stupid.'

Niilo continued, "The tension broke and I burst into laughter. He burst into laughter. We both laughed and laughed until they took him away. During my drive here, I resolved to name this joint in honor of him. So, that's why it's called the Bughouse Corner."

Babe and the other patrons laughed so hard that the ritual tire iron shook off its hook and smashed onto the cash register. That brought more howls of laughter and a round of drinks on Babe.

When he wasn't at the Bughouse Corner hanging out with the locals, Babe enjoyed the seclusion the tranquility of the Sudbury cabin which he called "Ihatetoquitit." He described the hectic pace of the last few years as a brass-buttoned, gold-braided atmosphere. Babe used the time to recharge.

Helen and Babe celebrated a quiet Christmas in Sudbury. Along with his Christmas card, Gunny included a letter to his friend expressing dismay. Gunny recounted a disturbing trend of discrimination against people of German descent. According to Gunny, the local pharmacist had accused his mother of being a German spy. Mrs. Gunther was terrified when uniformed policemen whisked her off the street in front of her home and questioned her for eight hours at the stationhouse. She was bed-ridden for weeks after this public humiliation and mortification. Babe replied by mail expressing his sadness and wishing Mrs. G. a speedy recovery and a Happy New Year.

Notwithstanding the triple whammy of November, the winter interlude had worked its magic on Babe. By the time spring training arrived, he was completely rejuvenated. He would need all his energy to navigate through the difficulties of the upcoming campaign.

In this tense atmosphere, the Red Sox returned to Hot Springs for spring training in 1917. Jack Barry, another Holy Cross alum like Carrigan, was named player/manager. When Red Sox broke camp they headed to Memphis for a series of exhibition games against the Brooklyn Robins. To boost interest in the teams, Robins' magnate Charles Ebbets suggested that the players wear numbered armbands for easy identification by the cranks. The Red Sox wore red sleeves with white numbers and the Robins wore blue sleeves with white numbers. The practice of putting numbers on the backs of uniforms during the regular season would not arrive for another dozen years.

With opening day for the 1917 season just days away, events leading toward war with Germany reached a fever pitch. George Ruth, Sr. was tending bar at his café when the telephone rang.

"Hi, Pops," said Babe over the telephone. "How are you?"

"I'm doing OK. All this war fever makes people thirsty. So, business is good."

"It's crazy here in Boston. The other day, over three thousand pro-war advocates descended on the Boston Opera House for a rally. Can you imagine? . . . a war rally at an opera house. Enrico must think we are barbarians.

"Mayor Curley riled them up something fierce. I'm sure conductor Muck stayed out of sight. I've heard from friends that Muck tendered his resignation to Henry Lee Higginson, the orchestra's owner and founder. Higginson refused to accept the resignation and pooh-poohed Dr. Muck's safety concerns, saying that no one in his right mind would attack a distinguished artist. Boy, does he have a lot to learn."

"If Muck's smart, he'll keep his head down," said George, thinking, and *you'd* better keep your head down.

"Hey, George, what's a guy got to do to get a drink around here," shouted one of his patrons over the din of patriotic slogans and inebriated singing.

"I gotta go, Jidgie. Good luck with the opener. That's a nice honor."

"Ok, talk soon, bye."

"Keep your pants on, Sam. I was talking to my boy. He got the opening day start against the Yankees," said George, as he poured beer into a tilted glass. Sam gave George a smiling, thumbs-up.

"You know George, we just busted up a meeting of the American League Against Militarism. We coulda used Babe – he pitches in the other American League, right?" interrupted Jimbo Anderson, grinning at his own cleverness.

With the foam teasing the rim of the glass, George slid the mug over to big mechanic. As the man gulped, George surveyed the back room. An hour earlier, one of his regulars knocked on the back door and asked if he could bring some thirsty friends into the back room of the Café. Usually, George was hesitant to admit customers on Sundays unless they were celebrating someone's birthday. But, given the mood in the city, he knew better than to stay closed.

"Come on, George, we all just came from breaking up the pacifist meeting uptown. We worked up a powerful thirst," said Sam Harris, a superintendent at the Fairfield Yard. George opened the door and a torrent of men burst in. Some wore bloody badges of honor on their faces; others proudly displayed knuckles scraped raw from pummeling an opponent.

"George, you should have seen Osborne. I didn't think that banker had balls. I was wrong," said Sam, his voice brimming with admiration.

"Yeah, there was about four thousand of us marching up North Howard. When we got to the Academy of Music, Ozzie was waving Old Glory for all he was worth. The mangy pacifists were inside holding a meeting to protest against the war against the Krauts. Osborne led us into the theater and right down the aisle to the stage. There was a cordon of police protecting the stage. That lily-livered Professor from Stanford, David Starr Jordan, was just about to speak when Osborne charged past the police and stopped Jordon in mid-word by pushing him with the staff of his flag. A cop clubbed Osbourne from behind. When he went down with the flag, our guys were blind with rage. The place erupted into violence," said Jimbo, with a faraway look as he re-lived the pandemonium.

George looked at the blood lust in the eyes of the men and poured another round.

"Jordan ran away. We were having a good time cracking skulls of those Kaiser sympathizers until we heard a shrill racket of whistles and sirens. Police reinforcements stormed into the theater. They was swinging billies like hellions. They didn't care who got clubbed. That was when we skedaddled and came here," said Sam.

Off in the corner, Carter Osbourne sat with an ice pack on the back of his head. George raised a glass and toasted the young banker.

"To Ozzie," echoed the crowd.

"Thanffs," whistled Osbourne through a broken front tooth.

A few days later, President Wilson asked Congress to approve a declaration of war against Germany. Congress voted overwhelmingly to go to war.

A few days after that, Babe was the winning pitcher in the Red Sox' 1917 season opener on the road against the Yankees. He went the distance and allowed only three hits.

Red Sox pitchers – Babe Ruth and Ernie Shore

June 23, 1917
Fenway Park, Boston MA

"I get by with a little help from my friends"
~ John Lennon & Paul McCartney

Under normal circumstances, to a professional baseball player in the early twentieth century the baseball season was like being part of an extended submarine voyage. The players were so focused on the grind of playing almost daily that they often lost track of the larger world outside of the playing field. In a letter to Gunny, Babe characterized the incessant travel during the season as akin to being homeless for eight months of the year. Teammates did almost everything together – they traveled, ate, played, and slept on the same schedule. Well, except for the sleeping part, because there were some members of the Red Sox who needed less sleep than others. Babe was one of those who, according to the old saying, liked to burn the candle at both ends.

The circumstances of 1917 were not normal. The declaration of war and ensuing war hysteria changed everything. As tension and fear about Imperial German spies and saboteurs escalated, official suppression of all things German such as newspapers, books, and mail, proliferated. While this effected Babe indirectly, he was to learn that abnormal times manifested in unusual ways. Like reality, the web of life cannot be denied. For Babe, this lesson started in New York City.

Going back to at least colonial times, New York City had a reputation as a wide-open place that was tolerant of a wide spectrum of beliefs, practices, and indulgences. As a Dutch colony, New Amsterdam was a cosmopolitan and multi-ethnic seaport where all types of vice and entertainment flourished. The temptations in New York City were considerably more diverse than those available in Boston its puritanical neighbor to the north. Coming from the cloistered environment of St. Mary's with an exuberant personality and unimagined disposable income, Babe was particularly susceptible. Ernie Shore, who knew Babe from the days he was first released from St. Mary's, liked to say, "You have to remember that when Babe was let loose, he wanted to do everything and experience everything." [xix] When he visited the City, Babe liked to navigate through the minefield of temptations in the company of Enrico Caruso, a friend and mentor who understood the nature of celebrity. Usually that meant that the fun did not start until after Enrico had finished performing at the Met.

"Hey, Hoop, what are you doing for dinner?" shouted Babe across the locker room. The Red Sox had beaten the Yankees at the Polo Grounds on a nifty three-hitter by Carl Mays. This would be their last night in New York City on this trip and the players were hustling to start the evening. Having sat the pines since his complete game victory a few days earlier, Babe was full of energy.

"What do you have in mind, big fella?" asked Harry Hooper.

"I'm meeting my buddy Rico at Reisenweber's after the opera, so I thought we could head over to the restaurant for an early dinner. I hear that Frazee is going to be there with his latest flock of chickadees," said Babe.

Located at Columbus Circle on 58th Street, Reisenweber's Café was a multi-level entertainment complex that combined excellent cuisine, music, and dancing for theater stars, celebrities, and the rich. One pundit described it as the intersection of glitz, glamour, and gelt, where pleasures, legal and illegal abounded, provided you could pay the right price.

"That sounds like fun. Our owner sure knows how to find beautiful young dames. Count me in," said Hoop.

Recognized as a team leader, the outfielder realized that his young teammate was prone to party to excess. Since Babe was his team's starting pitcher for tomorrow's game, Hooper hoped to tamp down the young stallion's behavior so that he would be at his best. Hoop knew that it would be a formidable task and searched the smelly room for help.

"Let's bring Deac along," said Hoop.

"Sure," said Babe. "Let's twenty-three skiddo. Our cab is waiting. It won't take us long to get to Columbus Circle where Reisenweber's is. They have a beefsteak special at the Rathskellar tonight - only $1.50 for an exceptional steak. Deleesh!"

After consuming the biggest steak Hooper had ever seen, and washing it down with a grand stein of Moerlbach Brewed Beer, Babe was just getting started. When their waiter realized that they were members of the Boston Red Sox, he offered to serve them a Boston Cream Pie.

"I love pie," said Babe.

"Babe, I'm sure that you know that the Boston Cream Pie is really a cake. It's not a pie," said Hoop.

"No, it's a pie – you can tell by the name."

"That's my point. The name is wrong. It should be Boston Cream Cake," said Hoop.

"Actually, it's not made with cream either. It's made with custard. It should be called the Boston Custard Cake," said Deac. Hooper looked at the shortstop and winked.

The waiter arrived and placed a beautiful, round, chocolate-covered disk on the table.

Babe took the serving utensil and placed a large piece of dessert on his plate. Savoring each mouthful, he speculated whether the filling was cream or custard.

"I can't tell. It's creamy, but looks custardy. I'll have to have another sample," he said while appropriating another healthy-sized wedge.

"The bottom layer is spongy like a cake, but the shape is definitely like a pie. More research is needed," he said, reaching for another piece. Hoop and Deac stared wide-eyed as Babe made the pie disappear, accompanied by a non-stop, faux-intellectual analysis of the Boston Cream Pie.

"Well, my friends, I think I have reached a proper conclusion. This is the prefect embodiment of Boston – a creamy, pie-shaped dessert slathered with chocolate signifying the various layers of Boston's baseball cranks," said Babe, emitting a loud belch. Slurping down his fourth cup of coffee, Babe rose and announced that it was time to move upstairs to the 400 Cabaret Club. Hoop and Deac inhaled and followed dutifully.

As they approached the entrance to the Club, Babe saw a sign announcing that there was a 25¢ admission charge to hear the hottest band in the country, Original Dixieland Jass Band. While they waited on line, Babe started dancing in place. He was humming "The Tiger Rag," the band's hit that was sweeping the nation.

"Hey, you, twinkle-toes," shouted a burly attendant. Hoop and Deac braced themselves for an altercation. Their over-exuberant teammate had apparently agitated the wrong guy with his antics. Babe looked his way, continuing his dance. The attendant scrutinized the object of his ire, probably gauging what it would take to remove him.

Another attendant who had been attracted by his partner's loud voice stepped forward from the dimly-lit cabaret.

"What's the problem, Johnny?" he said to the attendant. Johnny nodded toward the customer on line who was dancing while he waited. His two friends shrugged in embarrassment. Upon closer examination, the man asked, "Ain't you that Baby Ruth guy from the Sox?"

"The very same," said Babe, doing the sooey, a two-step with a dip.

"I thought so. There could not be another guy with a mug like that," he laughed.

"Johnny, this guy's a famous baseball player. Please follow me, Mr. Ruth," said the second attendant, beckoning Babe into the lounge where they proceeded to a table in the front.

With chagrined smiles, Hooper and Scott trailed along. The smoky café was jammed with stars of stage and screen and their champagne-sipping entourages. Babe meandered through the crowd shaking hands, ogling the ladies, and joking with one-and-all as if he were a Tammany Hall boss. He knew intuitively that a cabaret was a place of wild revelry and he was determined to uphold his responsibility to make the spectacle as entertaining as possible. Babe did not disappoint.

On the other side of the cabaret, Hooper spied Red Sox owner Harry Frazee who was surrounded by a bevy of showgirls. As of the 1917 season, Harry Frazee was the sole owner of the Red Sox. He had bought out his partner Joseph Lannin, incurring significant debt to accomplish the transaction. This strained his finances and his other vocation as a Broadway impresario. So far, Harry Frazee had mastered the art of enjoying the high life by using other people's money. That situation could not last forever and he would soon have to monetize some of his assets. But, for now, he was living life to the hilt.

Shortly after conferring with a waiter, Frazee raised his glass to Hooper. Moments later, their waiter brought them a bottle of champagne compliments of the owner. It was accompanied by a note that warned Hoop and company to stay away from Frazee's table, or face dire consequences. Obviously, Red Sox employees were prohibited from fraternizing with the owner and, more important, with the owner's beautiful showgirls.

176

Hoop could just imagine Babe intruding on Frazee's private party and scandalizing the showgirls with boorish behavior. Fortunately, the potentially volatile situation was averted by virtue of the quality of the entertainment which kept Ruth enthralled and disinterested in the goings-on across the room. The Original Dixieland Jass Band lived up to their billing as the self-proclaimed Creators of Jazz. The musicians hailed from New Orleans and were the first band to commercialize their form of music, marketing it as the musical idiom of jazz. After enjoying the cabaret act and numerous adult beverages, Babe checked his watch. Hooper and Scott were ready to call it a night.

"It's almost midnight; the big man should be arriving any minute. Let's head up to the Paradise Supper Club on the third-floor," said Babe.

Hoop gave Deac a look that asked, where does he get his stamina? Once again, they followed their teammate upstairs, this time to an elegant dinner club complete with the City's first ballroom dance floor. The ballplayers mingled with the sophisticates, especially Babe who was an accomplished ballroom dancer. It wasn't long before he was foxtrotting across the dance floor with a beautiful blonde named Nina. He was a natural with grace and style. The guys were amazed at how lithe he was on his feet.

The showmanship of Babe on the dance floor was about to be overshadowed by an even greater showman. As if on cue at the end of a string of lively tunes, the bandleader announced that they would return after a short break.

"However, before we do so, I am pleased to introduce the world's greatest tenor, the wonder of the Metropolitan Opera, *Signore* Enrico

Caruso. He has agreed to perform one of his arias for your listening pleasure. Please join me in welcoming *Signore* Caruso!"

Caruso entered the spotlight and with a flourish twirled his cape away into the waiting arms of a beautiful showgirl. He doffed his bowler and bowed deeply. The patrons roared with delight at this unexpected treat.

"*Mille grazie*, thanks. Maestro."

As Caruso serenaded the assemblage, the room swelled with patrons from the floors above and below until the crowd rendered the fire code limits obsolete. With sweat glistening on his face, Enrico reached unbelievable tonal heights with his beautiful voice. And then there was silence. It lasted a moment and the room filled with raucous cheering and Bravos.

The great singer shielded his eyes briefly and saw his friend clapping for all he was worth. Caruso walked over to embrace Babe.

"We are honored by your presence, *Signore*," said Babe, gesturing. Caruso sat down as the crowd buzzed with excitement. He gulped down a glass of water. Immediately, John Reisenweber appeared and inquired whether he would be having his usual dinner.

"Only if all my friends join me, eh?"

Babe nodded enthusiastically, while Hoop and Deac forced a smile that hid their unease. They knew that Babe and Enrico were about to embark on an epic eating binge and that they were being sucked into its vortex.

While they waited for their dinner, Nick LaRocca, the leader of the Original Dixieland Jass Band came to the table and introduced himself.

He wanted to know if Enrico could put in a good word for him at the Victor Talking Machine Company. Enrico promised that he would.

The next visitor was none other than the ballplayers' boss, Harry Frazee. He strolled over surrounded by several show girls. Babe was laughing and drinking when he recognized the girl draped tightly on Frazee's arm. As if by magic, Babe's laughter stopped and was replaced by a look of astonishment.

"Colina?"

"Jidgie," she said flatly. Her face wore an expression that dared him to judge her.

At that moment, Frazee shook hands with Caruso and turned to leave. The other girls stayed with Caruso's party, but Frazee guided Colina along with him. Babe noticed a flash of red light reflecting from a garnet ring on her right hand.

"You know her?" said Hooper. Babe nodded. With a grimace of regret, he grabbed the nearest bottle and drank.

"She's Frazee's main squeeze. Word is that he knocked her up a couple of times and forced her to take care of it," said Hoop.

"Don't you talk about her like that," Babe flared.

"Easy, big fella, I didn't mean anything by it."

"*Bambino, mi amico,* come here, so that we can catch up," said Enrico. Like a dutiful son, Babe complied. A healthy dose of comfort food helped assuage his mood.

Later, after a fine meal of Caruso's spaghetti and roasted capon, they enjoyed Cuban Partagas. The cigar smoke hovered over their table like a cloud of celestial nymphs.

". . . And so you see, my mother had twenty-two children. I am boy nineteen[xx]," said Enrico.

"You got me beat," said Babe. "How did you feed so many children?"

"Ah, that is the tragedy. Only three survived. That is why I carry these coins," Enrico said, reaching into his pocket and producing a huge handful of coins. "Whenever I see the *bambini*, the poor little ones, I give them coins to make sure that they can fill their *labanzas*, or as you say, their tummies. You should do the same, Bambino."

"Why?" asked Deac.

Caruso winked, "Because it's good for the soul and it's good for business. The *bambini* grow up and buy records."

"I think you are right. I'm going to start doing that."

"Excuse me, gentlemen, I can offer you some eggs and coffee before we lock up, the sun is up and we must close soon," said a gracious John Reisenweber.

"*Grazie.*"

Seven hours later, Babe entered the visitors' locker room to get dressed for the game. Deac had driven like a demon to get back to Boston on time with his teammates. Ruth was bleary-eyed, a little hungover and seriously perturbed. He could not shake the vision of Colina and Frazee. How could she lower herself to cohabit with such a repugnant toad? Babe was beside himself with helplessness. He could not eradicate the feeling of intense coldness that he experienced when Colina had stared at him over her shoulder while departing on Frazee's arm. Her eyes, once welcoming, now turned hostile. He felt like some sort of gelid ray emitted from her eyes had penetrated his chest and turned his heart into a cadaverous, inanimate pump. Even though it was a balmy summer day, he shivered.

When he bent over to tie his laces, he nearly keeled over. The trainer, Butch Lawrence, knew what was coming and leaped into action.

"Hey, kid, I need a bi-," said Babe.

"Coming right up," said Butch, as he puttered around the trainer's room preparing a bicarbonate of soda for his stricken pitcher. This routine with Babe helped to quell his upset tummy. Babe drank the concoction and emitted a loud belch that signaled that he was ready to pitch.

With Ray Morgan, the Senator's diminutive second baseman in the batter's box, Babe toed the mound in the top of the first. The Fenway crowd was still filing in at game time. He was still battling the image of his Colina with the weasel-faced Frazee. How could she? He ached. Such was his emotional state that he tried to throw the ball through his catcher. It sailed high and wide.

The affable catcher had acquired his nickname, Pinch, for his success as a pinch hitter. During this season, he had endeared himself to the manager by bringing out the best in Babe when behind the plate. Pinch was the catcher who worked best with the young pitcher. Pinch played with banter and bluster, but it was his scrappiness that Babe admired, probably because Babe, too, was scrappy – never one to back down.

The catcher sprang up to snare the errant pitch. He gestured with his glove facing down for Babe to calm down. The next pitch was better. It was crossed the black edge of the plate on the outside corner.

"Ball two," shouted Clarence "Brick" Owens, the home plate umpire. The umpire had received his nickname when, after an unsatisfactory call, protesting fans threw bricks at him. One hit him in the head and disabled him for a few days. When players called him Brick, he said that it was preferable to many of the other names he had been called.

Pinch held the ball in the position that he caught it.

"Are you trying to show me up, Pinch?" said Owens.

Pinch zipped the ball back to his pitcher. Babe snapped at the ball while glaring at the ump.

The next pitch was a foot wide of the plate.

"Ball three!"

As Babe entered his windup, the batter pivoted into a bunting position. With his shoulders squared toward the pitcher, Morgan waggled his bat. The ball crossed the plate high in the strike zone at the letters on the batter's jersey.

"Ball four," called the umpire.

"Open your eyes, Brick, and keep them open," shouted Babe.

"Shut your trap, Ruth, or you will be taking an early shower."

"You run me out and I'll come in there and bop you in the beezer!" responded Babe.

"You're outta here," bellowed Brick. "I hope Frazee fines your arse."

With that last remark, Brick sealed his fate. To the cranks in the stands, it looked like Babe had been shot from a cannon. Pinch Thomas was the only obstacle between Babe and the umpire. Babe leapt past the catcher and swung wildly at Brick with his left hand and missed. He followed with a right that caught Brick behind the left ear. The ump went down to his knees. Before Babe could inflict further damage, he was dragged away by manager Barry and several policemen. After just four pitches, Babe's day was done and he was back in the trainer's room lying on his back with his right hand immersed in a bucket of ice.

Back on the field, Jack Barry called for Ernie Shore to come in from the bullpen and signaled for Sam Agnew to replace the catcher Thomas who had also been ejected.

"Try to get through this inning," his manager told him.[xxi]

Brick Owens was still fuming when Shore entered the game. The umpire gave Shore only five warm up pitches to get ready. The game resumed. On the first pitch to the plate, the baserunner took off for second base. Agnew gunned him down with a perfect peg.

"Okay, that's one! Let's keep it going," shouted the husky catcher.

And that is exactly what the Red Sox did. Over the course of the next ninety minutes, Shore was literally perfect. He retired twenty-six batters in a row on the way to a 4 – 0 victory. The tall righty struck out only two Senators, but he was masterful with the location of his pitches. He needed only 75 pitches to retire all 26 batters that he faced. The reporters and cranks showered praise on Shore's remarkable no-hit, no-run, no-man-to-first performance. A perfect game in baseball is rarer than a white peacock and Shore was credited with one under unusual circumstances.

The team was exhilarated by the win and clambered noisily into the clubhouse to celebrate and get ready for the second game of the scheduled double-header. When Shore went into the trainer's room for some postgame treatment, he found Babe asleep on the trainer's table. Awakened by the noise, Ruth lifted his head and said, "So, how'd it go out there, East Bend?"

"We won," drawled the laconic Shore.

Babe yawned, rested his head on his arm and returned to his nap.

Babe Ruth posing with bat

June 1917
Boston, MA

"There are two tragedies in life. One is to lose
your heart's desire. The other is to gain it."
~ George Bernard Shaw

Delicate is the heart. Even a heart so muscular as to support the rigors of playing professional baseball at the highest level. Even one so muscular as to sustain a profligate lifestyle engaging in sexual escapades with myriad women. Even one so muscular as to absorb the incessant overindulgence in alcoholic beverages and binge eating. When Babe saw Colina draped on the arm of that weasel Frazee, all the guilt and pain that had been suppressed over the last few years surged to the surface in a manner more explosive and powerful than a great humpback whale breaching the surface.

The previous winter, the Ruths and the Thomases had gone on a whale-watching excursion to the Stellwagen Bank off Cape Cod. Babe had been awed by the way the forty-foot humpback whales would reach for the heavens, rising and twisting in acrobatic arches twenty-five feet into the sky. As miraculous as the breaches appeared, the thunderous slams and enormous splashes when the creatures returned to the ocean had most impressed Babe. Now, after seeing his first love so unattainable, he felt the thunderous slam of his heart returning, like the humpbacks to the ocean, into the reality of profound loss that cannot be restored. Following the encounter at Reisenweber's restaurant, Babe's usual joy evaporated and Babe drifted aimlessly on and off the field.

A few days after the strange perfect game, American League President Ban Johnson announced Babe's punishment for attacking the umpire. He was fined $100 and suspended for ten days. Babe was surprised and relieved at the lenient sentence. Although Ruth pitched well when he returned from the suspension, the season gradually slipped into a campaign of lost promise. In the last game of September, Babe pitched against the St. Louis Browns. He won his twenty-fourth game of the season, hurling a six-hit shutout. He ended the season with a team-leading .325 batting average.

For the Boston Red Sox, the 1917 season was a disappointment. Boston finished a distant second, nine games behind the Chicago White Sox. Losing the last two games of the season to the Nationals at home added to the team's gloomy mood when the players left Fenway for the last time. They were not used to going home this early. Having won the World Series in the last two seasons, the players had come to expect the handsome World Series shares which often exceeded their annual salaries. Jack Barry, their player/manager, made it official that he would not be with the team for the next season due to his commitment to the U. S. Navy.

The newly-enacted Selective Service Act mandated all men between the ages of 21 – 30 to register for military service. That meant that the vast majority of major leaguers were eligible for the draft. In the summer, 1917, Babe registered in Boston, listing the Red Sox as his employer and his home as 680 Commonwealth Avenue which was a few blocks from Fenway Park. Since he was married, Babe would be exempt from the military draft.

Occasionally, Babe's playful side would shine through the dark mood that engulfed him. One day near the end of the season-long grind, Babe emerged from the showers with a towel around his waist and a lit cigar hanging from his broad lips. His wet hair glistening black, hung over his forehead. Beads of water speckled his muscular torso. A rich, deep farmer's tan covered his neck, arms, and face, in stark contrast to the marble-whiteness of the rest of his body.

"Hey, Babe, you are the only guy I know who brings a cigar with him into the shower. How do you manage to smoke a cigar in the shower?" asked Pinch, deliberately egging on his friend.

The players waited for Babe to give the demonstration of technique that invariably brought howls. He mounted a bench and tied the towel around this neck like a royal cape. He grabbed a bat with his right hand and held it like a scepter.

"Well, you see my dear friend, you know that sticking the lit stogy where the sun don't shine, might keep it dry." At this point, he wiggled his bottom and pantomimed placing the cigar in that delicate orifice. Then, wagging his index finger in an exaggerated prissy fashion, he bolted upright feigning a hot seat. He fanned his fanny while shaking his head from side to side.

"Oh, no, that would be a bad idea for a number of reasons," exclaimed Babe. "Not the least of which would be the fouling of the taste."

Babe drew heavily on the cigar while adopting an angelic countenance, complete with fluttering eyelashes. The players guffawed and mimicked the antics of Babe who savored the attention and the cigar in that order.

"Oh, mighty Babe, please reveal your secret," pleaded Pinch, bowing and waving his towel from over his head. Hoop, Deac and several others joined in. Adopting a regal stance, Babe looked down on his subjects. The aroma of the cigar permeated the humid room.

"Please, you embarrass me with your begging. Rise, my friends and learn. Watch carefully and don't try this at home, kiddoes." He winked.

Babe turned and presented his profile. He drew on the cigar and exhaled a cloud of smoke. Then, he deftly twirled the cigar and put the lit end into his mouth. He clinched his teeth around the stub of the cigar. A grin creased his broad face as he simulated soaping and showering. When his phantom shower concluded, he withdrew the cigar and puffed it deeply. To raucous applause and laughter, he raised his arms triumphantly.

In mock amazement, Hoop asked, "How does he do that?"

"He's got a big mouth!" chimed in Pinch right on cue. Babe guffawed the loudest.

He placed his cigar on a shelf in his locker and sat on a stool to sort through a pile of mail. Since his rookie season, he had received mountains of mail containing letters of adulation, requests for autographs and, more than a few obscene propositions. Babe enlisted the help of the clubhouse boy to sit next to him and compile various piles depending on the response warranted. "Rubbish," "Autograph/ Picture," "Personal," "Business," and "Other." After reviewing the pile, Babe pulled two letters and gave the rest to the boy to handle.

The first letter was from Gunny. He told Babe that his job at the bank had become intolerable due to anti-German slurs from his supervisors and customers. Gunny explained that he was planning to quit, but, then, he received a notice from his local draft board. He had been drafted and would be leaving for basic training at the end of the month.

Babe slapped his forehead. His childhood friend was going into the Army. He had been assigned to a regiment in the 79th Infantry Division, nicknamed "Baltimore's Own." Babe wondered how many other young men he knew would end up in that unit. How many of them would not return home? The reality of the war struck home.

The second missive was on business stationery. Babe smiled as he read. His proposal to buy an interest in a cigar factory just outside Boston had been accepted. Soon Babe would be selling "Babe Ruth" cigars with his image on each wrapper. At a nickel a piece, the street kid from Baltimore was on his way to becoming a wealthy man. He had Rico to thank. His friend had counselled him to use his fame to create a stream of income outside of baseball. Babe was proving to be an adept student.

After the season ended, Babe needed to escape the gloom that had enveloped him. He and Helen spent several weeks enjoying the spectacular autumn foliage in New England. He loved driving through the mountain roads and gasping in wonder at the kaleidoscope of leaves dressed in reds, oranges, yellows, and purples arrayed before them. At certain times when the sun shone from behind the leaves, the brilliant translucent colors reminded him of stained glass windows he had seen in Catholic churches. On these occasions, he would pull to the side of the road and he and Helen would hike to the nearest summit. There, they would marvel at the rolling vista of color that blanketed the mountains and valleys. Feeling like he was purging the stale, humid air of the long, hot summer spent in stuffy railroad cars and hotels, Babe enjoyed inhaling the crisp, dry air of autumn.

Despite the sense of rejuvenation he experienced in the mountains, the painful reality of the loss of Colina was never too far away. It could be rekindled by a simple glance or gesture by Helen that brought to mind Colina. While driving aimlessly through New England, he wondered whether he would ever be able to free himself of the burden of guilt he felt over breaking Colina's heart that one stupid night in Wilmington. He blamed himself for his lustful interlude with a local beauty that was witnessed by Colina. He could not rid himself of the memory of her withering look of shock, betrayal, and pain. The memory of her piercing eyes haunted him. His hasty marriage to Helen who bore such a striking resemblance to Colina was a constant reminder of his perfidy. It was almost as if God mocked his guilty feelings by pairing him with an imperfect copy of his true love.

Still, his escape from Boston with Helen provided a much-needed tonic. When evening approached, they sought out small, rustic, bed-and-breakfast inns. With Helen navigating with ill-defined road maps, Babe barreled through the back roads. His attitude was that accurate directions were secondary to speed. We're making good time was his mantra. In response, Helen would protest that they were still lost. With a maniacal glint in his eye, Babe would laugh and flick his cigar out the window. On more than one occasion, they were so hopelessly lost that they slept in the car snuggled together for warmth. In later years, Helen would remember these as the best of times – times that she did not have to share him with the world.

In the morning after such a misadventure, Babe would take to the road driving like a madman to find someplace, any place that served breakfast. When he finally stumbled upon some family-run establishment, he would eat them out of house and home. With an endearing laugh, he would throw a one hundred dollar bill on the counter and tell them to go buy all the bacon, eggs, and bread they could carry and cook it up for him.

At the Tuckerman's Ravine Lodge, Babe entered a scone-eating contest and defeated the local champ by eating three dozen maple cranberry scones slathered with maple glaze and wild blueberry jam. The usually laconic locals cheered the irrepressible young ballplayer, who regaled them with all sorts of fantastic stories about life with their beloved Sawx. They were amazed at how he could eat and talk, only stopping to wash down the treats with cold milk.

Babe and Helen were refreshed when they returned to Sudbury to prepare for their annual pilgrimage to Baltimore to visit his father. In his red silk robe, Babe sat at the kitchen table while Helen packed. When she saw him shaking his head from side to side, she said, "Is everything alright, Hon?"

"Have you seen today's paper?" he asked.

"No, what's the problem?"

"There's a front page story accusing Karl Muck of being a Kaiser supporter. According to John Rathom of the *Providence Journal,* several women's groups requested that the orchestra play the Star-Spangled Banner when the Boston Symphony Orchestra played in Providence. The paper says that Dr. Muck refused to include the National Anthem because he is unpatriotic. And worse, he belongs in jail."

"In jail? Can they send you to jail for not playing a song?" asked Helen, her voice quavering.

"Apparently, there are some new laws that say you can go to jail if you are disloyal … what does that even mean?"

"Listen to Muck's response. 'To ask us to play the national anthem is embarrassing. It's almost an insult. Such an attempt would be destructive of the very thing the Symphony stands for – musical art. The public has no right to demand it.'"

"My friend Parker who works with the Orchestra says the government believes that there is a link between listening to German music and supporting the Kaiser's war," said Helen.

"That sounds silly to me. I remember at school, the brothers always told us that music was the universal language, that music does not belong to a country. I feel sorry for Dr. Muck. I hope this blows over, like the time I socked the ump. Over time, people forget. They move on to other things."

"I hope so, too. If anything happens to the orchestra, my friend Parker will lose his job. This Rathom fellow appears to be a real zealot. I'm not sure that he will ever let Dr. Muck rest," said Helen. She thought, hysteria, especially war hysteria, by definition is irrational. When scared people get together in mobs, innocent people get hurt. She prayed that her dear husband would be spared entanglement with war hysteria.

The couple drove from Sudbury to New York City where they spent the evening with Enrico at the Ansonia. During a sumptuous dinner in Caruso's suite, Helen asked Enrico what he thought about the controversy surrounding Dr. Muck. With a profound sadness in his eyes, Enrico sighed.

"I'm afraid that the best way for me to respond is to quote your William Shakespeare who was a man of great wisdom. 'All the world's a stage, and all the men and women merely players: they have their exits and their entrances. [xxii] I am afraid that it is time for Dr. Muck's exit, but he refuses to see it. Or, those around him refuse to see it is time for him to exit."

"What do you mean when you say those around him?" asked Babe.

"I mean Major Higginson, the owner, or whoever is making these foolish decisions. At the next concert after the debacle in Providence, the orchestra played the National Anthem and Dr. Muck announced his resignation from the podium. That would have ended the controversy.

But, no, Higginson refused to accept the resignation until the orchestra played in Philadelphia, Baltimore, Washington, and Brooklyn to conclude the tour. There was no problem in Philadelphia, but, there was a near riot in Baltimore. Major Higginson failed to take into account the fact that the Star-Spangled Banner was written in Baltimore and its citizens consider any slight to the anthem as a personal insult. The city of Baltimore rose up against Dr. Muck."

"What do you mean?" asked Babe, putting down his cappuccino with such force that a bottle of Anisette would have tipped over if Enrico's valet, Bruno, had not caught it in mid-air.

Ever the showman, Enrico flourished a newspaper over his head and fluttered it down on the table. The front page of the *Baltimore Sun* was in full display on the table. Babe caught snatches of the articles. "The best place for Dr. Muck is an internment camp." "A better place would be a wooden box." "Loyal Americans should officially prevent the performance of any such organization as Muck's." "Muck ought to have been shot." "Francis Scott Key should rise from his grave and haunt Muck until doomsday."

His shock at the vitriol gave way to disgust when he focused on the photo in the center of the page. The caption read, "At a rally to protest the musical director of the Boston Symphony Orchestra, Former Maryland Governor Edwin Warfield, draped in an American flag, (center) led an angry crowd of nearly two thousand patriots who convened at Baltimore's Lyric Theater in a chant "Kill Muck! Kill Muck!"

Babe's jaw nearly hit the table when he saw the most shocking part of the front page. He got up and walked to the window, staring vacantly at the lights of the City.

"What is it, Babe?" asked Helen. She had never seen her husband so in such a state. He was pale, sweating, and gripping the window frame so tightly that she thought his knuckles would explode.

She went to him and putting her hand on his shoulder, whispered, "What is it?"

With an uncharacteristic weariness, Babe plodded back to the table. He pointed at the grainy image to the right of the Governor's left shoulder. Helen gasped and looked at Babe. It was like looking into a bizarre mirror. The face that was distorted in rage was none other than the face of his father.

With the car packed to the gills with baseball equipment that Babe had bought for the boys at St. Mary's, he pressed down on the accelerator. Stone-faced, he drove in silence to Baltimore, an unlit cigar protruded from his clenched teeth. When Babe wheeled the big sedan into Cider Alley behind Ruth's Café, Helen breathed a huge sigh of relief.

Babe slammed the car door and entered the Café from the rear. He walked through the kitchen and storage area to the bar. His father's back was to him. Babe slid around and sat on a barstool.

"Hey, look who's here!" exclaimed George, Sr. "Is Helen with you?"

"She's upstairs unpacking. She is going to rest. You know how much travelling takes out of her," said Babe in a gruff voice. He waved to Martha,

George's second wife, who was at the other end of the bar by the cash register.

"Can we talk?" said Babe.

"Yeah, let's go to the office. It's quiet there," said George.

"Hey, Marty, take the bar for a few...," said George, gesturing toward Babe and the office. She nodded.

George sat down behind a desk and pulled out a bottle and two glasses. Babe sat and withdrew a newspaper from inside his jacket.

"Are you crazy?" blurted Babe, spreading out the paper.

George, startled by the intensity of Babe's question, spilled some of the liquor on the desk. He pulled a towel from his belt and sopped up the spill. Glaring at his son, he said, "What the hell are you talking about?"

"This!" Babe thundered with his fist slamming on the image in the newspaper.

"You're upset about the rally the other night?" said George, his voice rising incredulously.

"Have you seen this picture? There you are front and center with this ... this mob, screaming your head off, 'Kill Muck, Kill Muck!' You look insane. What do you call that?"

"I call that patriotism. You live in your bubble of professional baseball. The rest of us live in the real world where this country is at war. Unless people like me do our part here in the homeland, our brave boys fighting over there will have nothing to return to," said George.

"Don't you realize that your picture in this newspaper jeopardizes me? If you haven't noticed there is a resemblance. If the cranks think that I am a crazy person yelling Kill Muck at a riot, they might try to drive me out of baseball."

"Or, they just might think that you had a pair," said George with a malicious sneer.

"Where are you getting this from?" asked Babe.

"Several of my friends, Sam, Jimbo, and I have joined the American Protective League," said George, pulling out a badge from his pocket. Babe stared at the official-looking shield bearing the words 'Secret Service – Sergeant' encircled by the words American Protective League. It even bore a badge number.

"What the hell is the American Protective League?"

"It's a volunteer group operating under the direction of the United States Department of Justice Bureau of Investigation. We are the government's eyes and ears. We report suspicious activities by pro-German agents, like espionage, sabotage, and disloyalty."

"You can't be serious. And you think this piece of tin gives you the right to harass a fine man like Dr. Muck?"

"Damned right it does!"

"No, it doesn't. Not without proof and a trial," said Babe.

"This is all the proof I need," said George, holding up a newsletter with a goofy-looking masthead of the word Spyglass distorted by a lens as if seen through a telescope.

"This APL publication details the evil deeds of these pro-German scum who are like rodents crawling through the sewers carrying their filthy disease and trying to undermine our country. Here, read it for yourself. Some of them are sending diseased prostitutes into army bases.

Others are putting ground glass in Red Cross bandages. Our job is to flush out German spies and slackers. Read it. You'll see!" said George in a booming voice. Babe shook his head. He decided to bring the conversation back to a concrete reality.

"Dr. Muck is a fine man. He lives near my place near Fenway. I've been to parties at his place. He's harmless."

"No, he's not. He is buddies with the Kaiser and refuses to play the Star-Spangled Banner at his concerts. He and his traitorous band belong in the internment camp. If you don't watch yourself, you'll end up in a camp, too."

"That's it! We're outta here," said Babe, rising.

"Helen, get in the car. We're leaving. I can't stay with insane people!"

Dr. Karl Muck

Spring 1918
Hot Springs, AK

*"A mob is usually a creature of
very mysterious existence . . . .
Where it comes from, or whither it goes,
few men can tell.
Assembling and dispersing with equal suddenness,
it is . . . difficult to follow. . . ."*
~ Charles Dickens

Following the dust-up with his father over the accusations against Dr. Muck, Babe was so blind with rage that he nearly T-boned a trolley that emerged from around a corner. Only Babe's superior reflexes saved them from disaster. Several of the schoolboys on the trolley recognized Babe and they cheered after the car as it fish-tailed down the street with tires screeching.

In a world gone insane, Babe and Helen retreated to the serenity of Ihatetoquitit cabin in Sudbury. Babe spent his winter ice-fishing, snow-shoeing, and chopping wood to keep the cabin warm. He avoided the outside world and all its travails. When the time to travel to spring training arrived, he was in the best condition of his career. In his first few years as a professional ballplayer, he had learned to expect the unexpected. The Red Sox of 1918 exemplified this principle.

After the disappointing second-place finish in 1917, the Red Sox underwent a drastic restructuring. America's mobilization for war impacted the Red Sox more than any other major league team. By New Year's Day, 1918, twelve members of the 1917 team had joined some branch of the armed services. With one shaky season under his belt, team magnate Frazee recognized the need for professional baseball expertise. He hired Ed Barrow, president of the International League, to assist him in an executive capacity. When former manager Bill Carrigan refused Frazee's offer to return to man the helm again, the owner named Barrow manager for the upcoming season. In contrast to previous managers, Carrigan and Barry, Barrow's relationship with his star player would be combative and tumultuous.

At fifty years of age, Barrow was still vigorous, with a broad chest like a bulldog and a pugnacious temperament to match his large, strapping appearance. He was gruff, opinionated, and was not afraid to resort to fisticuffs if necessary. He sported thick, bushy eye-brows that concealed the scars of a short, youthful career in boxing. Baseball was his first and enduring love. He was devastated when his pitching career ended by throwing too many pitches in a cold, Iowa rain. Barrow made his mark in the game by excelling in all aspects of management. Frazee considered Barrow as the ideal person to rein in his high-spirited, and often out of control young star.

During his job interview, Barrow responded to a question about how he would handle Ruth by saying, "The first time he challenges my authority, I'll take him under the stands and kick his ever-loving ass!"

Frazee grinned and said, "You're hired."

When the time for spring training rolled around Babe boarded the train at South Station, heading to Hot Springs, Arkansas. This would be his fourth training session in the resort in the valley of the Ouachita Mountains. Aside from the sad memory of his fallen friend Yo-na, Babe loved everything about Hot Springs. He looked forward to the soothing baths, hiking the mountain trails and, of course, gambling at the casinos and Oaklawn Park Race Track. Babe was ready for whatever challenges the new year would bring, or, so he thought.

New manager Barrow knew that Babe was the premier southpaw pitcher in the game. He had racked up sixty-five wins in the last three seasons and, at only twenty-three years old, Babe was getting better. In 1917, Ruth won twenty-four games, starting thirty-eight times and pitching an astonishing thirty-five complete games. The sky was the limit for this young pitcher. Or, was it?

Babe had always shown the potential to be a devastating offensive force. However, in 1918, he would blossom. When the year was over, Babe would lead the team in most major categories: homers with eleven (no one else had more than one), batting average, on-base percentage, runs-batted-in, and slugging percentage. All this, while completing eighteen of nineteen starts as a pitcher. His performance with his bat would lead to constant friction with manager Barrow. As much as Babe loved pitching, he absolutely thrived on hitting and had the talent, temperament, and determination to revolutionize the game. Babe wanted to abandon pitching and play the field fulltime. Barrow resisted the transition with all his might. Babe was the irresistible force colliding with Barrow, the immovable object.

During spring training, Babe was a hitting terror. In batting practice, he crushed so many baseballs so far over the fences that magnate Harry Frazee complained about the expense and threatened to charge Babe for the lost balls. Then, came St. Patrick's Day when Babe surpassed even his own expectations. Against a Brooklyn Robins' pitcher named Norman Pitt, Babe connected with a fastball so ferociously that it cleared the wall at Whittington Park and landed 573 feet away in a pond at the neighboring Alligator Farm. One week later, on March 24th, Boston played Brooklyn again. Babe stepped to the plate in the third inning with the bases loaded and Brooklyn's Al Mamaux on the mound. Babe launched another homer that travelled well over five-hundred feet, again disturbing the gators. One pundit said that watching Ruth propel baseballs so far was as historic as watching Halley's Comet streak across the heavens.

Off the ballfield, the war continued to rage in Europe. Hysteria against German-Americans was fueled by the rhetoric of President Wilson and other national figures. On the eve of his war message to Congress Wilson said, "Once we lead this people into war and they'll forget there ever was such a thing as tolerance. To fight you must be brutal and ruthless and the spirit of ruthless brutality will enter into the very fibre of our national life, infecting Congress, the courts, the policeman on the beat, the man on the street."[xxiii]

Shortly after the declaration of war, Congress enacted the Espionage Act which was aimed at preventing interference with the war effort and to stifle support of enemies of the United States. The most direct impact of the new laws and regulations was the requirement that individuals residing in the United States who were born in Germany register at their local post office, report any change of address or employment, and have a registration card on their person at all times. Nearly one half million people complied by submitting forms, photographs, and fingerprints to the postal service.

In light of the war hysteria ginned up by the press, the law became a vehicle of abuse and harassment of anything German. Super-patriots organized efforts to eliminate the use of the German-language books and newspapers. The country was seized by a mean spirit of suspicion and prejudice against German-Americans. The law extended to criminalize what might be perceived as disloyal utterances. Statements perceived to be intemperate or disloyal led to the harassment of German-Americans at their jobs. Others were dragged from their homes to be interrogated, bullied, and tarred and feathered. Campaigns to remove German names from the public square were successful. In Chicago, the fervor to eliminate vestiges of German culture was particularly virulent. The Bismarck Hotel became the Hotel Randolph, the German Hospital became the Grant Hospital, Hamburg Street became Shakespeare Avenue, Lubeck

Street became Dickens Street, Frankfort Avenue became Charleston Street, and the Germania Club became the Lincoln Club. This xenophobia led to much confusion, but it also left a clear, indelible message.

As a consequence of this extreme atmosphere, there was a dramatic increase in law enforcement activity. Federal, state, and local authorities arrested over 10,000 German-Americans. Arrest became a tactic of intimidation and silencing. Attorney General Thomas Gregory acknowledged that German-Americans were taken into custody solely as a deterrent to enemy-alien activity. Eventually, 2,048 individuals were interned at Ft. Oglethorpe, Georgia and Ft. Douglas, Utah.

Babe's enjoyment of spring training was interrupted a few days later during lunch with Heinie Wagner.

"I'll have four frankfurters with sauerkraut and two hamburgers with muenster cheese on Kaiser rolls," said Babe, tucking a napkin under his collar.

Heinie raised his hand to the waiter and said, "My friend meant to order four hot dogs with liberty cabbage and two liberty steaks with white cheddar on bulkie rolls."

Babe's eyebrows crinkled and rose in a way that reminded Heinie of the time his puppy bit into a lemon.

"What gives?" asked Babe.

"Now that the federal government has declared open season on German-Americans, we cannot be too careful. The authorities are rounding up German-Americans who are suspected of being disloyal."

"What does that have to do with my lunch?"

"Babe, the Attorney General of the United States has authorized members of the American Protective League to find German sympathizers. They have recruited over 200,000 zealots to identify German-Americans who support the Kaiser. They are untrained, amateur detectives with rabid imaginations. They see spies behind every tree. The worst thing is that the real government agents listen to them and arrest people on their say-so. That's incredible power. Dangerous power."

"Heinie, I still don't understand what this has to do with my lunch?"

"You have to adjust your language and use non-German words. It's gotten so ridiculous that they even changed 'German measles' to 'Liberty measles.' All you need is one of these APL people to report you on a language slip and you'll have more trouble than you want."

"You know, my father joined the APL. He's got a badge and everything. I told him that he was crazy. My father was even at a demonstration in Baltimore where he led the chant 'Kill Muck.' Can you imagine?" Babe chuckled.

He shuddered to think of the picture of his father's face, his face, twisted into a demonic mask.

"Listen Babe this is serious. Here, take a look," said Heinie, handing a newspaper across the table.

Babe's jaw dropped when he read the headline about his friend.

ARREST KARL MUCK AS AN ENEMY ALIEN
Federal Authorities in Boston May Prefer Charges Under the
Criminal Code. CLAIMED SWISS CITIZENSHIP
Conductor Spends Night in a Cell—
Asked for Passports to Europe Yesterday.[xxiv]

Babe perused the article, the furrows in his brow deepening. He could not imagine the staid Dr. Muck incarcerated with common ruffians. The poor man.

Lunch arrived and Babe turned his attention to his meal. It sure looked like frankfurters, sauerkraut, and hamburgers with muenster cheese on Kaiser rolls. As he watched a few errant poppy seeds from the roll float into the pickle juice on his plate, he wondered whether his father had reprinted the menus at Ruth's Café to mollify his APL cronies.

Between bites of his roast beef sandwich, Heinie told his friend about the directive from league headquarters.

"I almost forgot to tell you the latest. Ban Johnson, the league president, has ordered all the clubs to begin devoting a portion of each practice to marching and other military drills. Get this . . . we'll be using our bats instead of rifles when we march."

Babe rolled his eyes.

"I know it sounds silly to you but the world has gone insane. Once that happens, once the hysteria takes over, it becomes mob rule. The thing about mobs is that they are unpredictable," said Heinie.

"I ain't worried about no mob. I play ball and don't worry myself about the other stuff. I don't do nothin' to rile up a mob . . . except of course, driving the horsehide outta the park," said Babe with a wink.

"Babe, trust me. That don't matter."

Heinie paused to think.

"Do you remember when we came to spring training here last year?"

Babe nodded.

"Well, then, you remember going past the south side of town and seeing all the debris from the houses that were wreaked by the tornado?"

"Yeah, it was a mess. The tornado was like a giant bowling ball that crushed and splintered homes on one side of the street. The other side of the street was spared. One of the waiters told me that a house landed right on the railroad tracks," said Ruth, shaking his head.

"That's right. Well, a mob is the same as a tornado. No one knows when they get started. No one knows which direction they are headed. No one knows what they will destroy. You cannot predict where or when a mob will turn and unleash its destructive force. You definitely would be wise to avoid a mob at all costs. Even if they start out as non-threatening, they can turn on you in an instant. You don't want to be caught in a gaffle."

Using his hot dog to slurp up the last dab of mustard, Babe replied, "I got it, Heinie, stay clear of mobs no matter what."

When the calendar turned to April, the team packed up and began the trek north – sort of. They were scheduled to play exhibitions in Little Rock, Austin, New Orleans, Birmingham, and Chattanooga. The abuse that Babe inflicted on baseballs during the spring fanned the controversy over how the Red Sox would use his skills. Would they take the best pitcher in the game and make him a fulltime player to take advantage of his powerful bat? Manager Ed Barrow pondered this question as the team barnstormed its way to Boston. The only thing he was sure of was that Babe would be his opening day pitcher.

Babe Ruth swinging

April 5, 1918
Collinsville, IL

"I hope that we shall have a few prompt hangings,
and the sooner the better."
~ Congressman Julius Kahn 3/25/18

By the spring 1918, the United States had been at war for a year. The initial euphoria over the adventure of war was sobered by the agony caused by news of rising casualties of young American boys. The government's propaganda apparatus warned of German spies and saboteurs, fueling xenophobia and paranoia. Speaking at the Union League Club in New York, former Secretary of State Elihu Root remarked that there were men walking our streets "who ought to be taken out at sunrise and shot for treason." Democrat Congressman 'Cotton Tom' Heflin and, later, Senator from Alabama, was a white supremacist who said, "We must execute the Huns within our gates. The firing squad is the only solution for these perverts and renegades." [xxv] Coming from the highest level of prominent Americans, this rhetoric created an atmosphere of distrust and animosity toward those of German heritage.

In many parts of the country, twenty-five percent of the population traced their ancestry to Germany. In southern Illinois, the percentage of residents of German descent was much higher. Each community had its own *verein* or singing society; its own *turnverein*, gymnastic clubs; and, a *Germania Bund* or cultural society. There was a concerted government effort to eradicate German influence. German books and newspapers were branded as implements of Imperial German conspiracy. Language teachers were prohibited from teaching German. There were campaigns to change the names of schools, parks, streets, and cities.

Meanwhile, throughout the country cranks were talking about two things – the war and the upcoming baseball season. In Collinsville, Illinois, Bart and Jeremy sat in their favorite watering hole speculating about how their teams might do in 1918. They had been patronizing the bar known as The Shaft since they left school to work in the coal mines. Collinsville was a mining town in the south of Illinois, but it was a short hop across the Mississippi River to St. Louis, Missouri. Both men worked in the Hardscrabble Mine and played on the mine team called the Horseshoe Bitters in the St. Louis Trolley League. Many of their teammates and players from the Dutch Hollow Ku Kluxers and the Caseyville Mutuals were also in the bar.

As far as The Shaft went, it was a local gin mill on Main Street that catered to a rough crowd of miners. When strangers to Collinsville asked Bart for directions to The Shaft, he would simply tell them to follow the bull. When they looked at him quizzically, he refused to elaborate. Upon arrival in Collinsville, they understood. On the side of the building was a thirty-foot high mural advertising the famous product of Bull

Durham. The central image of the mural was an enormous brown bull. When the mural first went up, outraged parishioners bombarded the priest at St. Raynald's Church with complaints about the accurate depiction of the bull's private parts. To assuage the parishioners, many of whom were regulars, Tuffy Bridger, the owner of the Shaft, painted a 'modesty fence' on the pasture depicted in the mural bearing the words Smoking Tobacco to shield sensitive eyes from the bull's offending anatomy.

"Do you think the Cardinals have a shot at the pennant this year?" asked Bart. He was tall, wiry, and the team's best twirler. Word was that he lost his shot at professional ball when he knocked up his third cousin once removed and became the guest of honor at a shotgun wedding.

"Personally, I think they are gonna stink to high heaven. The only reason they were respectable last year was on account of Huggins. That little bastard can manage. Now that he's gone, they don't stand a chance. You watch - last place, if they're lucky," said Jeremy.

Suddenly, a commotion out on the street drew their attention. An angry crowd surrounded a young man and hurled vile insults at him. When he tried to get away, they shoved him to the ground.

"Hey, isn't that Bobby Prager?" said Jeremy.

"Who is Bob Prager?" asked Bart.

"He's the squat, little guy who lives upstairs from us at the boarding house - the guy with the glass eye and handlebar mustache."

"You mean the baker? The guy who works at Bruno's Bakery down the road in Maryville?" asked Bart.

"Yeah, that's the guy. I wonder what he did to piss off these guys. It looks like he could use a little help," said Jeremy who cracked his knuckles in anticipation. As the team's catcher, Jeremy had the well-deserved nickname, the Anvil as much for his ability to guard home plate as for his physical presence. During the limited time he attended school, he was known for his willingness to wade into a melee to protect the underdog.

"I got your back, Anvil," said Bart, pulling on his thick, leather gloves.

Word that a German spy had been captured spread through the bar faster than shouts of 'Fire' at six-hundred feet below the surface. Dozens of slightly-inebriated patrons emerged from the Shaft. They were strapping, young miners who were underpaid, under-appreciated and mad as hell. Stories of German plans to sabotage the war effort by blowing up munitions factories and mines threatened them with every miner's worst nightmare – being trapped in a mine cave-in. Many of the miners were German-Americans who resented the media narrative that they were disloyal to the United States. In the current climate of war hysteria, they rushed to prove their loyalty by becoming super-patriots. As the rumor of a German spy spread down Main Street, other saloons emptied. In a flash, the original crowd swelled to 300 jeering men who jostled each other into a surreal frenzy.

Robert Paul Prager, a German immigrant, stood in the center of this toxic maelstrom. Born in Dresden thirty years before, Prager immigrated to America when he was seventeen. Prager loved America and tried to join the Navy when the war began. He was rejected. Since he had been a miner back in Germany, Prager applied for instatement in the United Mine Workers of America, Local 264. While his application was pending, the union president learned that Prager was overheard agitating the rank-and-file with socialist propaganda. Some of Prager's comments were considered to be seditious and pro-German. This enraged the union president who denied Prager's application. Prager responded by distributing an open letter to union members denouncing their president.

The controversy escalated and the union formed a committee to deal with Prager. They chased him four miles to Collinsville from his job at the bakery in Maryville. In Collinsville, several union members removed his shoes and stripped him down to his skivvies. They draped an American flag over his head and shoulders and demanded that he kiss the flag. Prager complied. That wasn't enough for Joseph Riegel. He decided that the crowd was having too much fun to end the humiliation of Prager.

"I'm not convinced that this Kraut is loyal to America," shouted Riegel. He was a twenty-eight-year old shoemaker who had previously served in the U.S. Army. Riegel took his cap off and stoked the crowd. "Let's hear him sing."

"Yeah, we want to hear the Star-Spangled Banner," shouted several voices from the crowd.

Prager cringed. He shivered from cold and fear. His eyes were clouded by tears as he anxiously scanned the crowd for a non-hostile face. A twitch jumped up and down on his face like a subcutaneous, hiccupping salamander. His mind raced.

"Come on, your Hun bastard, sing!" shouted Riegel, prodding the man in the side with the handle of a cobbler's hammer. The crowd picked up the last word and started chanting, "Sing, sing, sing!"

"I'm a Yankee Doodle Dandy ...," croaked Prager.

"I'm a Yankee Doodle boy . . . ," he continued, barely above a whisper.

"Boo, Boo. We want the Star-Spangled Banner!"

Suddenly, a savior appeared. Anvil stepped up to Prager and said, "OK, that's it. Come with me."

Riegel would have none of it. He raised his hammer to Jeremy's face.

"It's not over until we say it's over. Right, boys?" shouted Riegel. This stand-off darkened the mood. Two of the union thugs, Richard Dukes and Bill Brockmeier sidled up to Anvil intending to attack him from behind if the situation escalated. Bart, too, was surrounded by toughs carrying bludgeons and saps. Anvil calculated his next move. He figured he could neutralize the threat posed by Riegel and disable at least one of the clowns behind him. After that, he had no idea how he would survive the wrath of the crowd that was rapidly morphing into a mob.

"All right, all right, boys, this has gone far enough," shouted police officer Martin Futchek. He led a police-blue wedge composed of Fred Frost, Harry Stevens, and John Tobnick into the center of the mob. The surprise appearance of the cops served to defuse the situation. Officer Futchek grabbed Prager by the arm and announced in a stentorian voiced that he was taking Prager into protective custody. The four officers formed a cordon around Prager, loaded him into a paddy wagon and drove off to City Hall.

Jeremy and Bart breathed a sigh of relief and went back to the Shaft for a cold brew. They believed that the danger had passed. The mayor had been summoned to the scene and immediately ordered all the bars closed. Jeremy and Bart went home. However, the mob did not disperse, like a tornado it simply changed course. Riegel and Beaver concocted a plan. They rallied the union thugs and a dozen of the most blood-thirsty tormentors.

Collinsville became a mining town in 1857. Over the decades, the city prospered and grew. Gradually, mining operations were moved further and further from the city. Many of the inhabitants were unaware of the network of mining tunnels that snaked under the city. Riegel was not one of them. He led his group of vagabonds to the back door of the Hardscrabble Bar and went down to the cellar. His band of miscreants grumbled; until Riegel pried open a door that led to the labyrinth of tunnels. With miner's lamps lighting the way, they traversed the city underground and emerged across the street from City Hall.

When the police guard brought Prager to City Hall, Mayor J.H. Siegel thought that they were safe. With the taverns closed, he believed that the members of the crowd would go home; after all they had to go to work in the morning. Unfortunately, he underestimated the bloodlust of the mob and the ingenuity of Riegel. Mayor Siegel peeked through the curtains from his office and could not believe his eyes. The mob was re-forming across the street from City Hall. How did they find us so quickly, he thought? After consulting with his massive ego, he decided to reason with the malcontents.

Mayor Siegel tried to charm the mob. He appealed to their civic pride.

"Now, gentlemen, "We do not want a stigma marking Collinsville. I implore you to go to your homes and discontinue this demonstration."xxvi

There are various versions as to what happened next. The most reliable would appear to be the mayor's testimony at the coroner's inquest. He recalled telling the leaders of the mob that Prager had been removed from the building by police. At this point, Wesley Beaver, a saloon janitor demanded access to the building to make sure that Prager was not there. When the mayor opened the door to admit only Beaver, the mob surged forward and overcame the mayor and the policemen. It did not take long for Beaver to find Prager hiding in the basement under some tiling.

At the sight of Prager being manhandled on the steps of City Hall by Beaver, the ferocity of the mob returned. It dragged, pushed, and prodded the terrified German along St. Louis road to Mauer Heights, one mile west outside of Collinsville, and, more important, beyond the jurisdiction of the Collinsville police. At the city line, the police stopped following the mob and Prager, thereby sealing his fate.

To fortify themselves, the men passed around bottles of liquor. Guns appeared and anyone who tried to interfere was threatened. Someone suggested that Prager be taught a lesson by making him the object of a tar and feather party. But, when no one could find tar and feathers, the night turned tragic.

The headlamps of three automobiles illuminated the macabre scene. Riegel grabbed a tow rope and fashioned a noose. Then, he threw the free end of the rope over a sturdy limb of a hackberry tree. Rage twisted and distorted Riegel's face. He fitted the noose over Prager's head and shouted for the mob to join him at the rope, "Come on fellows, we're all in on this, let's not have any slackers here," [xxvii] At least fifteen people grabbed the rope and pulled Prager into the air.

Fortunately, for Prager, no one thought to tie his hands. He grabbed the rope and held on for dear life. As he gagged and struggled, someone suggested that the German should be allowed to say his last words. They lowered him to the ground. After praying for several minutes, he asked if he could write a letter to his parents. Once the short note was completed, Prager spoke his last words, "All right boys, go ahead and kill me, but wrap me in the flag when you bury me."[xxviii]

"We gotta tie his hands behind him," yelled Riegel.

Beaver performed the task. With that, Robert Prager was hoisted into the air. He died just after midnight at the hands of a vicious mob.

An armed guard with orders to shoot anyone who tried to cut him down was posted by the tree where Robert Prager hung through the night. The next day after the mob had dispersed; the coroner took the body down from the tree. Removing Prager's personal effects, he found a letter declaring his love for America, attesting to his loyalty and detailing his efforts to become a naturalized American citizen.

A grand jury indicted eleven men for the murder of Robert Paul Prager. They were: Joseph Riegel, coal miner and shoe cobbler; Richard

Dukes, Jr., coal miner; Cecil Larremore, coal miner; James DeMatties, coal miner; Frank Flannery, coal miner; Charles Cranmer, clerk; John Hallsworth, coal miner; Calvin Gilmore, plumber's helper; Wesley Beaver, saloon porter; Enid Elmore, coal miner; and William Brockmeier, coal miner. After several weeks of jury selection, the trial was conducted during the last week of May, 1918.

The trial lasted three days. James M Bandy was lead counsel for the defendants. The defense attorney argued that Prager's lynching was a "patriotic murder" because there was at present no law to punish those who made disloyal statements and, therefore, people who criticized America's war effort, or, who supported the Kaiser were subject to mob law.

Bandy was assisted at trial by D.S. Williamson. In his closing argument, Williamson said, "If you punish these men for gathering at City Hall, your verdict will stamp you as being opposed to men who are loyal, and in favor of disloyalty." [xxix]

It took the jury only forty-five minutes to reach a verdict of not guilty.

When Babe read about the trial and the acquittal in the *Boston Globe*, he retched.

If there was ever a contest for the year of death, 1918 would certainly rank high on the list. As the Great War entered its fourth year, a world weary of death, destruction, and carnage, seemed incapable of stopping the madness. With casualties exceeding the millions, military and political leaders prepared for another spring offensive. Where hope and new life should have been the order of the day, men planned for more death.

It was not surprising that the death of a prisoner in Bohemia would attract little attention. With all the casualties, what was one more? Yet, a sense of *schadenfreude* might have been justified. After all, the German word for satisfaction at the deserved suffering of another would apply to the assassin whose murder of Archduke Franz Ferdinand had triggered the war.

Three years after having been convicted and sentenced to twenty years in prison, Gavrilo Princip was confined in a fortress in Theresienstadt that housed political prisoners during World War I. It had been built by the Habsburg Emperor, Joseph II, and named in honor of his mother Maria Theresa. The cells were dark, cold, dank concrete that exuded a deathly chill even on summer days. Decades in the future when the world would resume its murderous madness, Theresienstadt would serve as a concentration camp.

Now, Princip reached the end of his short life coughing blood and gasping for breath. While in prison, he had contracted tuberculosis, a debilitating disease that seemed to consume him. Although parallels to Babe Ruth ended at their age and tumultuous relationships with their fathers, Princip probably would have envied the robust American, and, perhaps, rooted for him to succeed. As it was, they were worlds apart, with destinies as different as their circumstances.

Alone, in the prison sick bay, Gavrilo's life ended on 28 April 1918. At the time of his death, he was a bare skeleton of the youth that had assassinated royalty. Had he been made aware of the young man's death, Babe would have prayed a silent prayer for the repose of his soul. Princip's death never made it to Babe's attention.

Lynching victim – Robert Paul Prager

July 1918
Baltimore, MD

*"Baseball is a needed tonic and
diversion in such serious times as these."*
~ H.N. Hempstead, President New York Giants

For one disoriented moment, he panicked. Where was he? He squinted. His head throbbed. The noises of a weekday filtered into the darkened room. Drayers cracked their whips, men whistled and shouted, and machines whirred into action; all familiar sounds to a kid who grew up in the working area of Baltimore. The smell of rotting food and stale beer wafted into his room. Around the center and edges of dark curtains, three shafts of sunlight invaded the room. In this light, dust motes flickered and fluttered. He surveyed the room above his father's tavern. Small, sparse, and gritty summed it up.

Lying on his back, he stretched his left arm. The cracking of his elbow and the dull pain behind his shoulder reminded him of his situation. Although he was only twenty-three years old, he felt older. The rigors of playing professional baseball were beginning to take a toll. This season had been especially tough. Manager Barrow insisted that he pitch in the regular rotation, which he did. However, when he wasn't toeing the pitcher's slab, he played the outfield or first base. Now, one day before Independence Day he was alone in his father's spare room and without a job.

The last few months had been hell. It started with the arrest of Dr. Muck on trumped up charges for failing to register as an enemy alien and for violating the postal laws. If Dr. Muck was a spy, then Babe was a hippopotamus. Then, the awful news of lynching of Germans because some fink claimed that they were disloyal. The reports of the lynching of Robert Prager in Collinsville, a mining town near St. Louis, and not too far from Chicago, reminded him of the upcoming road trip to those cities and the abuse he would receive from the cranks.

Heading into May, the situation on the ballfield wasn't great, but it was tolerable. He was fourth in the American League in batting average. He chafed at the limited opportunities Barrow gave him to bat. The manager insisted that he was a pitcher first, and reluctantly played him in the field when he wasn't pitching. Being young and strong as one of the oxen that hauled the cargo from the port, he relished his role; anything to get more at-bats. Boy, did he love to crush baseballs with his fifty-four-ounce bat. The sound when he barreled up a pitch with that big old wagon-tongue was heavenly.

When Babe was given the opportunity to play a position he played hard and well; perhaps, too well. He loved to show off his powerful arm from the outfield and, frequently gunned the ball in to nail runners trying to advance. Whenever he whistled in a throw, he immediately saw bright points of light and his arm throbbed. On days after he pitched nine innings, these throws from the outfield took a great toll on him. Of course, not wanting to discourage Barrow from playing him in the outfield, he hid the pain.

As is often the case in life, Ruth got blind-sided by something he never expected. It started with the weekend series against the Yankees in New York during the first week in May. Babe pitched a complete game, but lost to the Yankees, 5 – 4. Even though he hit his first home run of the season, he blamed himself for losing the game because of two fielding errors that he had committed.

After a nice dinner with Rico at Rosina's Trattoria, he returned to the Ansonia Hotel in a restless mood. Since the following day was Sunday and there was no game to play, Babe decided to go on a bender. For the next twenty-four hours, he partied like it was 1899. Later, he would only recall being fished out of the Angel of the Waters Fountain at Bethesda Terrace in Central Park at sunrise on Monday by Police Officer Jay Harrington.

"Ruth, if I wasn't a lifelong Red Sox fan, you'd be spending some time in the pokey. Since you're a good lad, I'll show you the way to your hotel and avoid filling out all those nasty forms for public intoxication and indecency. It's a good thing that those hacks weren't around to take photos of your imitation of the Babe of the Waters Fountain," chuckled the cop, amused at his own witticism.

Babe's nocturnal escapade provided Harrington with a tale that he would use to regale his drinking buddies of the night he saved the Babe. He even had a signed baseball to show for it, a souvenir from Babe for bringing him back to the Ansonia. For his courtesy, the officer also received a couple of Babe Ruth cigars, including one he swore was marred with the teeth marks of the great Bambino himself. The bender left Babe with a sore throat that would have life-changing consequences.

Two weeks later, Babe entered the clubhouse at Fenway. His throat was inflamed and felt like he had swallowed a cactus. Through red, watery eyes he navigated through the locker room. As he passed the manager's office, a loud sneeze erupted from deep in Babe's chest.

"For the love of Pete, when did hurricane season start? Get over here, Ruth. Sit down. Let me see you," said Ed Barrow, emerging from his office.

"Hey, Doc, we need you over here right now," Barrow bellowed to the trainer.

Dr. Lawler felt Babe's forehead and announced, "Temperature is well over 100, he's burning up."

"Open your mouth, Babe," said the trainer. "Your tonsils are inflamed. Come into my office, I've got just the thing for you. We don't want an outbreak of that Spanish Flu that's been plaguing the Army boys."

Babe nodded dully and followed Doc. Once inside his private office that was slightly larger than a broom closet, the trainer pulled out a bottle of silver nitrate.

"This here is an antiseptic that we use to kill the germs in the throat. Now, lie back, OK," said Doc, as he swabbed the back of Babe's throat with the solution. Babe gagged and rasped, "Stop! That stuff is gonna kill me. My throat is burning up."

The solution was much too concentrated and caused severe injury to Ruth's throat. He went by ambulance to the hospital and spent the next week in bed with his throat packed in ice. Decades later when Babe was diagnosed with terminal throat cancer, he blamed the silver nitrate for his hoarse, raspy voice. [xxx]

The Selective Service Act was passed in May 1917, shortly after the United States declared war against Germany. This act authorized the draft and governed the registration, classification, and drafting of eligible males, ages 21 – 31 years of age. Generally, men were drafted unless they were exempt or engaged in productive employment. As more and more young men were drafted and went off to war, there was growing outcry about the privileged status of the young, healthy athletes who were playing major league baseball without serving their country.

The issue was whether or not baseball was an essential industry. The professional baseball leagues were in a limbo of uncertainty while Provost Marshall General Enoch Crowder who was in charge of administration of the draft waited for a determination by Secretary of War, Newton D. Baker. The issue of whether ballplayers would automatically be exempt from the draft was decided in July with a determination that major league baseball was a "non-essential" endeavor. Secretary Baker issued a "work or fight" order that mandated all eligible men to engage in war-related employment or risk induction into the military.

Babe registered with the draft board in Boston which granted him a "4" deferment as a married man. Nevertheless, to avoid the insults about being a slacker, he and a couple of the guys joined the

Massachusetts Home Guard. It didn't help stop the heckling much, but it made him feel like he was contributing to the war effort.

As is often the case, the devious seek ways to circumvent such an edict. Baseball leagues of teams sponsored by industrial concerns were an obvious solution for ball players who wished to avoid military service. Conceived as a morale booster and entertainment by executives such as Charles Schwab, president of the Bethlehem Shipbuilding Company, the Bethlehem Steel League was formed in 1917, fielding six teams from its east coast factories. Down the coast, the Delaware River Shipbuilding League had eight teams from shipbuilding plants in Pennsylvania, New Jersey, and Delaware. Naturally competitive, the rival plants recruited ringers to gain advantage. In the Bethlehem Steel League, Joseph P. Kennedy was appointed general manager of the team representing the Fore River facility. He recruited Dutch Leonard, a frontline pitcher for the Boston Red Sox. The addition of Leonard to the Fore River team would have a ripple effect in Boston.

After his hospital stay, Ruth returned to the Red Sox. Barrow rode him hard. The manager resented the young man's attitude and apparent lack of respect for his prodigious talents. He expected Babe to be perfect, which was impossible. The situation was exacerbated by the loss of pitcher Dutch Leonard to the Fore River club in the Bethlehem Steel League. Leonard's departure left the Red Sox short of pitching. When the manager badgered Ruth to pitch, the young man resisted. Then, centerfielder Amos Strunk injured his ankle and went on the disabled list. Barrow was forced to play Ruth in the outfield. Furthermore, Barrow was not the only one who respected Babe's hitting ability. Managers in the American League learned that often the best way to pitch to Ruth was not to pitch to him. At one point in May, Babe received five consecutive intentional walks. All of these circumstances led to mounting frustration.

On July 2nd, during a game against the Senators in Griffith Stadium, the tension erupted on account of an especially poor performance by Ruth. He arrived late to the ball park, committed a costly fielding error that led to a run in the first inning, and he had struck out on three straight pitches in his second at bat. When he came to the plate in the sixth inning with his team trailing 3 - 0, Babe swung and missed at the first pitch and eventually stuck out again. Barrow was fuming at Babe's lack of patience. When Babe returned to the dugout, Barrow made a sarcastic remark chiding him.

"Why don't you go to hell old man?" snapped Babe.

"You could use a good kick in the ass, that's what I think. You won't pitch, you show up late, and now I have to watch this. That was a bum play."

"Don't you call me a bum," said Babe. "I'll give you a punch in the nose."

"That'll cost you $500!" thundered Barrow.

"The hell it will. I quit!"[xxxi]

Babe stormed out of the dugout and was gone from the Stadium before the game was over. He escaped to Baltimore, the first place that came to his mind. Unfortunately, St. Mary's was shut down for the mid-summer holiday; so, Babe ended up at Ruth's Café.

It was unusual for Babe to lie in bed with nothing to do. If he were still with the club, he would be in the clubhouse joshing with the guys while preparing for batting practice. A natural showman, Babe enjoyed the freedom during batting practice to swing as hard as he could to drive cookie pitches to the farthest reaches of the ballpark. The cranks came early to ooh and aah at his blasts. That was fun.

The smell of fried bacon in the kitchen downstairs made his stomach rumble. Time to eat and make some decisions. The remnants of breakfast lay strewn across the counter. He would have to make his own breakfast. His hand glanced across a pot of coffee; it was still warm. Sitting down with his coffee mug, he fumbled with the newspaper. Big George emerged through the trapdoor from the basement carrying several boxes of liquor.

"Hey, lookee here, sleeping beauty is awake. Nice to see ya champ," said George.

"Hi, Pops. I had a disagreement with that monster Barrow and quit the club,"

"Yeah, I read about it in the paper. Now, what are ya gonna do?"

"I'm not sure. I don't know what I'm going to do."

"Well, since you are here, give me a hand getting ready for the big celebration tomorrow. The local chapter of the American Protective League is holding their America First shindig here. Governor Warfield will be here hawking Liberty Bonds. It's going to be great."

"Sure, Pop."

Babe thought what the heck he might enjoy some mindless physical work and stop worrying about his next move. That was before he unfolded the paper and saw the headline.

Crackerjack Babe Ruth Agrees To Play With Chester Ship

"What the heck," he shouted. Babe stood, almost upturning the kitchen table in the process. The plates and silverware rattled and the coffee sloshed from the mugs. Frantic, his eyes flashed across the room in the way that a trapped sparrow searches for escape. His heart pounded. He stumbled, trying to make sense of the headline. He never agreed to play for the Chester Ship industrial baseball team. This would definitely complicate any possibility of a gracious return to the Red Sox. Now what? Then, a bolt of clarity struck. This could only be the handiwork of one person.

"You," he screamed. "This is your work, isn't it?"

His father stiffened, unprepared for Babe's violent reaction.

"I thought that you could earn a few bucks while you hang around here."

"What!? Is that what you think this is about – a few bucks?" said Babe, trying to steady his voice. He wiped a glob of spittle from his chin.

"Aw, shut your trap, junior. You don't know nothin' about business. When I read about your fracas with Barrow, I figured that you would come running here with your tail between your legs. Then, I thought that you'd be lookin' for a new gig."

"So, then, what?" said Babe in a challenging tone.

George gave him a look as if he were about to explain how to tie shoelaces to a toddler. Babe bristled.

"So, then, I sent a telegram to Frank Miller, the manager of the Chester Ship team, asking him if signing a star left-handed pitcher and batter might interest him. I signed it George H. Ruth."

"You, what? You sent a telegram under my name?"

"Not exactly, in case you forgot, I had the moniker first before I gave it to you."

"You arrogant son of a b - -," said Babe, making an obvious effort to restrain the impulse to knock his father into the middle of next week. For his part, George stood there with his chin jutting out, daring his son to lash out. His right hand gripped a shot-filled sap that he kept in his pocket for emergencies.

"You sniveling ingrate. I will not let you talk to me in that way in my house!"

"Your house!? Ha! You forget who paid for all this with my first World Series check!"

"That's it. Get out! Get out!" said George, shaking with rage, his fists clenched.

"With pleasure . . . I won't spend another minute in your presence. You never let me be myself. You're jealous of my success and want to sabotage me just like the Kraut bastards you pretend to hate want to sabotage the country," shouted Babe. He grabbed his duffel and stormed out the door, leaving it open in his wake. A final thought entered his head.

"Oh, yeah, I'll make my way back to the Sox. When we get to the World Series, don't ask for any tickets and when I win the World Series again this year, don't expect any money from me!"

"Don't let the door hit you in the butt on the way out," George taunted, in a sing-song voice.

These were the last words he ever heard his father utter.

August 1918

"But if anything is certain it is that no story is ever over, . . . and it isn't the game that is over, it is just an inning, and that game has a lot more than nine innings. When the game stops, it will be called on account of darkness."
~ Robert Penn Warren

"Is this stool empty?" said a man's voice.

Babe nodded, without looking up. He was sitting in a nondescript breakfast dive across from the train station going over his options. A plate of congealed eggs sat half-eaten in front of him. His meddling father had really done it this time. Babe knew that the shipbuilding league was not an option. When Leonard left the team, Barrow had called a team meeting to remind "each and every one of their sorry asses" that they were under contract with the Red Sox and that if they tried to jump to another team he would tie them up in court for so long that even their grandkids would not be able to play ball.

Barrow . . . he still did not know how to deal with the tough, old bird. The manager did not like him and the feeling was mutual.

Barrow could care less that Babe's throat still burned and his shoulder barked the day after he pitched. The manager showed no concern for his welfare. The old man just expected Babe to perform like a machine.

The young man could deal with the physical aspects of the game, but he worried about the war hysteria. There was a growing volatility throughout the country. Sometimes when he was in the outfield, he heard threats aimed at him because of his German heritage. Every player must learn to ignore the nasty jeers from opponents and the cranks; otherwise, they get run out of the league. The tenor of the taunts was changing to something sinister. It was not uncommon to hear threats of shooting. The last time the team played in Philly, the bugs kept threatening to shoot his Kraut butt and then popped balloons. Only his superior discipline kept him from ducking for cover.

The constant drumbeat for players to join one of the branches of military service wore on him even though he had a marital deferment. One thing he knew for sure was that he would not be a slacker like Leonard and take a no-show job at a shipbuilding company to avoid serving. As much as letters from his friend Gunny railed about the miserable conditions in the Army, Babe would definitely do his patriotic duty and serve if called. Right now, his problem was how to get back to the Red Sox without having to kiss the creepy old man's butt.

"It looks like you could use a friend."

Lost in thought, Babe tried to ignore the insistent stranger.

"Hey, would you mind passing the sugar, bud?"

This guy was annoying. Babe considered leaving for the train station and wait there. Something triggered in his mind - there was something familiar with that voice. Could it be? He turned to face the smiling face of Heinie Wagner.

"I thought you'd never look up."

"What are you doing here?"

"Babe, I could ask you the same question. We both belong in Philly with the team. The skip asked me to come to Baltimore to bring you back to the team."

"I like to pitch, but my main objection has always been that pitching keeps you out of so many games. I like to be in there every day. If I had my choice, I'd play first base. I don't think a man can pitch in his regular turn, and play every other game at some other position and keep up that pace year after year,"[xxxii] said Babe.

"All we want is for you to help us get through this year. We'll worry about the future in the future. We have a great opportunity to win it all this year, but we can't do it without you. Whatta ya say?"

"I can do it this season all right. I'm young and strong and don't mind the work, but I wouldn't guarantee to do it for many seasons."[xxxiii]

"We need you now, and want you back, no questions asked – all's forgiven," said Heinie, giving Babe his most sincere look.

"Really?" said Babe, with an exaggerated exhalation.

"Yes, we have a train to catch and a pennant to win."

"Damn right," said a grinning Babe.

They made it to Philly in time for Babe to play centerfield and bat third. The next day he pitched a complete game victory and batted cleanup. As Heinie had promised, Barrow acted as if the incident never occurred. For his part, Babe agreed to pitch every fourth day. Over the rest of the season he won nine of his eleven starts, including the pennant-clincher in Shibe Park, Philadelphia at the end of August.

Back in Baltimore, George shrugged off Babe's volatile exit, chalking it up to just another tantrum by his immature, and unrealistic son. One day he would learn how the real world worked. Thankfully, he thought, business at Ruth's Café had never been better. Since Big George had aligned himself with the boys in the American Protective League, the saloon was always crowded. It seemed like the APL held rallies every week – whether to sell Liberty Bonds, to raise money for widows and orphans of the fallen, or to round up disloyal Germans, the patriots were always thirsty.

Although the adage taught that time heals all wounds, sometimes there isn't enough time.

Over the ensuing weeks, father and son were extremely busy and there had been no opportunity to reconcile the lingering hard feelings. It had been six weeks since his dustup with his son and the Red Sox had been in Boston for an extended home stand. The Red Sox were about to embark on a long road trip to play in St. Louis, Cleveland, and Detroit. After that, the team was scheduled to return from Detroit for another long home stand, and George figured that he might surprise his son by taking a trip of his own to Boston. Anyway, from his vantage point in Baltimore, it seemed to George that his son's difficulties with Barrow had been resolved. Since Babe had returned to the team, the Red Sox had moved into first place by virtue of winning two out of every three games. It was a good bet that they were going to stay in first place and return to the World Series.

"Good evening, George," said Jimbo, "pour me the usual."

"How's my favorite mechanic?" said George as he slid a sudsy mug across the counter. Jimbo Anderson was a towering figure who had been a pretty fair country ballplayer in his day. That is, until an elevator he was repairing accidentally slipped and sheared two toes off his right foot.

Nowadays, Jimbo worked as a mechanic at the Fairfield Yard. He had two passions – keeping America safe from German spies, and baseball. Somehow, in his mind they blended together.

"Just dandy . . . just dandy. On my way, here I stopped in at the offices of the *Baltimore Evening Herald* to catch today's scores. Our boys did it again," said Jimbo.

"Come on, out with it. How did my boy do? I know it was his turn to pitch. How'd he do?"

"Let's see. . . I think my memory could use a little refreshing," he said, pushing his empty mug toward George who obliged, chuckling and shaking his head.

"On the house, Jimbo."

"Okay, the Red Sox three, Browns one. The home town lad pitched another complete game. No home runs for the kid . . . (an exaggerated pause) but, he scored the Sox' last run by stealing home. Yeah, and he got up with a limp, but gutted out the rest of the game for the victory."

"That's twelve wins for my boy," said George, puffing his chest in a way that made him look like a bullfrog in heat.

"I guess he got his speed from his mother," joked Jimbo.

George started to join the good-natured laughter when his eyes fell on a dark figure, who had entered the saloon. It was his second wife's brother Benjamin, a ne'er-do-well if there ever was one. He was a sullen and devious man in his late twenties. After Katie's tragic death, George married Martha Sipes. Her older brother, Benjamin, visited Ruth's Café frequently and expected to drink for free. When employed, he was a blacksmith and, to George's chagrin, Benjamin was the reigning arm-wrestling champion in the saloon. Needless to say, George and Benjamin were like oil and water; the two men barked and snarled at each other whenever they were in the same room.

The animosity between the two men had reached its peak a few months earlier when Ben took a shift behind the bar and was caught selling drugs to a soldier from Fort Meade. Not only did Ben's transgression jeopardize George's liquor license, it resulted in a file being opened by the APL. The saloon-keeper banned Benjamin from the premises.

George was embarrassed and appalled at what APL's investigation revealed. Benjamin was consorting with unsavory German merchant sailors who were stranded in Baltimore as a result of the wartime embargo. Captain Harris, George's superior officer in the American Protective League, suspected Sipes of conspiring with Paul Hilken, a known German sympathizer who ran the North German Lloyd Lines, a front for an espionage/sabotage ring.

George sidled over to Martha and, through clenched teeth, said, "Get your brother out of here."

Hours later, as a weary George was preparing to close, he saw Sipes loitering outside the front of the Café. Incensed, George rushed out of the bar, removing his bartender's apron as he went to confront Sipes.

"You no-good piece of crap; I told you to get away from my place. You are polluting the neighborhood. Get outta here!" George screamed, with veins popping from his neck and forehead.

"Ha, looks who's calling me a piece of crap. Where's your slacker son? Is he still hiding behind your apron? Anyway, Mr. Big Shot, you don't own the street. It's a public street, and I'm gonna stay here as long as I want," replied Sipes, defiantly, flicking his still-burning cigarette into the gutter.

"We'll see about that," said George who threw a haymaker at the taller man.

Sipes went down. George pounced on him, kicking him in the side and screaming obscenities.

The bar emptied. Sipes deflected George's kicks and regained his feet. The crowd urged on the combatants. Filled with bloodlust, George bull-rushed Sipes. The younger man sidestepped the charge, and delivered a thunderous blow to George's head. His momentum stopped, George teetered back and then fell. The back of his head slammed against the curb with a sickening, squishy thud. At that moment, all sound, motion and, even the breathing of the on-lookers, stopped – frozen in an instant of horror and disbelief.

Jimbo was the first to break the inertia.

"Get back," he shouting lifting up his immobile friend and carrying him inside.

"Somebody call an ambulance!"

To Be Continued

BONUS

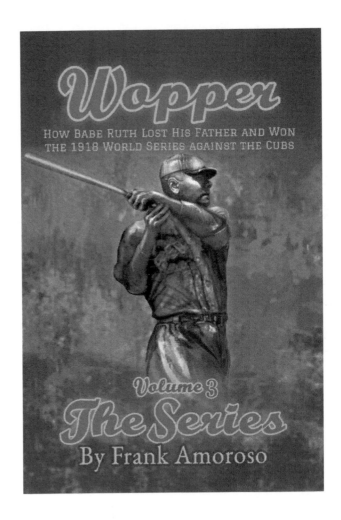

Wopper

HOW BABE RUTH LOST HIS FATHER AND WON
THE 1918 WORLD SERIES AGAINST THE CUBS

Volume 3
The Series
By Frank Amoroso

August 25, 1918
Boston, MA

"I hope that real love and truth are stronger in the end
than any evil or misfortune in the world."
~ Charles Dickens

Situated in Boston's Back Bay at the corner of Boylston and
Exeter Streets, the Lenox Hotel was a short cab ride from
Fenway Park. The hotel was named after the wife of King
George III. Built in the Beaux Art style, it was the tallest
building in Boston, at eleven stories. Hotelier Lucius Boomer
cultivated the hotel's reputation for elegant splendor by
welcoming famous personages of the day. Boomer was an avid
baseball crank. With penthouse suites overlooking the Charles
River and Boston Commons, the Lenox Hotel became a
favorite post-game hangout for the fun-loving Red Sox. On
this night, they were celebrating their victory over the Browns.

It was Babe's twelfth win and the team was steamrolling toward another pennant. The intoxicating fragrance of World Series bonus money filled the air.

"Ecco, Bruno. Here is his room."

A barely distinct rainbow reflected from the crystal chandelier onto the brass numerals on the door to the penthouse suite. He raised his free hand and knocked. Suddenly, the door swung open. The man with his lips set tightly over his handsome features recoiled.

"The ice is here," yelled Boston outfielder Harry Hooper who stood in the doorway with his mouth agape, a cigarette dangling from his lip. He was wearing an under shirt, his trousers were held up by suspenders. His free hand clutched a bottle of liquor.

"Excuse me, sir," he stammered to the imposing figure before him. They stood eye to eye, quiet for a second.

"Babe, ya got company," Harry barked over his shoulder with an ever-so-slight Canadian lilt. He back-tracked into the room to admit the visitor. He mumbled, "Eh, nice to see ya."

The suite was filled with smoke, partially disrobed men and women, and a cacophony of noise. Babe sat semi-reclined on a sofa on the opposite side of the penthouse. Lights from the Charles River twinkled behind him. His left ankle was encased in an ice-filled towel.

"Hey, everybody, quiet down," bellowed Babe. When the noise subsided, he hobbled over to his new guest.

"Everybody, this is my dear friend, Enrico Caruso!" The assemblage applauded, some cheered.

Babe kissed Rico on both cheeks. Grinning, Babe informed them, "We are especially honored to see him here because he is on his honeymoon. That's right; this rascal got married last Tuesday in New York."

With this announcement, hoots and lascivious howls filled the room. Enrico bowed in comedic fashion.

"Champagne, champagne," chanted several of the showgirls.

Several hours later, when the festivities were winding down, the phone rang. Heinie Wagner who was clearing the tables of various bottles, answered.

"Babe, call for you."

"Who's calling at this hour? It's nearly two in the morning."

"Hello," said Babe.

"Hey, sis, what's going on?" said Babe, simultaneously whispering to Rico that it was his sister Mamie.

Suddenly, Babe's smiling countenance disappeared. His face turned ashen.

"What!? When? Where are you?"

After listening intently, he returned the earpiece to the cradle. There was a dumbfounded expression on his face, as if he could not comprehend the message he had just received.

"What is it?" asked Rico.

"My father . . ." Babe said, in a voice so quiet that it was barely a whisper.

"What about your father? *Bambino*, what happened to your father? *Diga mi*, tell me," pleaded Rico.

Babe slumped, shaking his head in disbelief.

"My father was severely injured in a bar fight. He was knocked to the curb and cracked his skull," said Babe. "He's at University Hospital in Baltimore in a coma. The damage is so extensive that they don't expect him to live until dawn."

Several of the girls gasped, hiding their faces behind mournful hands.

Enrico hurried to the younger man, embracing him with a hug that enveloped like a protective cloak.

"Oh, *mi Giorgio, mi Bambino*, I'm so sorry. *Chi terrible*," he whispered. His large hands encircled the *Bambino's* moon-face and stared into the moist brown eyes of his friend.

"Rico, I . . . I . . . I'm so glad you are here. I don't know what to do. What to say. It hit me like one of the Big Train's steamers."

Enrico's eyes widened and his shoulders lifted in the universal sign of lack of understanding, "Who is this Big Train, and what is a steamer? Do we eat it?"

His younger companion burst into a loud guffaw. The gloom of a second ago, dissipated into unself-conscious hilarity. Babe and the other ballplayers heaved and rocked with paroxysms of laughter. It infected Caruso whose chest emitted a deep rumbling laugh. When the cacophony abated, the Babe chortled, "Eat a steamer!" and the raucous laughter erupted again until they could hardly breathe. They clutched their sides, fearing that to stop would bring back the hurt.

The Babe said, "So, what do we do now?"

"We drink," Enrico exclaimed. "We drink to dull the pain, we drink to celebrate life, we drink because we deserve it, and we drink because we can."

"Bruno, open the prosecco and order some cabernet from the sommelier. Tell the kitchen to bring up some Caruso spaghetti and roasted chicken. *Velocemente,* quickly."

The short man in the grey suit who had blended into the background bolted into action. Glasses were lifted and salutations in various languages entoned.

"To life!"

Tears glistened at the edge of Babe's eyes, restrained only by the barricade of his eyelashes. Damn him, thought Babe. How could he abandon me? How do I move forward now?

Learn what happens next in
WOPPER: How Babe Ruth Lost His Father and Won the 1918 World Series Against the Cubs
Volume 3
The Series

GLOSSARY OF EARLY 20TH CENTURY IDIOMS AND BASEBALL SLANG

Agate, n. – baseball; apple; horsehide; the pill

Aggregation, n. - team

Annie Oakley, n. – base on balls

Bingle, n. – a well-struck hit, a single

Bop in the beezer, v. – punch someone in the nose

Box artist, n. – pitcher; ball tosser; or twirler

Bush, bushes, n. – lower level baseball, minor leagues

Busher, n. – term of scorn for a low class player, prone to rinky-dink or unprofessional actions

Butterfinger, v. – error, fielding muff, as in Max Flack admitting that, "I butterfingered the play and am unanimously elected as the goat."

Cake, n. - dandy or vain ball player who obsesses over his personal appearance to the detriment of his game

Candy kid, n. – swatter who drives in a run

Circuit drive, n. – home run

Coachers, n. – base coaches

Cudgel, n. – baseball bat

Emery ball, n. – when the pitcher scuffs a ball with sandpaper or an emery board to cause the ball to move erratically

Fade, n. – screwball, pitch that moves away from the batter, perfected by Christy Matthewson

Fans, n. – cranks; bugs

Flivver, n. – small car with a rough ride

Frank, n. – walk, ball on balls

Fumble, v. – to commit a fielding error

Get his alley, v. – find weak spot in a batter's swing

Get your nanny, v. – be irritated, as in "Don't let him get your nanny." Derived from nanny goat.

Horse collar, n. – when batter goes hitless, he wears a horse collar.

Horse-hide, n. – name for baseball based on the leather covering used

Hoodoo, n., v. – jinx, superstition that player or object has unnatural mastery

Hot stove, hot stove league, n. – off-season when fans gather around hot stove to discuss baseball and potential personnel changes

Jape, - a practical joke, a jest

Jinegar, n. - term for pep or spirit

Jounce, v. – to jolt or bounce, as in, he jounced a hit through the infield

Kalsomine, n., - whitewash, shut out, as in, he put the kalsomine on the Cubs

Knuckle party, n. – fight, fisticuffs

Lamps, n. – a player's eyes

Leather, n. – baseball glove or defensive ability, as in, he's good with the leather; or, he can really flash the leather

Lemonball, n. –leather baseball handstitched with two circumferential rows of stitches

Magnate, n. – owner of a baseball club

Mauler, n. – power hitter

Necktie party, n. – a hanging bee, lynching

Outfield, n. – garden

Outfielder, n. – gardener; garden tender

Piffle, n. – nonsense, as in "Don't hand me that piffle."

Pinch, n. – a difficult or pivotal part of a game

Pink slip, n. – refers to the action of a manager removing a pitcher from the game, as in, with a disgusted grunt, Huggins gave Thomas the pink slip and signaled for a reliever from the bullpen.

Platter, n. – home plate, as in, he crossed the platter for a tally

Policeman of the diamond – umpire

Shineball, shiner, n. – when the pitcher rubs a ball vigorously to create a shiny area to cause the ball to move erratically

Slab, n. – the mound; rubber

Slabman, n. – pitcher, boxman

Slants, n. – pitches

Snake's hips, adj. – something excellent

Snuggle-pupping, v. – making out, passionate kissing

Southpaw, n. – left-handed thrower

Stepping in the bucket, v. – when the lead foot of the batter pulls away from the plate

Striker, n. – batter; swatter

Throng, n. – large crowd of fans or bugs

Trolley-wire, v. – to strike a baseball with such force that its trajectory appears as straight and true as the wire that provides electricity to a trolley car

Wagon tongue, n. – baseball bat

Whiff, n – a strikeout, often by virtue of a swing and miss

Willow, n. – baseball bat

Yannigan, n. – a rookie, a player not on the regular team

Zeppelin, v. – To hit the ball high and long; *esp.* to hit a home run. Now apparently *disused*

Zipper, n. – fastball

ENDNOTES

i   Smelser, Marshall, The Lie That Ruth Built, Quadrangle/The New York Times Book Co. (New York, New York 1975) p. 176.

ii   Kathia Miller, "Guest Commentary: Unassisted Triple Play was One for the Record Books," *Naples* (Florida) *News*, July 20, 2009, drawn from SABR Bioproject "Neal Ball" written by John McMurray, http://sabr.org/bioproj/person/32998a44 .

iii Westcott, Richard, *Philadelphia's Top Fifty Baseball Players*, University of Nebraska Press (Lincoln, NE 2013) p. 56.

iv Adomites, Paul and Wisnia, Saul, *Babe Ruth His Life and Times*, Publications International, Ltd., (Morton Grove, Illinois 1995).

v   Steelman, Ben, *Wilmington Star News Online*, "North Carolina has complex history with liquor" posted March 6, 2010.

vi Parrott, Edward, Sir, *Allies, Foes, and Neutrals: A First Sketch of European History from the Age of Pericles to the Eve of the Great War*, Ulan Press (Neuilly sur Seine, France 2012) p. 358.

vii C. Starr Matthews, *Baltimore Sun*, July 10, 1914, quoted in Millikin, Mark R., *BABE RUTH Star Pitcher of the 1914 Baltimore Orioles*, p. 25, Mark's Bayside Publishing, Chesapeake Beach (2014).

viii *Burns, Robert, To a Mouse, on Turning Her Up in Her Nest with the Plough, Country.*

ix *Babe Ruth a hit in R.I. before he became baseball legend,* Providence Journal, August 9, 2014, retrieved June 26, 2016. http://www.providencejournal.com/article/20140809/SPORTS/3080 99834

x   New York American, May 7, 1915, Damon Runyon

xi Meany, Tom, *Babe Ruth* (New York: Bantam Books 1947), 58.

xii SABR, http://sabr.org/bioproj/person/dca1fee6, quoting Murray Robinson, *New York World-Telegram*

xiii SABR, http://sabr.org/bioproj/person/400b2297, quoting Murray Robinson, *Journal American*, September 10, 1965.

xiv Creamer, Robert, BABE the legend comes to life.

xv F.C. Lane, Baseball Magazine, quoted in SABR

xvi Roosevelt, Theodore, Hyphenated American speech given to Knights of Columbus at Carnegie Hall on Columbus Day 1915, "*Roosevelt Bars the Hyphenated*" New York Times, October, 13, 1915.

xvii Wilson, Woodrow, Flag Day Address, June 14, 1917

xviii Wilson, Woodrow, Third Annual Message to Congress, December 7, 1915.

xix Gibbons tape #110, June 11, 1981

xx EC boy 19

xxi http://sabr.org/bioproj/person/6073c617

xxii Shakespeare, William, As You Like It, Act II, Scene VII

xxiii Cobb, Frank and Heaton, John L., *Cobb of "The World"* (New York: E.P. Dutton & Company, 1924), 270.

xxiv *New York Times*, March 26, 1918, p.3, col. 5.

xxv Okrent, Daniel, *Last Call: The Rise and Fall of Prohibition,* (New York: Scribner a division of Simon Schuster 2010), pps 100-101.

xxvi *The St Louis Globe-Democrat* (April 5, 1918), *GERMAN ENEMY OF U.S. HANGED BY MOB ST. LOUIS COLLINSVILLE MAN KILLED FOR ABUSING WILSON*

xxvii The WWI Home Front: War Hysteria & the Persecution of German-Americans, Authentic History.com (last accessed August 9, 2016)

xxviii *Id.*

xxix Prager Lynch Murder Trial Ends in Miscarriage of Justice [event of June 1, 1918] 1 Unsigned article in *St. Louis Labor*, whole no. 905 (June 8, 1918), pg

xxx Gilbert/Rothgerber, *Young Babe Ruth*, (McFarland & Company, 1999, Jefferson, North Carolina) p. 176

xxxi Wood, Allan, *Babe Ruth and the 1918 Red Sox*, (Writers Club Press, New York 2000) p. 159.

xxxii Babe_Ruth_Thread, www.baseballfever.com (accessed August 17, 2016) http://www.baseball-fever.com/showthread.php?21998-*Babe-Ruth-Thread*&s=526fc45b9eb4174abofde6f6d8b327b5

xxxiii *Id.*

Acknowledgements

The creation of a work of historical fiction requires assistance from many people and sources. *Wopper* is no exception. Without the amazing capabilities of the Internet, this series would have taken much more time to research and write. Similarly, without the generosity of Babe Ruth scholars this series would not have been possible. Mike Gibbons, executive director of the Babe Ruth Birthplace Museum, was exceptionally supportive and generous with his time and materials. Fred Shoken and Bill Jenkinson provided excellent information and leads to fascinating Babe Ruth sources.

I was blessed to have the insight and editorial suggestions of several talented people. I am most grateful to Dr. Robert Kuncio-Raleigh and Shaun Cherewich for their dedication and insightful edits. Larry Keith, former neighbor and top executive at *Sports Illustrated* provided a unique perspective and wealth of experience that greatly improved the final manuscript.

The biography project of the talented members of SABR (Society for American Baseball Research) was a constant source of anecdotal and background information that helped to provide depth and authenticity to this work. I am proud to be a member of this august organization.

Last, but not least, I wish to thank my family for their never-ending support and guidance. My children Valerie, Jenna, Jason and Louis inspire me. Words cannot suffice to express my love and gratitude to my wife, Rhonda for everything she does to make me a better writer and person.

Made in the USA
Middletown, DE
03 June 2017